Raw Feed Stories
A collection of short novellas

MICHAEL WHETZEL

RAW FEED & all contained stories
Copyright© Michael Whetzel 2012, 2013

All rights reserved.

All stories are works of fiction. Names, characters, businesses, organizations, places, events, and incidents are either the product of the author's imagination or used fictitiously.

For more information on Michael Whetzel, including news and announcements, please visit www.michaelwhetzel.com

*For my parents,
For their support and help in fostering my love of books.*

TABLE OF CONTENTS

The Pied Piper of the Undead	1
BOOM	55
Punchy	102
Bandwidth	127
Cube^3	170
Special Black Rain Preview: The Student	289

THE PIED PIPER OF THE UNDEAD

I.

Peter looked out from the platform of the water tower. He grabbed another handful of chips from the bag sitting next to him and slammed them into his mouth. He was 13 years old; slightly pudgy for his age, with fair skin and shaggy blond hair. He wiped the grease from his fingers on his shirt. The shirt was one of his favorites, a worn blue T-shirt with the Batman logo starting to flake off. He had only brought four shirts from the house and was thinking he might go back and get some more of his clothes. But that would have to wait for another day. Today he was heading elsewhere.

He munched another handful of chips. They were salt and vinegar flavored. It was his favorite kind and part of today's themed meal plan: Crunchy Chip Day. This morning for breakfast he wolfed down two small bags of Ranch Doritos with a large can of lukewarm Mountain Dew. Lunch would be the rest of the bag he was working through. Supper would be tortilla chips and hot corn chips.

The previous day had kicked off theme week. Peter decided he would start with Cookie Day and had enjoyed copious amounts of chocolate chip, oatmeal, and snicker doodle treats. It had gone well and the only discomfort he felt was a bit of indigestion before bedtime. It was worth it. What the hell else was he going to eat? It was going on three months up on the tower and it wasn't like a McDonald's was still open down the street.

He finished the chips and crumpled the bag up into a small ball. Standing at the safety railing, he flung the ball out into the open air. He watched it flip and turn; the bag beginning to un-ball itself. It landed a few yards from the base of the tower.

Right at the feet of Sandy Kramer.

She was looking up at Peter through her one working eye. The other was nothing but an empty socket, located above the rotting hole of her cheek. Something white glistened in the sunlight, and Peter realized it was Sandy's teeth reflecting through her destroyed face. She stood unmoving, in a ratty summer dress, flies buzzing around her face.

"Hello, Sandy," Peter said. She did not respond. Zombies could not speak. Or maybe they chose not to.

Sandy was considered the prettiest girl at Nathaniel Turner Middle School. The other young men in Peter's grade fawned all over her, offering to carry her books home from school or buy her ice cream at lunch. It made Peter sick inside. He was attracted to Sandy, but he did not want his "balls in a sling." Carter told him that one. They got a good laugh during lunch at every poor loser running to the ice cream cooler.

"She's got his balls, Peter. Wrapped tight." Carter pointed at the love struck teen. Peter always laughed at his friend's snide comments. He missed Carter.

Sandy was pretty. Key word being *was*. Currently, Sandy Kramer was running for the most unattractive thing Peter had seen all week. The rot on her face was disgusting. Pus oozed from the eye socket and her nose was little more than two holes in the middle of her face. The glistening teeth were proving to be hypnotic.

"What do you want, Sandy?" Peter spoke again. It was not unusual for the zombies to come and visit. It was always the same thing though. They just stood and stared up at him. Waiting for something interesting to happen.

The whole wide world is probably full of zombies. And I got stuck with the dumb ones. The thought popped into his head a lot when he was canvasing the town. They were incredibly stupid. They moved slowly, lumbering around like overdosing drug addicts, drooling all over their stained clothes. They were only dangerous if you got close enough or were overwhelmed by sheer numbers. But even then they were really slow.

He was sure they wanted to eat him. He witnessed plenty of zombies eating humans when the shit had gone down. That was before anyone knew what was happening. By then it was too late.

Sandy stood and stared at Peter. He sipped some cola from a bottle and belched loudly.

"Hey, Sandy, show me your tits!" Peter smiled. Sandy hit puberty hard last fall and her developing breasts were a popular subject around the hallways then.

Peter looked at her chest. They were lopsided and one seemed to be....missing?

"On second thought, never mind," he said. "Why don't

you go over to the ice cream shop with the rest of your friends? I got things to do." The zombies seemed to be attracted to the bright colors of the shop. It sucked for Peter. He wanted to check the freezers to see if they were still working. Ice Cream Day would be an epic treat. He would make it Ice Cream Week if it ever happened.

Peter heard Sandy grunting and turned his attention back to her. She was trying to climb the water tower's ladder. The zombies barely had any motor skills, besides walking and eating, and watching the dead girl trying to climb the rungs was entertaining.

Her leg slipped through the bottom of the ladder and before he knew it, she was stuck. He watched as she struggled to free herself. It was disastrous. The zombie began ripping violently at the ladder to no avail.

"Better calm down," Peter said. Sandy stopped her struggles and looked back up at the boy. Then she turned back to her trapped leg. "You know what's going to happen!"

Sandy started twisting her body back and forth at the bottom of the ladder. Peter watched in fascination as her leg began to twist off at the hip. The undead flesh could not hold up to the physical punishment the girl was exerting on herself.

Finally with a loud grunt, Sandy pulled her body from the trapped leg. Peter shook his head as he watched the girl fall to one side and the leg fall to the opposite side.

Sandy crawled away, heading back towards town. The stump where her leg previously was attached trailed dead skin and muscle, and bits of blood and sticky stuff. Peter was pissed.

"Hey! Get back here and pick up your leg!" He watched as she pulled herself down the small bluff the tower sat on. "Dammit! Get back here!"

Great. Now he would have to clean up the mess. If he left it there, it would start to smell.

Peter frowned and slapped his forehead with his hand. "Stupid zombies."

He looked out at the town. The zombies, hundreds of them, shuffled back and forth on its streets.

He looked down at Sandy's leg.

It was going to be a long day.

II.

Rockville sat in the northwest corner of Oklahoma. It was a small rural town boasting a population of over 1200. It had a very small school system, a volunteer fire department, and a municipal library. Although small, the town council had taken great pains to expand the town limits and make Rockville more enticing to new residents. The council made agreements with several notable business chains and retail stores began to pop up on Route 54, the main highway passing near Rockville.

Already the town boasted a new CVS Pharmacy with a fancy drive-thru, a Krystal Burger and Fries, and a huge Chinese buffet that the residents fawned over immediately. Even Peter had to admit the sushi there was pretty good.

The town was beginning to really come into its own. And then the Zombie Apocalypse began. Peter figured if the council knew that was going to happen, they would have simply said "Screw it" and watched American Idol during the monthly meetings. That's what he would have done anyways.

After the Zombie Apocalypse, the quiet residents of Rockville became the undead residents of Rockville. All except for Peter. He was the lone survivor. And he had found the safest place in town: the water tower.

The tower was ideal to live on. It was old and showed its age through its rust colored spots. But it was built sturdy and strong. Standing eight-five feet tall, the upper platform had a safety railing circling the huge steel water tank and plenty of room for a young boy to stretch out on. Peter had erected a tent with tarps he found at Dickson's Hardware Store. A large sleeping bag made up the floor of his new home. He found two small bookshelves which furnished the tent and held CDs and his handheld GamePak video games. A large box contained all the food he had brought back from town, everything from soda to chips to canned goods.

Peter strapped on his book bag and started to climb down the ladder. He was heading into town to pick up more food and his special items. As he stepped off the ladder, he glanced around. Zombies were pretty stupid, but it always paid to be careful. He had learned that the hard way.

At the bottom of the ladder, he stood over Sandy's lost leg. It was probably an attractive leg at one time, but now it was crusty and rotting. The leg ended in a dirty pink sock. There were holes forming in the toes of the sock and Peter spotted a red painted toenail. He stared a few seconds at the red nail, thinking of Sandy sitting on her bed, listening to the radio and applying the paint with the tiny nail brush. She was smiling, nodding her cute face to the beat of the stereo, flipping her hair away from her beautiful blue eyes.

He kicked the leg away from the ladder and down the small bluff, cursing Sandy and her big boobs the whole way.

At the bottom of the bluff, he turned right and proceeded up Main Street. Even with the growth on Route 54, Rockville still maintained a small commercial district. Stores sat on either side of the street, built right next to each other. This made skirting danger pretty easy. Peter could climb the fire escape at Susie's Gift and Thrift and simply roof-hop over to whatever destination he had in mind. Everything he needed could be found on Main Street.

Where the businesses ended, the suburbs began. Peter stayed away from the rural houses. It was not a good thing to be caught in a house with a hundred zombies trying to break in. He had learned that one the hard way too.

As he headed towards the thrift store, the shufflers began to catch sight of him. This was how it always happened. They saw him and they followed. When he climbed up on the roofs, they would follow along the street, trying to keep him in sight. Usually he would lose them once he entered a building or doubled back. For the zombies, it was out of sight, out of mind. It was a game, sometimes dangerous, but mostly just tiring.

The disturbing thing about it was that Peter, like in most small towns, knew almost everybody.

The first zombie to approach Peter was Mr. Myers, the custodian at his school. Myers was sporting a particularly gruesome scowl today, and Peter was sad to see the man had lost his other arm sometime during the past week. The armless zombie snapped his jaws open and closed in anticipation of a meal.

"Hello, Mr. Myers," Peter quipped. He easily dodged the zombie and whirled to the right. The dead man, trying to keep Peter in sight, twirled with the movement but it proved too difficult for his stiff legs. Mr. Myers tangled his feet up and went down. Hard. His face smacked the asphalt of the road with a meaty THUNK.

Peter stopped and looked at the janitor. Half the zombie's face was smashed flat from the fall, giving him a very unusual look, like an abstract painting. *Poor Mr. Myers. The guy just can't get a break.* The kids always picked on the janitor, saying mean things behind his back. They would cover the hallway walls with dirty graffiti and stop flushing the toilet. All to make the old man's life hell.

Good thing they can't see you now, Peter thought.

He closed in on the thrift shop, passing one of the local mailmen and Mr. Roberts, Rockville's dog catcher. Mr. Roberts looked pretty good for being undead. But he was sitting on the curb; chewing on a small mutt Peter could not recognize (Miss Nettle's yorkie?). He threw the carcass aside when he saw Peter and began to follow.

There were about twenty following him now. Grunting and shuffling behind the boy, the ones with arms reached out for Peter but to no avail. They were just too slow.

The smell emanating from the group was horrible. It was a mixture of rotting flesh with an undercurrent of blood and pee. Peter scrunched up his nose and hurried into the alleyway next to the thrift store. This was a tricky venture. He had to be careful there were no zombies waiting in the alley. He could easily be trapped before he reached the fire escape.

Fortunately the alleyway was empty. Peter ran down to the dumpster and hopped up on the lid. From there he could jump up and grasp the last rung of the fire escape ladder. As he climbed the side of the building, he looked back down at the growing mass of undead bodies. There were about thirty now, and more entering the alley. Once he disappeared over the edge, they would grow bored and begin to disperse.

Peter climbed to the top and slipped over the edge of the roof. Like many of the stores on Main Street, the thrift store was a straight brick and mortar store with a flat roof structure. There were a few roofs that sloped or angled crazily, but the town council had prided itself on making downtown look pretty uniform. Lucky for Peter.

He peeked over the edge at his admirers. Some were looking straight up at him, a wanting need in their gruesome eyes. Peter watched in awe as one of the zombies tried to climb up on the dumpster. This was the first time he had ever seen one of them try to follow. He recognized the brave dead soul. It was one of the bag boys from the hardware store.

The boy jumped up on the dumpster, but only managed to roll back off and hit the brick wall. Some teeth fell from the boy's mouth and Peter watched with fascination as the zombie tried over and over again to pick them up. The task proved tedious and the zombie's hands were not dexterous enough to grasp the lost molars. Soon the boy disappeared under the clamoring mass of flesh. All the rotting faces were looking up at the rooftop now.

Peter ducked back out of sight and headed across the roof. At the far side he jumped the three feet across to the next building, a small apartment complex. He had entered the roof access of the building to explore once before but found zombies still inhabited the apartments. He knew the power was still working, even after all these months, and wanted to try using the phones.

He had entered the hallway of the first apartment and found a landline. But after dialing 911, all he got was a weird screeching sound full of white noise. He tried his grandmother in Wisconsin, but the phone rang and rang.

After listening to it ring for about five minutes, Peter then realized he was not alone in the apartment. He heard a noise in the next room and opening the door, glanced into a living room.

A small television was on; its screen displaying the emergency broadcast symbol over and over again. A large fat dead man sat in the chair, focused on the TV screen. When the man's chubby face turned to look at Peter with its green bloody eyes, Peter sprinted from the apartment. Another zombie was coming up the hall towards him. He ran back up the stairs and slammed the roof door shut, locking it from the outside.

His thoughts turned back to the next jump. This one was a bit more difficult. The next building was the Morris Inn, a fine dining restaurant. It had a sloped roof and some of the tiles were coming loose. He would have to be extra careful when landing.

Peter took a deep breath and hitched the book bag tighter. This jump was about six feet wide and the inn roof sat a good four feet lower than the apartment building. He counted to ten and raced off the roof. He landed with a dull thud and started to slide backwards. He quickly grabbed the top edge of the roof and scrambled back to safety. A few tiles hit the ground below. Some of the zombies took notice and looked up at Peter.

Now they will follow me until I get to Swanie's. He wished they would leave him alone. It was hard jumping from roof to roof with an audience taking in your every move. He picked his way across the inn and jumped to the next building, the movie theater. Swanie's was still three buildings away. The remaining jumps were a piece of cake.

Peter could hear the zombies scrabbling along the street. He peeked out quickly. There was Miss Jacobs, the old lunch lady from school, her gray hair lying in patches on her fleshy head. Following behind her was Greg Stein and Michael Reese, two kids who were a grade ahead of Peter. Stein was walking on one foot. The other foot was twisted up behind his ankle. He dragged the broken leg behind him. Reese was sporting a huge hole in his stomach, which was now empty of organs. Peter gagged a bit as he watched the boy stick his hands into the hole over and over again. His fingers came out covered in slime.

Disgusting, he thought. Neither one were considered friends. In fact, they acted like big jerks on the bus all the time. Reese constantly pulled girls' hair and Stein was always laughing heartily ay Reese's antics. Interesting to see they were still together, even in death.

Peter made the last jump onto Swanie's Convenience Store. It was a large building, two stories tall. The bottom was the grocery store and the top part housed a pharmacy and toy store. He climbed down the fire escape and went in one of the second floor windows.

The lights were still on inside. It was weird to see the power still working and no one around to take advantage of it. Peter stumbled into the store and slid down the stairs to the first floor. He walked to the cereal aisle and grabbed two boxes of his favorite, Fruit Loopies. Then it was over to the soft drink aisle. A six pack of Lightnin' Energy disappeared into the backpack. He grabbed beef jerky from the front counter and a handful of candy bars from the rack.

Outside the large windows in the front of the store, the zombies piled up against the glass. They stared into the store, watching Peter wander between the shelves. The front doors were locked and the glass was pretty solid. So far, the horde was not able to break in like they did the ice cream shop or the carpet place. *It's only a matter of time,* Peter thought. *When enough of them pile up out there, anything can break.*

He passed the produce racks. Even though the coolers were still working, most of the fruits and vegetables had spoiled over time. He hated veggies anyways. The first few days of coming here, Peter ate all the apples and bananas he could carry, but now they lay in ruins as well. He turned the corner and grabbed a box of fruit rollups. In his mind it was a good substitute. The book bag was now full and weighed a good bit more than before.

He walked back up the steps and turned into the toy store. This was where he really wanted to go. Food was important but his excitement grew as he headed towards the back of the store.

Shattered glass littered the floor in front of the video game case. Peter had broken it open the first time he came here. He looked past the XBOX Infinity and PS6 games. The GamePak discs were towards the top of the display. It was half empty. Peter had taken most of them back to the tower. Those games were old news. Already beaten over and over again.

He looked over the titles carefully. He would choose two for now. He was trying to ration them out. He could try and set up something to play the other game consoles, but did not want to take the chance of being trapped in a room somewhere with zombies storming down on him. Maybe if he could find a super long extension cord and a light enough TV to haul up the tower's ladder that would be an option. But that was a lot of hard work. And the GamePak was portable and still very entertaining.

He pulled a box from the display. *Slug Wars 3*. He had played 1 and 2 a great bit over the past few months, but was growing bored with the whole Slug conflict. But this one looked different enough to garner a try. He slipped it into the outside pocket of the bag.

After glancing over and reading a few more game descriptions, he settled on *Innocent Bystander 2*. It was one of the most violent games ever produced and his mother would have a fit if she knew he was playing it. But she wouldn't care now. The undead were not really into censorship.

Peter grabbed his stuff and headed for the roof.

III.

He was getting ready to jump back towards the inn when he noticed the street was pretty empty now. He slowly moved to the edge of the roof and looked over. The majority of the zombies were down the street a ways, hovering around the front of the movie theatre. There were only a handful of shufflers standing around on this side of town. He could drop to street level and make a dash for the tower without any problems.

He slid down the fire escape and hit the concrete ground softly. Looking around, he edged out onto the street. The remaining zombies immediately began to notice him and follow. He walked quickly back towards the tower, easily leaving them behind.

Up ahead he noticed a small group of three zombies hitching towards him. He dodged towards the right and then dashed back to the left. The zombies tried to follow his movement but the front two walkers ended up tripping into each other and falling to the hard asphalt. One of the zombies began to hit the other in the head with slow, weak thumps. The bottom zombie answered by biting his attacker on the face. Peter watched as the biter tore the other's nose off and chewed it up in his broken mouth.

"Good grief," he mumbled. *What a sorry state of affairs.*

He slowed his walk a bit. The third zombie was still a few yards away. Peter glanced up at it, and then did a double-take. The zombie was a young boy, Peter's age, wearing a tattered *Guitar Zero* shirt and ripped up cargo shorts. Even with half the boy's skull uncovered, Peter still recognized his former best friend, Carter.

"Oh shit! Carter!" He laughed with glee. He had not seen Carter since the attack began and Peter found that he sorely missed his friend. Forgetting exactly what he was talking to, he began to run towards the zombie boy. When Peter got close, Carter began to swipe at him, trying to get a hold of the living food in front of him. Peter deftly dodged the swipes and continued talking up a storm.

"Damn, you look terrible, man."

Swipe

"You stink too."

Swipe

"Dude, it's so good to see you. Guess who I saw this morning?"

Swipe

"Sandy Kramer! And her tits look horrible, dude!"

Swipe *Swipe*

Peter glanced over Carter's shoulder. The horde of zombies lost interest in whatever was in front of the movie theatre and were heading their way. He ducked Carter's lunge and laughed.

"I'll find you tomorrow, you undead monkey." He ran up the street and looked back at his friend. Carter stood looking at him, dripping gobs of pus from his lips.

Good old Carter, he thought. He ran to the water tower.

It was corn chip time.

After dinner, he grabbed a fresh pack of batteries from one of the shelves and fired up the GamePak. *Slug Wars 3* was different from the first two, but he found himself bored within minutes. The slug war had grown stale, and even the sight of slug guts painting the battlefield did little to keep him interested. This would be a game he could play late at night. Something to help him fall asleep.

He ejected the game disc and loaded the other one. The title screen for *Innocent Bystander 2* came up. The title was written in blood that dripped down the tiny screen. The intro movie began to play. Peter watched as a young man and woman walked hand and hand down a busy city street. Suddenly, a car sped from around the corner and began to spray machine gun bullets all over the side of the road. The young couple watched in terror as people were riddled with bullets and their bodies were spun around on the sidewalk.

The young man went to push the woman to the side, only to scream when her head exploded into a million pieces. The man was shot in the arm and dropped to his knees on the bloody sidewalk, cradling the woman's headless corpse in his lap.

"Holy crap, this is awesome!" Peter swigged some Lightnin' Energy and stared at the tiny screen.

The young man's name was Trevor and as he lay in the hospital bed, mourning his girlfriend, he began having visions of death and destruction. When Trevor is released from the hospital, he goes home, dresses all in black and grabs his handy shotgun. He was going to get revenge on the people who killed his love and the rest of the innocent bystanders.

Peter was enamored for hours by the game. He was at

the part where he was torturing a Korean shopkeeper with a clothes hanger and pliers, looking for information regarding the killers, when he heard a strange noise from below.

Quickly he saved his game and looked over the railing.

Sandy Kramer was pulling herself from the bushes. Her dress was ripped completely in half, displaying her bottom very prominently. She pulled herself forward with her arms. Dirt and leaves clung to the upper part of her body. The stump that had once held the rest of her leg was dried and clotted with green pus.

She crawled a few feet and turned her head towards the tower. Peter stared at her.

"I don't have your leg anymore," he quipped. *What the hell does she want?* "I kicked it down the hill, Sandy." She stared unmoving. Peter's eyes traveled over her naked bottom half. The curves of her buttocks were still very interesting to look at, even for a dead girl.

He felt a nervous tension develop in his stomach. Sandy blinked her one working eye. Peter glanced at the shreds of her dress.

He swallowed.

Sandy began to crawl away under the tower. The spell was broken. He tried to catch his breath, wondering what was wrong. He ran to the other side of the tower and watched Sandy disappear into the undergrowth. Her bare bottom was the last thing he saw.

He ached all over and was aware of the hardness in the crotch of his shorts. He slowly walked back to the tent and crawled onto the sleeping bag. He started the game back up and played for 2 more hours. The sun set on the horizon and the moon began to rise. It was a ¾ moon, glowing bright against the metal surface of the tower. Peter stopped playing and looked out over the town.

The zombies were still during the nights. Most of them wandered slowly on Main Street, but quite a few would stand in place staring at the street lights or the blinking neon of George's Ice Cream and Soda Shoppe, or the show lights at the movie theater. Sometimes Peter would stare with them, looking at the bright pink and green neon, thinking about before when everything was normal.

Tonight he looked at the moon instead. And thought about Sandy. It was ironic that in school, Sandy was desired by all the boys. She was the ultimate fantasy. Someone leagues above Peter in the social order. He doubted she even knew his name then.

But now things were different. Sandy was just another victim, her glamorous traits falling off every day. And Peter was the desirable one now. He was desired by the whole town. It was unique, to feel wanted, to have all the attention pointed right at him. Sometimes it could be tiring, like when climbing the roofs, but it was a different feeling to be wanted, to be popular. He found he liked it, just a little bit.

He peed over the edge of the railing and went to get his toothbrush. As he dry brushed his teeth, he studied the undead people staring at the lit signs, recognizing classmates and neighbors. He watched his spit fly the long way to the ground and rinsed his mouth from a bottle of water. And then crawled into the tent and fell asleep.

Peter dreamed.

In his dream, he was walking down Main Street. The whole town was there, all of them zombies. But they were not trying to attack Peter. Instead, they were cheering for him. He smiled as many of the townspeople came forth and patted him on the back. There was the mayor and the chief of police, grinning ghastly smiles of death, hugging him and telling everyone how great Peter was in their guttural voices. Peter's classmates were cheering him and pushing in to touch him, talk to him, and be near him in any possible way.

Peter surged to the front of the crowd and a parade began to take place. He was the head of the parade and the zombies followed behind, shuffling and cheering. On the either side of the street were more of the undead, and Peter realized they were from all around the world, and had gathered to pay their respects to him. He marched proudly, his head raised, waving at the onlookers.

They shuffled past the movie theatre. He looked to the right at the ice cream shop and saw Carter standing there. Normal Carter, alive and well. His friend looked at him and Peter motioned for him to join the parade. Carter ran out and clapped Peter on the back, smiling. They marched together down Main Street.

At the end of the street, a large bandstand was erected, and zombies were gathered in huge crowds awaiting the arrival of Peter. He saw the mayor at the podium addressing the audience, and then he pointed to someone in the crowd. Immediately the group parted and Peter saw Sandy Kramer standing tall, smiling and waiting for him. She was normal too. And nude.

He walked to her, Carter nodding his head in agreement. Peter took her nakedness in as he got closer. The curve of her neck, the fullness of her breasts, each one topped with a small pink rosette. His eyes traveled across her flat belly to the dark patch of hair, waiting, inviting. He took Sandy in his arms and felt her breath against his ear.

His hands traveled over her warm skin and the crowd cheered even more. He reached in and kissed her and felt her hot tongue dart into this mouth. When he pulled away, he realized he could see her teeth through the hole in her cheek.

Peter staggered backwards. Sandy's face was changing to the zombie version. He turned to Carter only to see his friend being attacked by the hordes of the undead. They ripped Carter's flesh from his arms and began to bite into his best friend. Peter shook his head and turned back to Sandy. She was still smiling but now blood dripped from her rotting lips. Quickly zombies grabbed the young girl and began to tear her apart. Peter tried to punch his way to her but found himself being grabbed by rotting hands.

He kicked at the zombies and wretched himself free. Now Peter was running as fast as he could back up the street. The dead followed, no longer slow, but running fast with newfound energy. He felt the rush of wind as several of the followers tried to grab him, just missing catching onto his clothes. He saw a car parked on the side of the road and sprinted for it.

Desperately he snapped at the handle and found it unlocked. Quickly Peter ducked into the car and punched the locks closed. The horde covered the vehicle, pounding on the glass and roof, rocking the vehicle back and forth. Peter started to cry.

He watched in horror as one of the dead climbed up on the hood of the car. He recognized it as Miss Swanbee, the eighty year old lunch lady from his school. The old woman was completely nude and he tried to close his eyes as she began to push her body against the windshield. His eyes would not respond, and when Miss Swanbee pushed her naked, rotting, old bottom against the glass, causing green bloody smears to appear, Peter began to vomit on the floorboard of the car. He passed out on the seat…

...and woke up in a dank pool of sweat.

It was still night and the moon was almost full, creating a brilliant white radiance to the tower's surroundings. He lay awake, shuddering, feeling the cool night air against his skin. Slowly he got up and went to the railing and vomited into the open air.

Finished, he rinsed his mouth with a swig of water, washing the taste of potato chips from his lips. He lay back down in the tent but was not able to fall back asleep. He kept seeing the transforming face of Sandy Kramer appear in the canvas fabric.

Sometime during the early morning, he finally drifted off. As the sun began to rise into the sky, Peter slept peacefully on. Eventually, he awoke to the sound of shuffling feet and slowly realized one of the zombies was passing below the tower.

He sat up and stretched. Looking over the railing, he glimpsed Mr. Twigg, the owner of the hardware store, stumbling down the bluff. The zombie stopped briefly, and Peter saw that he was missing his mouth and jaw. Mr. Twigg turned and looked back at Peter and the boy waved to the dead man. The zombie reached for him, and finding he could not stretch the ninety feet between ground and tower, proceeded to shuffle back to town.

Peter got up and changed into a fresh shirt. He drank some water and looked in the food box. Today was going to be Candy Bar day. He stocked up over the week on his trips out and now a huge stack of chocolate bars covered the bottom of the box. Peter selected one: Choco Nuts.

He stared at the wrapper and found his appetite had left him. Instead the remnants of the dream came back to him. He tried to push the images away, but it was hard. He glanced back into the box and saw a Sticky Peanut bar. It was Carter's favorite. Immediately his thoughts turned to the dream and the normal Carter that appeared.

Peter reached into the box and grabbed the candy bar. Stuffing both bars into his pocket, he climbed down from the tower.

IV.

Main Street was quiet this morning. Peter walked slowly down the side of the street, ducking behind parked cars and into doorways, keeping out of sight of the undead. Most of the zombies were on the other side of town, standing in groups, bumping into each other. They almost seemed normal, walking amongst themselves, like they were attending a large public gathering of some sort.

Peter suspected Carter was somewhere else though.

Many zombies, although not bright, seemed to be drawn to familiar places and objects. One of the places Carter and Peter loved to go was the basketball court next to the car wash. It was a private place, normally shunned by the other kids. Many of the area kids preferred the courts located at the school, where a lot of the girls could be found hanging around. Carter and Peter were not the greatest players, so they gravitated to the more empty court to prevent embarrassment.

The basketball court was actually two courts joined side by side and surrounded by a large chain link fence. Peter snuck down the side of the car wash. He was a block over from Main Street, near the suburban part of town. There was zombie up the street, but it was heading the opposite way. He slowly peeked around the corner of the building and looked at the courts.

Carter was standing underneath one of the far baskets,

staring at the chain link basketball net. Every few seconds, he would sway slowly back and forth. Suddenly, the dead boy reached back and scratched his ass.

Peter walked around and entered the gate. He closed it shut behind him. Carter turned at the sound of the rattling metal. As soon as he saw Peter, he began to walk forwards, reaching outwards with his rotting hands.

"Hey Carter," Peter greeted his friend. He took the Sticky Peanut bar out of his pocket, unwrapping it as he walked. He approached Carter slowly. "Hey buddy, remember me? It's your best friend, Peter."

The zombie began to snap his jaws in response. Peter grimaced as a tooth fell from Carter's mouth and bounced off the asphalt. The zombie was close now and took a swipe at Peter. He ducked quickly and spun back around. Carter opened his mouth wide unleashing a mournful groan and Peter stuck the whole candy bar into the black rotting hole.

Carter froze. His mouth snapped shut over the gooey chocolate covered peanut bar.

He worked the bar slowly between his putrid lips, large gobs of melting chocolate and peanut butter dripping from the sides. Peter watched as the zombie reached up and tried to take the sticky mess from his mouth, but the peanut butter was proving to be a challenge.

Carter began to choke on the candy. He started spraying small drops of pus from his nostrils and peanut butter drool dripped onto his torn shirt. The dead boy gagged harshly, once, twice, and then on the third time swallowed the whole bit. A surprised look crossed his pale face and with a large thump he fell backwards on his rear.

A large fart escaped the dead boy and Peter started to laugh hysterically.

"Oh my God! That was awesome!" He danced around the zombie while Carter stared up at this new interesting distraction. As the zombie tried to regain his feet, Peter ran to the far side of the courts. There was a large plastic box that sat against the fence. He opened the bin and grabbed one of the basketballs stored there for the neighborhood to share.

Peter dribbled down the length of the court and bounced the ball off the board. It swished through the metal links of the basket. Two points.

Peter rebounded the ball and threw it over to Carter. Carter was just about to stand back up when the ball hit his chest and he landed back on his rear again. Peter grabbed the ball and shot from twenty feet out. It clanged off the rim. The zombie grunted and began to snap his jaws again.

"Alright Carter, we play to ten. Winners take outs." Peter dribbled around his friend, dodging the swinging arms that were trying desperately to grab him. He waited at the foul line for Carter to approach, and then he deftly drove the ball around the zombie and laid it in for the score.

"2-zip."

Peter went to grab the rebound but it bounced off his foot. He watched as the ball smacked off the pavement and landed in Carter's hands. The zombie looked surprised at his catch.

"Nice. You can still move it, buddy. Now try and shoot it," Peter urged.

Carter hefted the ball up and looked at the basket. He stared a few seconds and then snapped his mouth into the ball. There was a loud pop as his teeth punctured the rubber hide. Angry, he threw the remains aside and shuffled towards Peter.

"Why did you do that, stupid?" Peter quipped. He looked at the flat ball. It was the only one that had been inside the box.

Carter reached out and grabbed Peter by the shoulders. Peter pushed him off quickly.

"Stop it!" He backed a few steps away. "You're supposed to be my best friend. So stop it now." Carter grabbed the young boy again. Peter tried to throw him off, but the zombie's grip was stronger. He screamed and punched his friend in the face. The flesh was slimy against his small fist, and he felt his fingers slide off of the skin.

Carter pushed Peter against the fence and tried to bite him in the neck. Peter yelled and started to beat both hands against the pale face. The zombie grunted in rage and tried to grab Peter's hands. Peter ducked to the right and escaped the fence.

He stumbled over something and scraped his knees on the asphalt. He felt tears begin to fall down his cheeks. Turning, he saw the large chunk of concrete he fell over. Carter was approaching quickly now. Peter grabbed the rock and stood up to meet his friend.

This time when Carter grabbed for him, Peter smashed the rock against his head. There was a solid crunch and the side of the zombie boy's face flattened. But Carter continued forward. Peter hit him again. And then again. Bits of skull and brain peppered his face and arm. One final time he smashed the concrete piece against the zombie's head.

Carter fell to the court. He did not move.

Peter, gasping for breath, braced himself against the fence. He dropped the rock to the ground. He was crying and shaking uncontrollably. He glanced over at the body of his dead friend. Still shaking, he left the basketball court.

Peter walked back to Main Street. The street was beginning to fill up with the dead. He was still blurry-eyed from crying and walked into the back of one of the zombies. The dead man turned around with a snarl. It was Mr. Roberts, the dog eater. Peter jumped back as the man made a grab for him. He ran out on the street, stopping suddenly when he realized he was surrounded.

The zombies all turned and looked at the young boy. Peter sprinted towards the water tower as the horde of undead began to follow. Stumbling, he reached the ladder, hitting his head on one of the steel rungs. Quickly he scrambled up and looked over the railing.

Every zombie in town was heading for the tower.

Already a small group was jostling for position at the foot of the ladder. Peter was not too worried about them climbing the ladder. In the months he was camped out on the platform, many of the zombies had tried to climb the ladder, but failed to get past the first few rungs. They were not coordinated enough to make the climb. He was more worried about them not leaving. If they stayed around the tower, he would not be able to leave. And with limited food and water, that could be disastrous.

As much as he wanted to watch them, to make sure they would not climb up, he needed to be out of sight for them to lose interest. Peter summoned all his courage and left the railing. He knelt in the tent and grabbed a small towel. He wet the towel from a bottle of water and gently wiped the blood and gunk from his face and arms. His head was tender from the steel ladder rung and he felt a small knot already forming there.

He threw the towel from the tent and leaned back against the water tank. Grabbing his GamePak, he turned on *Innocent Bystander 2* and began to play. He could still hear the grunting and groaning of the zombies at the foot of the tower. He concentrated on the game, trying not to think about the nearby horde, or the death of his best friend.

V.

Peter was pretty far into the game now. He had worked Trevor through most of the city's criminal underground, torturing and killing all those who stood in his way. Now he was closing in on the kingpin, the head drug lord of the entire East Coast. The drug lord had issued a bounty on the unknown person who was disrupting his business, and now Trevor was killing bounty hunters too.

He was in a large warehouse, waiting for all the hired hunters. They were converging on this spot to take Trevor out once and for all. What they did not realize was the warehouse was one huge trap waiting to be sprung. Peter spent the first part of the level, erecting and joining gas lines that connected huge tanks of propane throughout the building. Now he was at the very end of the gas line, waiting for the hunters to enter.

As soon as they were all in, Peter flipped a switch, sparking the gas and setting off a chain reaction of explosions destroying the building. Quickly he directed Trevor to the main entrance of the warehouse. He grabbed a large axe from the parking lot and waited for anyone to escape from the towering flames.

As the hunters exited through the main doors, Peter had Trevor chop them down quickly. Blood splattered the small game screen and Peter became lost in the rhythm of the chaos on display.

When he finally looked up from the game, the sun was beginning to set on the horizon. Quickly he saved his progress and raced over to the railing. The horde of moving dead was gone. There was only one zombie down below. It was Timmy Sommers, a boy who was one year behind Peter at school.

Peter watched the young boy. Timmy shuffled from place to place, and it was a few minutes before Peter realized the young zombie was chasing a butterfly back and forth. The butterfly landed on a branch of a bush and Timmy tried to pick it up with his whole hand, snatching and grabbing a fistful of leaves when the butterfly escaped his grasp. Finally Timmy proved too quick for the butterfly, and he watched as the boy popped the bug into his mouth and began to chew.

Peter sighed and went back to the tent.

He grabbed a handful of candy bars from the box (making sure to skirt the Sticky Peanut bars) and sat down to a late dinner. Looking towards the city, he watched as the neon lights of the ice cream shop began to glow brightly. The marquee over at the movie theatre clicked on; the automatic timer set to go off when the sun was all the way down. The zombies began to move in small groups towards the bright glows, like moths to streetlamps.

Peter looked towards the car wash and basketball courts and on out towards the suburban part of town. His house stood someplace among all the other homes. He thought about his room. It probably looked the same as before, his Utah Jazz poster on his closet, a flat screen TV with a large shelf of video games sitting against the wall collecting dust. He missed his bed, the goose down pillow his mother gave him that used to be hers when she was a little girl.

His mother…..he pushed her away from his thoughts. He did not want to re-live that day ever again.

He threw the half eaten candy bar over the railing. Timmy the zombie scooted over to where it fell. He sniffed the strange smelling object. Then he wandered down the bluff, his rotting face recoiled in disgust from the smell of chocolate and the neon lights calling his name.

VI.

Peter slept soundly that night. It had taken a while to finally feel the tendrils of sleepiness ease around his mind, but after two hours of repetitive *Slug Wars* he was ready to turn in. After a few minutes, he drifted off. No dreams came to him under the moonlit sky.

In the middle of the night, shadows shuffled under the tower and staggered down the bluff. They paused at the rough asphalt of Main Street, glancing around slowly, and then joined the rabble watching the lights of the town pulse and glow in the darkness.

Peter rolled over, still asleep, and pulled the sleeping blanket over his head.

If he had been awake, and looking down at the shadows crossing underneath the tower, he would have been overwhelmed (and probably very scared) to see his parents shuffle out onto Main Street.

He had not seen them since the day he left for the tower.

Peter woke late the next morning. The sun was already high in the blue sky, and the air was warm and refreshing. He stretched and grabbed a clean pair of shorts from the bag. He went to the railing and looked down the bluff.

There was no one in sight. Out towards Main Street, he saw a few of the dead straggling around the sidewalk.

He tied his shoes and grabbed his bag. He scurried down the ladder and glanced cautiously around. Today was going to be a scorcher. He was already beginning to sweat through his shirt. Usually when it grew hot, the zombies became sluggish and timid, as if the heat emptied their energy reserves.

Peter walked out on Main and kept to the store fronts. Most of the horde was standing around the small community park located down next to the Rockville town offices. He could see the bent silhouettes walking beneath the trees. The majority of the undead would have headed back to the rural area of town, seeking shelter in many of the empty houses there.

One thing was for sure, the heat did not help the smell any. He could almost taste the rotting stench in his mouth, and his eyes started to water a bit. He walked down the street, trying to breathe through his mouth.

The heat would make the tower almost inhabitable today, with all the metal surfaces reflecting the sunlight. On days like today, there were two places Peter could seek shelter from the humidity. One was Swanie's. But the thought of staying in the convenience store all day became boring. The other place held some promise, and he ventured up the fire escape to climb over to the roof of the movie theatre.

The theatre was closed on the day the dead rose from the earth. Whenever he saw the double front doors, Peter would glance inside the darkness, wondering what could be salvaged there. Today would be ideal in exploring the cool interior of the building. He never saw any evidence of zombies in the theatre and knew he would be relatively safe in the dark interior. As long as he kept a low profile.

Peter jumped from the apartments and landed on the flat roof of the theatre. He edged up to the roof entrance and tried the door. Locked.

Reaching into his bag, he took out a hammer he managed to salvage from the hardware store. One, two, three strikes against the door jam and it started to give. Peter dropped the hammer back into the bag and kicked out with his leg. The door smacked open against the interior wall. A dark stairway greeted him.

He waited a few minutes to see if the noise of the broken door brought any visitors. When he was sure he was alone, he entered the stairway.

He brought out a small flashlight, clicking it on. The stairs went down one flight to another door. This one was a heavy duty swinging door. If it was locked, he would be stone "shit out of luck" as Carter would always say. He pushed the thought of his friend away quickly.

The door was unlocked. He swung it open and saw that it led to the main lobby. Quickly he darted in and turned off his light. The front glass doors where directly across the lobby. Sunlight shone brightly through the glass, lighting the front counter and candy display. It was not a large theater, containing only one screen and the main lobby.

The theater usually showed two movies during the summer and changed out the movies on a weekly basis. Mostly they were movies that were a few months old, having already run nationwide, but not yet debuting on home DVD. The week the outbreak happened, the theater had scheduled *Jurassic Park: The Return* for its matinee hours. The evening shows were for *Black Rain Chronicles: Episode 1*.

Peter loved science fiction movies and he originally planned to see *Chronicles* with Carter before the disaster. He had already seen *Jurassic Park* twice at the colossal Twin Peaks theatre out near Hampton. It was good, but *Black Rain* looked way better.

He eased his way to the glass doors and looked outside. There were a handful of zombies nodding around the entranceway. The rest had taken up cooler shelter elsewhere. The doors were locked and as long as he stayed away from them, he should be safe.

Peter walked back through the lobby and looked behind the counter. He filled his bag with gummy bears and Milk Duds and then headed for the large screen room. The screen room seated about fifty people when at capacity. He eased through the door and headed right. Here there was a small set of stairs that led up to the projection room.

He opened the door to the small room. There were little lights embedded into the ceiling that lit the interior, bathing it in a comfortable glow. He went to the projector and saw that *Black Rain* was loaded and ready to watch. He looked over the switches and cut the screen room lights on. The soft glow of the small lights appeared around the rows of seats in the cavernous theater.

He found the right switch and turned the projector on. Peter hurried out of the room and into the theater. He found the best seat, right smack dab in the middle. He took note of the red 'EXIT' sign down front (just in case) and tore open a bag of Milk Duds. It felt great in the large room, nice and cool.

The green screen announcing the previews came on. The first one was for some awful romantic comedy that Peter was glad would probably never be released. Then a trailer for the *Justice League* exploded onto the screen. Peter cheered with excitement. He watched as Superman zoomed over Metropolis and Batman and Wonder Woman fought off a swarm of weird monsters. It ended with the whole league (including his favorite, Hawkman) facing off against a villain calling himself Darkside. It looked great.

"Dammit," Peter cursed into the empty theater. "Why's the flipping world got to end before *Justice League* comes out? God, that fucking sucks." He threw his remaining milk duds at the screen and opened a pack of gummy bears.

The movie was pretty good. It was about a mysterious alien voice that killed almost everybody in the world. The survivors were running around trying to figure out what was going on while dodging wild bug aliens and huge glowing ships. There was a kid named Everett, who had lost his parents in the devastation, and found himself on his own and trying to survive. He managed to hook up with another survivor, an old woman, and they were being chased by crazy cannibals. There was also a guy who was trying to mount an offensive against the aliens and form an army from all the survivors. He was gathering military gear and training people how to shoot guns and such.

The movie ended with the kid and woman crossing a huge dam with the cannibals chasing right behind. At the same time, the aliens were attacking everybody and to top it off there was some crazy tennis player with a sword on the other side of the dam.

Peter was enthralled. Right after the huge action sequence, the credits began to roll, and *To be continued in Episode 2* came up on the screen. Peter cursed again under his breath. Stupid Hollywood, didn't they know better than to spread their movies so far out over different releases? God forbid, the world really did end and no one would get to see how the story finally unfolded.

Peter decided that going to the movies sucked. *Black Rain* would always be unfinished to him and previews would always be previews. They would never grow into their feature film potential again.

He swallowed the rest of the candy and went to the projection room. Shutting the projector off, he looked around the room and saw there was another film canister nearby titled *I only Die Hard*. He could always come back and try that movie out. Maybe it was a one and done deal. It would be something to do.

Peter walked up the stairs to the roof and exited into the hot evening sunlight. His eyes blinked heavily, trying to get used to the bright glare. Finally able to see again, he edged to the side of the building and looked out over the town.

Many of the zombies were still under the trees at the park but he could see a large swarm heading up Route 54 towards the interstate. He squinted, trying to see what had caught their attention. When he heard the gunshot, he could not identify it at first. The large bang ricocheted off the rooftops and reverberated through the town.

Peter ducked instinctively. He peered over the roof edge looking for the source of the sound. In his book bag, he found another thing he salvaged from the hardware store: a small pair of binoculars. He put the glasses up to his face and scanned the horizon.

At the highway, he found the swarm of zombies walking rapidly towards something. Turning the binoculars to follow their path, he found two men crouched down on the side of the road. Both men were armed with handguns and were firing into the mass of undead. Peter held his breath, watching the two men and listening to the sound of the guns going off, over and over again. Zombies fell to the side of the road as bullets tore through their brains.

There are people, he thought. *There are others who are alive.* Peter could not believe it. There were other survivors, not just him!

Quickly he stood up and started waving both arms towards the highway.

"HELP! HELP!" he screamed. "I'M HERE. I'M OVER HERE!"

Peter ran towards the fire escape, deciding to try and make his way to the men. Before he could start climbing down, he heard one of the men screaming in pain. He raced back to the roof edge and looked through the binoculars again.

The zombies were beginning to overwhelm the other survivors. One of the men was racing backwards up the road, firing into the horde. He saw the other trying to fight off zombies from where he had fallen. Peter cried out as a zombie bit the fallen man in the neck.

He circled the glasses towards the second man. The man fired his gun, and a nearby zombie fell to the ground. But he was out of ammo now, and as he tried to reload, Peter watched as the zombies grabbed him and tore into his body.

Peter dropped the glasses to the rooftop. The glass shattered and fell from the heavy plastic frames. He stood still, staring out towards the highway.

Just like that they were gone. He had seen other survivors. Survivors who tried to enter Rockville.

And now they were gone.

Peter dropped to his knees. The gravel on the roof dug

into his bare legs.

He cried and cried heavily, and finally passed out.

VII.

He did not remember climbing back up the tower at all. But somehow he managed it.

His body was aching all over, and he wondered if he was getting sick. His eyes burned from crying. He glanced over the railing, realizing there was no recollection of dodging zombies or trying not to be eaten. The zombies were still there, shuffling back and forth. He had traveled the past twenty minutes from the theatre roof in blackout mode. It was a wonder he made it back home.

He slid down the rail and sat on the platform. Reaching into the food box, he brought out some warm water and took a large drink. His thoughts turned towards the men he had just seen.

If they were alive, there were bound to be more survivors. And anyone traveling by would want to swing by Rockville to check it out for supplies. He was not sure about the rest of the country, but the town still had electricity, and the town lights would attract more visitors.

But there were too many dead roaming the streets. Anyone not prepared would soon meet the same fate as the others. *The damn zombies are screwing up everything,* Peter thought.

He lay down on his sleeping bag, a headache slamming through his skull.

There are people out there. Alive. Just like me.

He drank the rest of the water and passed out. The sun sank over the horizon, and the lights of the theatre and ice cream shop glowed brightly under the stars.

He woke needing to pee really bad. His bladder was on the verge of exploding. Crawling out of the tent, he saw that it was late night. The moon provided a steady glow across the tower.

Peter walked to the rail and pissed into the bushes. His head still hurt and he wished he had some aspirin to ease the pain. He zipped himself back up and looked toward Route 54. There was no movement or any sign of the men from earlier in the day.

He eased himself back onto the platform. His whole body ached and he definitely felt like he was coming down with something. He leaned his forehead against the middle rail. The metal was cool and comforting to the touch.

It was a few minutes before he realized he was not alone. Someone was standing in the clearing at the bottom of the ladder. There was no movement since he had woken so he was sure whoever it was had watched him piss.

He walked to the ladder, looking down at the figure. The tower's tank cast a large shadow over the figure, making it hard to see any features. Peter grabbed the top handrails of the ladder and looked down.

He stopped breathing.

It was his mother.

Most of her hair was gone, fallen out from decay. The skin on her face was pulled tight across her cheeks and the white glow of cheekbone flashed in the darkness. Her nose had caved in and her eyes (both still there) leaked drops of pus and blood from the tear ducts. She stared at her son.

Peter was speechless. The last time he saw his mother she was running from the house trying to find his father, who was looking for bullets for his rifle in the truck. She still wore her red sweater, although now it hung in patches around her sunken chest. She placed one hand on the side of the ladder and continued to stare at Peter.

"Mom."

It was a small sound and he finally realized it had come from his mouth. Tears came back into his eyes and he watched as one fell from his face and landed on the ground in front of where she stood.

"Mommy." He placed one foot on the ladder and turned to climb down. A rustling sound came from the brush. Quickly, Peter turned. His father stumbled from the undergrowth and stood behind his mother. His mom's eyes never wavered from her son.

His father looked far worse than his mom. The top half of his skull was missing and his jaw hung loose from one hinge. The only clothes he wore were his pants, gratefully covering his crotch area. He shuffled up to his wife and looked around the clearing. His jaw kept clacking shut on its one hinge.

Peter continued to steady himself on the ladder. His parents had come back. They came back to get him. He crept down two rungs of the ladder and looked back towards the ground. His mom let go of the ladder and reached both arms up towards Peter. A low groan escaped her green lips.

"Mommy, I'm so scared. Please…."

Three more rungs down the ladder and now he could hear his dad usher his own groan, full of hurt and pain and wanting.

Peter flashed back to the last day he saw his father. The zombies were attacking the surrounding neighborhood. His dad grabbed his rifle from the closet and headed outside to the truck. He had turned to his mother and Peter and said:

"I'll be back. Stay here. Don't let anyone in."

As they watched his father struggle to load the gun, a zombie was shuffling across the lawn towards the truck. His mother ran out to warn his dad and bring him back inside. She squeezed Peter's hand and closed the front door behind her. Peter watched from the window.

They never saw the three undead come from around the corner of the house. As his mom and dad fought off the first dead man, the others swarmed them. Peter had screamed and screamed, beating his fists against the window. Then he ran to his room and hid in his closet.

A week later he was on the tower. His parents had disappeared from the front lawn.

Now they were here and everything would be alright. They could be together again. Peter continued down the ladder. His mother waited with open arms.

When his feet were close enough, he felt her grab his ankle in both hands and pull. Hard. He looked down and saw his parents snarling up at him. His mother was drooling as she held his ankle tight.

"Please mommy, don't," Peter pleaded. His eyes filled with tears and snot ran from the tip of his nose. The snarling intensified as his father now tried to reach for his other ankle.

Peter kicked out with his foot and caught his mom above the eye. She let go, falling back a step. Peter climbed out of reach and hung there, looking down.

His parents continued to look up greedily. His father grabbed the sides of the ladder and tried to shake Peter off. But the ladder held tight and did not budge.

"No, Dad. Please let me come down." Peter watched his parents and slowly realized they were not his parents anymore. They would never be his parents again.

Slowly he climbed up the ladder and settled on the platform. He wiped his eyes with his shirt tail, leaning against the safety rail. Below, the moans grew louder. Peter closed his eyes tight and wished them away.

After about twenty minutes, he heard the zombies shuffle off into the underbrush. Peter crawled back into the tent and cried himself to sleep.

He woke to rain slapping the tent roof. Wiping the sleep from his eyes, he peeked out from under the shelter and studied the murky day. The sky was a dark gray and he watched as puddles of water gathered on the tower platform.

Peter grabbed a jacket from the rear of the shelter and went to the safety railing. He looked out towards the town. The zombies walked the street here and there, looking miserable in the wet precipitation. Their skin was even more mottled and rotted from the dampness.

He was relieved to see no sign of his parents anywhere. Wrapping the jacket around himself tighter, he went back into the tent. He lay on his back, studying the roof, deep in thought. *I'm not alone. There are others out there. I can get help. Others will come and I can be rescued.*

This was the first time Peter ever entertained the thought of rescue, ever thought he needed to be rescued. The past few days helped him recognize exactly what his situation was. He could not keep going on like this forever. Eventually supplies would run out, or worse, he would finally be caught. He shuddered, thinking back on his dream. The vision of Carter being ripped apart flashed before his eyes.

What do I do? How can I get rid of them all? He picked up his GamePak and turned on *Innocent Bystander*. But after a few minutes, he grew bored with the game and turned it off. He stared out into the daylight, and watched the rain fall.

A seed started to grow in his mind. By the time the rain stopped falling and the sun began to peek out from behind the dark clouds, Peter was preoccupied with a plan, one that could change his situation for the better.

As night fell, Peter finally made himself eat. Crunching down a bag of chips, his stomach was full of butterflies at the thought of all he needed to do tomorrow. He finished the bag and threw it over the side. He crawled back into the tent and got ready for bed.

A long time passed before he fell asleep.

He was up bright and early the next day. Grabbing his pack, he threw two bottles of water, a handful of cookies, and some candy bars into it. He scrambled down the ladder and carefully headed for Main Street.

The zombies were still grouped around the glowing lights of the theatre and ice cream shop. He knew it would only be a few minutes before the sun would be up and they would lose interest in the incandescent glows.

Climbing the fire escape, he thought about his plan and where he needed to go today. The first stop would be the supply shed that sat behind the town offices. It held the lawn equipment the maintenance crews used for yard work. But Peter was not looking for weed eaters or leaf blowers. He hoped to find the red cans he always saw sitting next to the equipment trucks.

He jumped to the roof of the theater and double checked that the entrance was still open. Satisfied, he jumped across to the inn. His sliding feet knocked a few roof tiles to the ground again. He heard the low groans of zombies startled by the falling debris.

Ignoring his dead audience, Peter made his way onto

the roof of the town offices. There was no fire escape or ladder, and no door with access to the interior. He walked around the edge looking for a way to get down. He saw the supply shed sitting in the shade of a large oak tree. There were two lawnmowers, retired under tarps, waiting to be fired up to trim the town medians. He was so close.

I can't stop now. I just started, Peter thought to himself. He noticed a drainpipe hooked to the corner of the building. Looking down, he saw that it passed about two feet from one of the office windows. Cinching his backpack tight, he dropped his legs over the side and grasped the drainpipe.

Slowly he inched his way down the pipe. The windowsill was only a few feet away now. He would have to kick the glass in before he would have anywhere to put his feet.

Halfway down, Peter heard groans from the ground beneath him. A group of the undead gathered below, watching his progress intently. A few of them reached their arms up, trying to grab the boy, but he was a good three stories up.

Great. Can't they leave me alone?

He was to the windowsill now and reaching out with his foot, kicked at the glass. It took a couple of tries before the window gave. With a huge crash, the glass shattered, raining down onto the zombies below. One of them opened his mouth to catch a few of the shards.

Carefully Peter sidled into the broken window. But to no avail. When he dropped to the floor of the office, he noticed drops of blood falling to the bright cream-colored carpet. He had cut his arm on a large sliver of glass.

Grasping it tightly, Peter sucked in his breath. *Damn, it hurts.* Looking around he tried to find something to stop the bleeding with. The office was furnished with a desk and file cabinets and a few comfortable looking chairs.

He saw a scarf hanging from a coat rack and wrapped it around his arm. The cut wasn't deep but large enough to be a nuisance. Waiting a few minutes for the bleeding to slow, Peter tried to think about the layout of the building.

He had visited the town offices only once before, with his dad. His father picked up a small parking fine; and after much grumbling and procrastinating finally headed down to pay. Since it was on a Saturday, Peter got to ride along. He remembered the smiling female clerk who helped his dad and the cold white linoleum floors of the hallway.

He only got to see a bit of the first floor, but he did remember seeing the stairway. Now he sat on a third floor office. He needed to find those stairs and make his way to the bottom floor and out the rear entrance to the supply shed.

He crept to the office door and opened it a few inches. The corridor was dark. Quickly he eased out the office and into the hallway. He wasn't sure if there were any zombies inside or not. It was better to be safe than sorry.

He crept down the hallway, passing closed office doors on either side. The hall ran into a second corridor and Peter peeked around both corners of the T-Intersection. One way held more offices but the other path ended with the stairs he was looking for.

He raced up to the large double doors and quietly slipped into the stairway.

Peter gagged as the horrible smell engulfed him. He fought his urge to vomit and pulled his shirt up over his mouth and nose. Sunlight drifted in the small windows of the stairwell, leaving enough light for Peter to make his way down to the other floors.

He climbed down to the second floor. The smell grew

worse and his eyes began to water heavily. The doors to the second floor were closed, but Peter could make out the garish large streaks of blood and gore that covered the windows. Flies buzzed incessantly around the doorway.

Quickly, Peter slipped past the doors and headed to the first floor. The smell began to lighten a bit but still was heavy even on the first floor. As he stepped off the stairs his foot kicked something against the wall of the small corridor.

His heart skipped a beat as he made out the shape of the hand his foot hit. Peter could see something glinting on one of the fingers and a few seconds later he realized it was a diamond ring. The fingernails were painted a nice pink, but most of the flesh was past rotting. *A woman's hand,* he thought. He wondered if it belonged to the smiling clerk from his memory.

Peter snuck up to the first floor windows and peeked through. He could see the treasurer's office his dad had visited and beyond that where the hall turned the corner. He was sure that the rear entrance would be found there. He opened the door and entered the hallway.

It was cooler here on the first floor, and darker. This floor held the least amount of offices, but Peter was surprised to find every single door open. As he passed each office, he quickly scanned the interior for movement. Even the supply closet was open. Peter glanced at the cleaners and scrubbers in their brightly colored packaging. He was about to move on when something else caught his eyes. There was a hammer leaning against the bottom of the closet. Quickly Peter grabbed it and held it tightly in his fingers. He felt safer with the newfound weapon.

He was past the treasurer's office and almost to the turn in the hall when he came upon a *closed* office door.

This one was marked "MAYOR REGINALD TURNER" in large black letters on the smoked glass. He recalled the Mayor, a nice jolly man who always gave a small speech before the Fourth of July fireworks and could be seen reading classic literature in the park on the weekends.

Why is this the only door closed? Peter wondered. He leaned close to the door, trying to pick up any sounds from inside the office. After a few minutes of silence, he decided to move on. He tightened his hold on the hammer and ducked past the door.

Now he was at the turn in the hallway. The young boy knelt at the corner of the wall and peered around it. *There was the rear door!* He could see the yellow shaded supply building through the small glass window.

The hall looked clear and Peter stood up to make his way to the door.

A large crash echoed in the hall behind him. He heard a loud growl and realized the sounds came from the Mayor's office door banging into the wall. He peeked behind him.

Mayor Reginald stood in the middle of the hall, his large distended belly swelling behind his dress shirt and tie. He was covered in gore from head to toe. Peter was horrified as he watched the Mayor lift a rotted leg to his mouth and take a large bite. As the Mayor chewed on his constituent's hearty donation, Peter stifled a scream.

Reginald saw the young boy. He dropped the drumstick to the floor with a loud *PLOP* and started after Peter. He sniffed the air, catching a whiff of something enticing.

He smells the blood from my arm! Peter's heart started hammering in his chest.

Peter turned and ran for the door. Reginald was fast, faster than any of the other zombies outside.

Maybe he has more energy from all the food he's been eating.

Peter now understood why the second floor doors were covered in so much blood.

He hit the release on the rear door and pushed with all his might.

The door was heavy and Peter had to put his full weight on it to open it. And the Mayor was coming on fast. Peter could hear the large man licking his chops in-between heavy footfalls. The hall was full of loud snuffles as the man smelled the blood soaked scarf.

The door flew open and Peter felt the large girth of the man slam into his back. Both bodies stumbled through the doorway and out into the daylight. Peter rolled over onto his side. His breath was ragged now and his back hurt. It hurt a lot.

He stole a glance at his quarry. Reginald had landed face first, sprawled across the wide cement sidewalk that traveled around the side of the building. Peter tried to catch his breath as the Mayor's head rose, revealing the mess of his busted face. The large man's eyes were shut tightly and his mouth let out a large snarl of pain.

Peter stumbled to his feet, looking for the hammer. He saw it lying next to the doorway, behind the mass of dead man who was getting to his hands and knees.

Peter willed his young legs to move and dashed around the Mayor. Too late. He felt a large hand grab his ankle and he fell back to the ground.

But not before his hands found the hammer.

The Mayor was pulling himself up, using Peter's leg as leverage. Peter spun around and kicked out with both legs. The Mayor fell back to the earth, landing right next to his prey.

Peter rolled fast on his back and buried the sharp end of the hammer in the Mayor's ear. There was a meaty

THUNK, and the hammer stuck deep. He watched as the zombie shuddered violently and finally quit moving.

He pushed himself away from the fat man and leaned against the cool brick wall. *Stay calm. Deep breaths.* He was on the verge of hyperventilating, but managed to stay in control.

Focus on what needs to be done. He was starting to calm down. *This is why you are going to do this.*

This is why you are going to kill them all.

VIII.

The red cans sat right inside the shed door. There were three of them. He picked each of them up and shook them. He could smell the sweet metallic scent of gasoline coming from inside. Two of the cans were full, but the third was empty.

He thought about trying to get more of the cans and filling them from Lucky's Fill-Up. But the station was located right in the center of town and he could not roof jump to it. By the time he even got the nozzle in the can, he would be overwhelmed anyways.

This will have to be enough. He would have to be smart with it. Make sure he got the most out of the little bit of fuel.

Getting the cans back out to the street was the challenge now. They were heavy and the extra weight would be a death sentence if he tried to roof jump or carry them in his hands.

Peter looked around the interior of the small supply building. It was packed with equipment and tools. Back in the corner he spotted something that could prove useful. A large red radio flyer wagon sat full of empty flower pots.

It was rusting out on the sides and peeling paint but would suffice for what he needed to do.

It took quite a bit of time before he managed to work the wagon out of the shed. He flipped it over and dumped the trash and rust from the inside. He sat both cans in the bottom of the wagon and threw his backpack down next to them.

I'll have to go the street way. It'll be dangerous and I'll have to be very, very careful. The street was crowded with cars, most of them parked on either side. He could use those for cover and hopefully work his way to his destination.

"I need some weapons," he said aloud. His voice sounded weird, and a bit awkward in the quiet afternoon. He glanced back at the hammer stuck in the Mayor's head. He really did not want to try and retrieve that bit of nastiness. He looked back in the shed. After careful thought, he settled on a medium sized shovel that was perfect for his size and a heavy duty crowbar. He placed the weapons into the wagon.

Grabbing the handle, he pulled the wagon around the building and settled in behind a stalled mini-van parked out front. Peter studied Main Street.

The zombies were spread throughout the town. They were hovering around in small groups. Fortunately they were staying towards the middle of the street. He could pretty much stay out of sight by keeping behind the parked cars. The key was to be as quiet as possible. Peter reached back and grabbed the crowbar in his free hand.

He started up the street.

The wagon was quiet and he was grateful for the small rubber tires. He saw a zombie stumble across the sidewalk and make its way into one of the alleys. He glanced down the alley, watching the zombie carefully as he pulled the wagon past.

So far, so good. Then Miss Swanbee stepped from between two cars and stood in his way. His mind instantly flashed back to the dream, and he could see her pushing her hips against the car's windshield again. He stopped in his tracks.

The old woman stared at him for a second. Then she pitched forward to grab Peter. He stepped back and swung the crowbar, catching Swanbee in the neck. There was a loud gurgle and the woman moaned. Peter brought the crowbar around again and connected with her head. She went down.

But not before every zombie on the street noticed the commotion.

He grabbed the wagon and started to run up the sidewalk as fast as he could go. Zombies were shuffling quickly towards him. He would need to be quick or he would be overwhelmed. Someone grabbed his arm from behind and Peter swung around with the crowbar.

The metal smacked into the head of a man he vaguely recognized. Peter ducked as the man's head exploded. Blood and gore rained down on the concrete. More zombies were crowding the sidewalk now and Peter swung out wildly with the crowbar, connecting every time.

He spotted a hole form in the small crowd and pushed his way through. Once he was clear of the zombies, he sprinted up the street with the wagon bouncing along behind him. He could hear the horde following him.

I need to get to the tower. But first I got to stash the wagon. He ran around the rear of a pickup truck and glanced back to his pursuers. He had put some distance between him and the horde. Peter threw the gas cans into the bed of the truck and grabbed the crowbar. He ran for the tower as fast as he could.

Peter slung the crowbar into his backpack and climbed the ladder quickly. The zombies (now twice the number than before) arrived at the tower just as Peter pulled himself up on the platform. He slid into the tent and flipped over on his back. His breath came in ragged gulps as he tried to catch his breath from running.

So close, so close. He stared at the tent roof and listened to the moans and growls of the dead below.

It was close to three hours before the dead citizens dispersed. He waited another forty-five minutes after the last zombie had left before climbing back down the ladder. He needed to get the cans from the truck and move them to the theater.

Peter snuck back down to the street and grabbed the cans from the pickup's bed. He needed to be fast so he left the pack and crowbar at the tower. It was getting later in the afternoon but the air had grown more humid than this morning. Most of the zombies were gathered around the trees in the park or seeking cooler shelter elsewhere.

Peter walked quickly down to the movie theater and placed the cans at the front entrance. He ran to the side of the building and climbed the access ladder to the roof. Moving fast, he opened the front doors from the inside and brought the cans into the cool lobby, locking the doors behind him.

I made it. Oh shit, I actually made it. Even with everything that happened today, Peter managed a grin in the dense light. *Now to get everything ready.*

He went up to the projection room and got the reel set up. He also looked over the controls, turning the lights and the surround sound all the way up. Then he brought both gas cans into the large screen room.

He poured gasoline down each aisle and across the aisle that ran in front of the stadium. The smell began to make him feel lightheaded as it collected in the large room. He poured the last of the fuel up the steps to the roof door, ending in a large puddle at the foot of the door.

He covered his mouth with his shirt and walked back to the lobby. He took anything flammable he could find in the lobby, the manager's office, and the projection room and stuffed it all into the aisles and seats of the screen room. Old movie posters, company papers, and dusty flyers made their way into the twisted stacks of tinder.

After he was finished with setting up everything, Peter snuck to the front entrance. The street in front of the theater was clear. He unlocked all the glass doors and propped them open. Then he ran back to the roof and waited for nightfall.

As soon as the sun disappeared behind the horizon, the lights to the theater and ice cream shop cut on. The zombies gathered in the street, hypnotized by the bright glow. Peter ducked back down the stairs and hurried to the projection room. Already he could hear a handful of undead searching the lobby for food.

He made it to the projector and flipped the switch. As he ran back to the stairwell, he could hear the first preview fire up on the big screen. He smiled as he heard how loud the surround sound was in the large room.

Peter ran across the roof and looked down to the front entrance. He was relieved to see the doors fill with undead bodies as the zombies crowded inside. He could hear gunfire erupt as the next preview began to play. He had chosen *Jurassic Park: The Return,* figuring the thunderous soundtrack would grab the most attention.

He glanced across the street. The zombies at the ice cream shop were heading this way and there were several more coming from the suburban side of the town. Peter whooped and yelled from his vantage point on top of the building, trying to garner more attention to the theater.

"C'mon you bastards. Every single one of you, get your asses over her!" A few of the crowd glanced up at him, but then turned their attention back to the noisy theater.

Peter heard glass breaking as one of the front doors finally gave way. He looked down and saw some of the zombies had fallen in the doorway and were being trampled. The night was filled with the roar of dinosaurs as the movie began.

He walked back to the roof door and opened it slightly, making sure there were no wanderers on the stairs. The smell of gas was thick in the enclosed space. Quickly he ran back to the edge of the roof and checked on the front doors. Almost all of the zombies were either in the theater or trying to get in the theater. It was time.

Calmly he walked back to the door. He stooped down at the edge of the gas puddle and reached into his pocket. Peter opened the pack of matches and struck one. He dropped the match on the fuel and jumped back. The gas caught instantly and raced down the steps into the theater.

Peter jumped across to the next building and climbed down.

He ran to where he had abandoned the wagon and grabbed the shovel. He crossed to the far side of the street and stood in front of the theater. Smoke was already pouring from the front entrance. He could hear something breaking in the lobby area. The smoke and fire only served to drive the zombies at the front entrance into more of a frenzy to get in.

One of the zombies stumbled back away from the theater into the street. It was Roberts, the dogcatcher. Peter ran up behind the man and slammed the shovel down on his head. Roberts dropped to the asphalt. Peter slammed the shovel down again and the dogcatcher stopped moving.

Flames were heard crackling in the theater and smoke poured from the top of the roof now. Two more zombies staggered back from the entrance and Peter quickly dispatched them with the shovel.

A dinosaur screamed from the building, which now licked flames from around the windows and doors. Gunfire erupted as someone tried to kill the dinosaur that was still roaring into the night. Peter caught a whiff of something burning, and realized it was rotting flesh.

Zombies began to back from the entrance and Peter ran and smacked them with the shovel. Most of them fell quickly as the heavy metal connected with their soft flesh. He found himself swinging two or three times to take down some of the tougher foes; and soon his arms grew tired.

He could no longer hear the movie playing over the sound of the fire as it ate the building whole. Zombies were now fleeing, covered in flames and falling to the street where they lay burning until they stopped moving.

Peter watched as the fire grew bigger and bigger. Embers floated into the still air and he shouted in vain as the inn caught on fire from the neighboring theater.

"Shit!" He did not want to burn the whole town down. He watched anxiously as the roof of the inn began to burn.

The theater's front entrance began to collapse and Peter backed up a few steps as debris began to fall from the walls. The roof of the inn was burning heavily now.

Need to get back to the tower. Safest place to be now. He wasn't sure how to access the water in the tank, but the thought of sitting next to several thousand gallons of water comforted him. He looked around one final time for any moving bodies. He could see burning shadows bumping into each other in the confines of the theater.

Peter walked back towards the tower.

As he passed the alley next to Susie's Gift and Thrift, movement caught his peripheral vision. He glanced into the dark alleyway. Something was crawling quickly towards him. He stepped back a few paces into the glow of the fire. Sandy Kramer crawled from the darkness and glared at Peter with her good eye. Her clothes were completely worn away now and Peter stared at the pale skin on her back and buttocks.

She pulled herself towards him and grabbed his ankle. As she turned to sink her teeth into the bare flesh above his sock, Peter brought the sharp edge of the shovel down on her neck. The blade cut halfway through the muscle to the bone. Sandy's head plopped, face first, against the rough sidewalk. Peter left the shovel sticking out of the dead girl's neck and climbed the ladder of the water tower.

IX.

He stayed up all night watching the fire burn. About two hours in, the theater collapsed and smoke and dust billowed in the air. The roof and top floor of the inn continued to burn, but early in the cool morning, the fire lost its momentum and started to flicker out.

Peter saw several zombies crawl from the wreckage of the building. They moved a few feet, smoldering like bright campfire embers on a summer night, then would collapse among their fellow un-dead, never moving again.

The smoke drifted over the tower a few times and he smelled the stench of burnt flesh and film negatives. Sandy Kramer still lay with the shovel saluting the night sky.

He tried not to think about his parents. But wondered if they perished in the theater with the rest of the town. *At least everyone went out watching a good movie,* he thought. The sun began to creep over the horizon, casting soft morning rays on the devastated buildings.

Peter stood up and grasped the railing, surveying the town. Nothing moved and the only sound he heard was the crackling of burning wood. No birds stirred. No zombies marched to and fro. No one shuffled underneath the ladder. The underbrush and surrounding trees stood still as statues. Life had ceased for Rockville.

He blinked his eyes in disbelief. *I did it. I can't believe I did it.*

There would still be a handful of zombies around for sure. But it wouldn't be anything he could not handle. Peter would be able to walk the streets of his town again. He would be able to explore the houses and find more supplies.

He could go back home.

He felt happy. He felt surprised at his accomplishment. He felt hungry. He felt safe.

And after all those feelings finally abated….

…..he felt *alone*.

Peter reached for his bag. He grabbed the GamePak, throwing it inside and climbed down the ladder.

It was time to start a new game.

BOOM

I.

(tick tick tick tick tick)

Ulee was pissing on his car. Jeffrey Walls looked at the young man and his shoulders dropped. Every morning Ulee and Pierce met him at his car, and every morning he caught them doing something gross on or around his car. Well, except for that one morning when the only thing that greeted him was the steaming pile of dog shit that was sitting right next to the driver's door. He didn't see anyone near the vehicle that morning, but he knew it was them. It was always them.

Ever since he bought the silver Nissan Altima, Ulee picked on him about. He just had to say something. At least that was how it began. Now they knew Walls wasn't going to do anything about it, and they had taken their actions up a notch. And Walls wasn't going to fight. He just was not one for confrontation. He couldn't seem to find the strength to stand up for himself. He usually felt numb to those around him.

Ulee turned at the sound of the vehicle's owner striding up the sidewalk. Jeffrey had left the apartment a little earlier for work, thinking he could bypass this whole experience. He glanced at Pierce as he walked by. Pierce had a little gleam in his eye to match the multiple piercings tattooing his face. A smile crept across his lips as Jeffrey walked by.

"Morning, Walls," he said. Jeffrey nodded slightly his way, than turned his attention to Ulee.

"Shit, Walls." Ulee was zipping up his fly. "I'm really sorry. I had to go so bad, and....well, ya know." Ulee grinned his big stupid *What the fuck you going to do about it?* grin. Pierce stepped behind Jeffrey.

"I mean, its okay? Right, Walls?" Ulee flexed his muscular arms, covered with black inky designs of dragons and half dressed women. Even though Jeffrey was a head taller than both men, he seemed weak and complacent in his white shirt, striped tie, and khaki pants.

"It's fine. I need to get to work, Ulee." Jeffrey barely mumbled the words. He didn't make eye contact, only shuffled towards the driver's door. Ulee stepped out of the way with a slight bow.

"It's such a nice car, Walls. Silver, man, that's a tight color on those Nissans." It was the same thing all the time. They always complimented him on the car. It was brand new, a graduation gift to himself, the only thing he owned that was worth something. "What do you think, Pierce?"

Pierce slid up beside Ulee, the chains connecting his bling rattling slightly.

"Well, I'm not much on those Jap cars. Seems like a bunch of rice eaters wouldn't know anything about precision performance. But hey, it is a nice looking automobile." Ulee nodded his head in agreement.

Jeffrey grabbed the door handle. He quickly let go of it when he noticed it was wet. Ulee and Pierce were rolling on the grass laughing hysterically.

"Just a little joke! I swear no harm!" Ulee was cackling like a hyena. "Shit, his face, Pierce."

Jeffrey held down the bile trying to escape from his stomach.

Ulee had pissed on the door handle.
(tick tick tick tick tick tick)

Jeffrey pulled the car out of the apartment complex. He stopped at the small gas station on the corner and went to the bathroom to wash his hands.

He scrubbed hard under the water, rinsing the soap suds down the rusty drain. Once he was satisfied the piss germs were gone, he splashed water onto his face and slicked back his hair. Jeffrey stared in the mirror at his reflection. His eyes seemed hollow. They were bloodshot from lack of sleep. The bones stuck outward from around the sockets.

He rubbed the high cheekbones he had inherited from his father. He frowned at the pale skin stretched across his tight forehead. *At least I got rid of the glasses.* He hated the black horn rims, and opted for contacts his sophomore year of college.

Jeffrey looked down at his shirt. There was a wet stain above the belt, slowly drying a soft yellow color. It was where he wiped his hand after getting into his car. Good thing he had an extra dress shirt at work in his locker.

Those fuckers. I hate them. I hate them so much.
The faucet dripped steadily in the sink.
drip drip drip (tick tick tick)

Jeffrey dried his face and brought out a small bottle of aspirin from his pocket. He hadn't even made it to work yet, and the headache was already in full swing. He emptied half the pills into his mouth and slurped water from the faucet.

(tick tick tick tick)

He slammed the paper towels into the wastebasket.

"Please fucking go away!"

The door slammed against the cement wall as he stalked back to his car.

II.

It was going on three months since the noise had begun. The incessant countdown in his head, drumming away sleep and sanity inch by inch until it wore Jeffrey down to another level of numbness. After two weeks of no rest and throbbing headaches, Jeffrey finally went to the doctor for some help.

He sat in the white observation room, looking over the diagrams describing particular illnesses he was sure he had or was surely going to get in this horribly unlucky life he led. When he had memorized all the posters in the room, he stared numbly at the white walls until the doctor arrived.

(tick tick tick tick tick tick tick tick tick tick tick)

Like ants marching to the beat of the devil's drum.

The door opened and a short, balding man entered, stethoscope draped around his neck.

"Hello, Jeffrey. I'm Dr. Neese." Neese was reading over the notes and information gathered from Jeffrey by the nurse earlier.

Jeffrey nodded his head slightly in reply. The doctor sat

on a small stool and rolled over to the examination table. He looked at the young man seated in front of him.

"What seems to be the problem?"

Jeffrey sat up a bit straighter on the table.

"You see, uhm, I'm having a little problem sleeping." Neese nodded his head as if he already knew all the burdens that Jeffrey carried on his shoulders.

"Tell me about it."

"I really haven't slept in about two weeks. I keep hearing things."

"What kind of things?"

"Noises."

"Like voices?" Neese started jotting notes in a small pad.

"What? No, no, nothing like that." Jeffrey was a little surprised at the question. But he understood the underlying meaning of it. *I'm not crazy. No matter what you think, I'm not losing my mind.*

"It's like a ticking. A clock ticking all the time." He closed his eyes, feeling the lack of sleep weighing on him, but when he re-opened them the feeling softened.

Neese shook his head and made a few more marks with his pen.

"Let me ask you. Is the "ticking" more in your ears or in your head?"

"Both. And it's not just at night. I hear it all the time. At work, at home. I can hear it right now."

Dr. Neese rolled the stool back to the small desk and looked over the file folder. "Is there anything else you're noticing with the sound? Fever, nausea, anything like that?"

"No. I just hear the noise and can't sleep. I mean, I'm not tired, or not as tired as I should be. I still go to work and everything." Jeffrey took a large breath and let it out. "It just won't stop. All day long I hear it until I almost forget about it. And then I notice it again."

The doctor nodded. He returned to the file folder.

"It says here, Jeffrey, you just graduated from college. Architecture degree." Jeffrey nodded. "It also says your parents died in a car crash your sophomore year. Neither one survived." He looked up sadly at his patient.

Jeffrey nodded again. Neese continued. "You don't have any other family. You're not married. What about work? How's being an architect?"

"I'm not. An architect that is."

Neese seemed confused.

"I couldn't get a position. The economy is shit, I mean, excuse me. No one is looking for new architects right now."

"I see. The economy's been crappy to us all." The doctor smiled. "Even to us doctors."

He took out a prescription pad. "Here's what I think. Physically you check out super healthy. So I'm thinking this is a mental thing."

Jeffrey began to object. Neese stopped him.

"I know what you're going to say. I saw the notes on the counseling you had after your parents' death. I'm not talking grief related or depression mental thing. I'm talking more of a stress related condition."

"Oh." Jeffrey nodded. "You know, I do feel stressed out a lot. I feel like a lot of pressure is always bearing down on me."

"Exactly. And that can lead to loss of sleep, which in turn can lead to the body experiencing even more stressful tendencies. In this case, the sound you keep hearing. It's like a ringing in your ears."

Jeffrey watched as the doctor wrote out a prescription. "I am going to give you a powerful sedative to help you sleep. Do not drink alcohol with it and do not take more than what is prescribed. But it should fix you right up."

Jeffrey leaned back. "Thank you, doc. I'm glad you can help."

Neese smiled. "That's what I'm here for." He handed the slip of paper over to his young patient. "So it sounds like a clock, you say, ticking down to something?"

"Yeah, like that stopwatch they always showed before 60 minutes."

"Huh," Neese laughed, "I wonder what it's counting down to?"

There was a long pause before the patient responded.

"I don't know."

(tick tick tick tick tick)

III.

The pills did not work. He took the prescribed amount the first three nights, hoping upon hope he would finally sleep. Nothing. He doubled the amount the following night and then tripled it. By the end of the week he was taking six at a time and nothing changed. He spent most of his nights parked in front of the television, watching whatever late shows were lucky enough to get the 3 a.m. slot. After another week of no sleep, no rest, he began driving around the city and stopping at whatever happened to be opened.

Jeffrey spent many nights walking the aisle of Big Mart, looking at clothes he could not afford or the big screen TV he dreamed of owning. One night he came upon a small set of workout weights that were heavily discounted. On a whim, he bought them. That night he started a steady routine of pushups, crunches, flies, and curls. *I'll wear myself out until my body has no choice but to pass out.*

It didn't work. He never felt tired. But he found he did like the feel of working out, of pushing his body as hard as he could. He would sweat out the wounds of the day: Ulee and Pierce, work, bills and student loans, and gasping for breath almost forget about the sound. He would turn the water to burning hot in the shower, and there under the stinging droplets, it would come back from the depths of his mind.

(tick tick tick tick)

Jeffrey thought over all of this as he turned into the parking lot of High Tec Stereo & Sound. He had worked at High Tec for the past six months. It was the only job he could find after graduation. He garnered a nice windfall from the life insurance his parents had taken out, but it was almost gone having been swallowed up by the student loans needed for Georgia State. The electronics store wasn't the ideal place Jeffrey wanted to be, but it paid the bills.

He pushed open the glass door of the store and walked into the sweltering showroom. It was going to be a hot day, but Donovan never turned on the air conditioning.

"We're not one of those corporate box stores. This isn't Great Buy or Stereo City. I'm small fish," Donovan gritted between his nicotine stained teeth. This was the response whenever someone asked him why they never turned the air on. Jeffrey always wondered how much air conditioning they could have if Donovan didn't own a brand new Lincoln Continental.

He walked through the rear of the store to the employee locker room and grabbed the extra dress shirt in his locker. While he was changing, he heard Griffin come in.

"Hey, Walls. Damn, you been working out." Jeffrey quickly buttoned up his shirt in embarrassment. Griffin was the senior salesman at High Tec. He was a few years older than Jeffrey, but where Jeffrey lacked self-esteem, Griffin more than made up for in bravado.

Griffin was very popular with the employees and customers, as proven by his being top salesperson every month for the past year. He also dated Allison, the store secretary, and the most beautiful woman Jeffrey had ever seen.

"You ready to go out there and make some money, brother." Griffin grinned maniacally at Jeffrey. "Let's go find some suckers, yeah. Make some money and then bang some pussy, hey Walls?" Jeffrey looked at Griffin and tried to return his smile. It came out looking like a half-crazed leer. Griffin never noticed.

Griffin fixed his hair in the mirror and winked at his reflection. He smacked Jeffrey on the shoulder and headed for the door.

"Got to go see my bitch. See you out there, Walls." Griffin strutted out of the room.

Jeffrey slammed the locker door closed.

(tick tick tick)

They started every day with a store meeting, going over yesterday's sales numbers and tracking the monthly quota. Donovan always leaned to one side, usually reading the paper while Darryl, the assistant manager, led the meeting. Where Donavan was overweight and balding, Darryl was fit and tan. He looked at each one of the staff: the four salespeople, two warehouse workers, and Allison. The meetings were usually short and sweet with Griffin always getting praise for setting some sales record.

Jeffrey stood trying not to look at Allison. She was next to Griffin, who was patting her ass softly as Darryl yelled at one of the warehouse workers for checking in shipments wrong. She was wearing a nice pair of black slacks and a blue blouse. She was stunning with her blue eyes and blonde hair.

Jeffrey watched as Griffin leaned over and whispered something into her ear. Allison giggled and slapped his wandering hand away.

How could something so lovely be with something so horrible? Jeffrey stared at the curve of her neck, the soft luminescence of her skin. *I'm not horrible. I'm a good guy.*

"Walls!"

He looked up quickly. Darryl was speaking to him now.

"I need you and the rest of the crew to step up today and sell something." Jeffrey watched as small drops of spittle flew from Darryl's lips. Donovan flipped a page of the newspaper.

"Yes sir," Jeffrey replied.

"Remember, everyone who walks through our doors is a sale waiting to happen. It's up to you guys to convince them of that. Watch Griffin. Watch how he talks to people and imposes his will on them." Darryl nodded at Griffin. "You can learn a lot from watching him. And it would be nice if somebody else was salesman of the month for once."

"Not happening, boss," Griffin chirped. There was laughter all around.

"Now here is the new list of special offers. We got several coupons appearing...." Darryl droned on but Jeffrey looked out the front windows, wondering when exactly his dreams had started to fade away.

His eyes began to flit as they shook from the noise calling out behind his sockets.

(tick tick tick tick tick tick tick)

IV.

"What do you mean I can't use both of them?"

"Well, it plainly states on the ad, sir, you can only use one coupon per store visit." This was the third time Jeffrey had been through this with the older gentleman. The man was trying to buy a new DVD player and wanted to use double coupons, which was not allowed. Jeffrey could feel his patience beginning to turn.

"Tick."

"What?" The old man looked up at Jeffrey. Jeffrey looked back confused.

"What?" *Now what is this guy wanting.*

"What did you say?"

"I was saying that we cannot accept both coupons for the same...."

"No. I want to use both of them. I cut them both out of your ad this morning." The man's face was beginning to turn crimson, contrasting heavily with his white hair and bushy eyebrows.

"Jeffrey, can I see you for a bit?" Jeffrey turned to see Darryl standing close by. Griffin was next to him, smirking.

"I can't right now. I'm with a customer."

"Griffin will take over. Come back to the office with me. Donovan and I would like to speak with you."

Jeffrey sighed and turned to follow. *The office meant a lecture. Great.* He heard Griffin already charming the customer.

"Don't worry, sir. I'm going to take real good care of you."

"I hope so. That young man just doesn't get it."

"I get it, sir. Believe me I do."

Darryl opened the door to the office. Donovan was seated behind the large oak desk. He grabbed a handful of jelly beans from a small glass bowl sitting next to a picture of his wife. Jeffrey sat down in front of Donovan and Darryl took a seat beside the door. Donovan threw back his head and shook jellybeans into his mouth.

Jeffrey looked at the picture of the pretty wife. She was a sandy blond who looked ten years younger than she really was. Jeffrey had met her one time before at an office function. He remembered she had the body to match the pretty face.

Donovan swallowed his candy and cleared his throat.

"How's it going today, Walls?" The boss started drumming his fingers on the desktop.

"It's okay, I guess."

"What was happening with that customer? The old man? It seemed like you were having some trouble there." Donovan stopped drumming and leaned back in his large plush leather chair.

"Well yeah, he wanted to use double coupons. He can't do that." Jeffrey looked straight at his boss. "You always said never take double coupons. It's in the fine print and loses the store money."

Donovan laughed and Jeffrey heard a snicker in reply from Darryl.

"You are right. We did say that, didn't we Darryl?"

"Yep, that's how we train you."

Jeffrey nodded. *I was doing the right thing. They'll back me up.*

Donovan leaned forward, very serious now. "But...we have to remember the customer is *always* right too. You remember that golden rule in business, don't you Walls?"

"Well yeah but..."

"Because if the customer does not feel taken care of they will not spend money with us and they will not come back to spend more money with us and they will not tell all their friends and family to come spend money with us."

"Yeah."

"So do you think that gentleman felt like he was being taken care of out there?"

Jeffrey paused. *What the hell? I was doing the right thing.*

Donovan raised his eyebrows, questioning.

"Did you want me to take the double coupons? If we changed the policy, no one told me that," Jeffrey replied.

"Hell no!" Donovan's chair squealed on its small plastic wheels.

"Oh God no" came from Darryl.

"What was I doing wrong?" *Because I have no flippin' idea what you are expecting from me.* A headache formed in the front of Jeffrey's head, compounded by the dreadful sound rolling in his ears.

(tick tick tick tick tick tick tick tick tick)

"I want you to take care of the customer because they are always right." Donovan flashed a mighty grin and ran his hands back through his thinning hair.

"Even when the customer is wrong?"

Darryl piped up from behind Jeffrey. "Especially when they're wrong."

"Yes!" Donovan slapped his hand hard on the desktop. "Right on, Darryl."

He turned back to Jeffrey.

"That's when you show how strong you are, how

hungry you are. That's when you become the fucking animal."

Jeffrey was quiet. He wasn't sure what to say. So he said: "I don't understand."

"You see, Walls, I want every customer to feel that they're always right when they walk into my store. If they feel they are 'safe', they will be more willing to open their pockets and dig deeper for that big money we want." Donovan waved off Jeffrey's objection. "Now we both know a customer being right all the time is complete bullshit. But a salesman who can impose his will on a customer can turn bullshit into gold. Right, Darryl?"

"That's right, boss."

"A salesman who has the ferocious, confident nature of a beast can silence the questions and insecurities of a paltry little piss ant customer. A customer would never ever question a beast. They would only accept what they are told, and trust that the beast is going to lead them to the promise land. Because, fuck it, customers are the weak animals. They are the ones coming to us for their needs. And I'll be damned if they are going to dictate to us the terms of a sale." Donovan pointed his finger at Jeffrey. "You must become an animal."

What the hell are they talking about? Jeffrey gazed at Donovan.

Donovan reached into his desk and brought out a small folder. He flipped it open and began studying the contents.

"You've been here going on six months, Walls. And you have been the bottom salesperson every single month." The big man glanced up at Jeffrey and leaned back in his chair again. "Now I know you went to college and got a fancy pants engineering degree in whatever. But that don't count for shit around here. They don't teach you about the real world in college, about human nature. Look at me and Darryl. We didn't go to college and we're your boss, son."

Jeffrey nodded in agreement.

Donovan continued. "College makes men into sheep. And sheep are weak animals. We have no need for sheep around here." He leaned forward again. "I'm going to help you, Walls. I'm going to make you into something better. Because I don't think you want to be a sheep all your life, now do you?"

Jeffrey shook his head no.

"No one ever does. It's just the hand we're dealt," Darryl added solemnly.

"That's right, Darryl. It's just the hand you're dealt. I know you have had a hard couple of years, with your parents and all. But you can change all that. You can make yourself into the beast."

Donovan clasped his hands in front of him on the solid oak desk. "Look at Griffin. That young man is a tiger. Relentless and smart. He controls the customer's whims from the get go and they have no idea what is happening to them. He's a machine. He's even fucking that good looking broad, whatever her name is."

"Allison." Darryl again. Jeffrey perked up at the sound of her name.

"Yeah, he has it all because he's not a sheep. Now Darryl, Darryl is a bear. The wise old bear. Mean when he has to be but always watching and waiting. And when one of the cubs gets out of hand, he whacks the shit out of them and they get straight quick. And me..." Donovan grinned. "I'm the king. I'm the lion. And this store is my jungle and I control all of it. The lion is the boss. I bring all of you under my wing and protect you here in my store.

But the store is only as strong as its weakest link. And you don't want to be the weakest link, do you Walls?"

Donovan clapped his hands together. Darryl stood up behind Jeffrey.

"What kind of animal are you, Walls?" Donovan asked.

(tick tick tick tick tick) The headache was getting worse. Jeffrey looked up at his boss and shrugged his shoulders.

"I'm not sure, sir," he squeaked.

"Well, that's okay. That's fair. It's a big step. A brash move, especially when you've been a sheep most of your life." Donovan looked sympathetic. "Why don't you think on it a bit? Observe Griffin and Darryl out on the showroom. Sleep on it. We can talk more later."

Darryl opened the door and Jeffrey got up to leave.

"Oh one more thing, Walls," Donovan added. "I hate asking this of you, but you are the lowest on the seniority ladder. The shitter is clogged again. Take care of it please."

Jeffrey nodded his head and looked at the floor as he walked out the door. Darryl clapped him on the back as he closed the door behind him.

"Tick, Tick."

V.

The showroom was quiet. Usually in the middle of the day, business slowed down as many people were on lunch breaks. Jeffrey was leaving the bathroom with the cleaning supplies and met Donovan heading in with a magazine under his arm. Donovan spent much of his lunch break on the can, reading whatever he could find, which usually consisted of whatever nudie book was lying around in the rear warehouse.

Jeffrey walked towards the front of the store. It was

time for his break but he had no appetite. Lack of sleep had also led to lack of hunger. Besides the protein shakes and what little bit of dinner he nibbled at home, he hardly ate anything throughout the week.

He was getting ready to hop in his car and go for a drive when he heard his name being called.

"Jeffrey!"

It was Allison. She walked up to the car, a kind smile on her face.

"Hey. Do you want to go to lunch with me?" Jeffrey was not sure if he heard right.

"What about Griffin?" He shuffled his feet back and forth.

"He said he has to run a bunch of errands and won't have time for lunch today. We can go wherever you were heading. I just don't have a ride and I'm starving."

"Okay." Jeffrey opened the driver's door and got in. He thumbed the lock switch and Allison jumped in next to him.

"Wherever is fine," she said. Jeffrey nodded and pulled out of the parking lot.

They had Chinese for lunch. He wasn't that big on Chinese but it was close and Allison had mentioned before how she loved it. They sat waiting for their orders. Jeffrey stirred the straw in his drink and looked at the paper placemat. He wanted to talk but had no idea what to say. Allison looked around the restaurant and waved at a few people she knew.

"Work is so boring today."

"I'm sorry, what?" He did not realize she had spoken.

"I said work is so boring today."

Jeffrey nodded. "I think it's boring every day." Allison giggled at this and sipped her water.

"I heard you studied architecture in college." Her eyes were so blue and Jeffrey tried hard not to fall into them.

"Yeah, fat lot of good it did me. I'm still paying off student loans for knowledge that I'm currently not using."

"I know how that feels. I studied art in college. I was going to be the world's greatest painter. Now I'm the world's most mediocre secretary." Their food arrived and Allison dug into her beef and broccoli with relish.

"I don't think you're mediocre." Jeffrey hadn't touched his food yet. He just sat looking at this beautiful woman who he very much wanted to hold.

Allison smiled. "That was sweet of you to say. Whoa, Jeffrey Walls has got a sweet side."

Jeffrey smiled down at the table. "Don't get an occasion to show it much."

Allison reached over and touched his hand lightly.

"You should. It's nice to see a man who knows how to treat a woman." Jeffrey kept looking down at the table, hiding his blushing cheeks.

"What kind of art do you do?" He looked at her now, wanting her to really see him.

"I paint. I like drawing too but painting is my passion. I can really release a lot of things through my painting."

"That's good," he said. "It's good to have something that is just yours and yours alone. To be able to….express yourself."

Allison licked her lips and wiped her mouth with a napkin. "Yeah well, I need something. Working at Hi Tech isn't the most emotionally rewarding thing ever. Especially with Darryl and Donovan running the show." They both laughed. It was easy to laugh together. Comfortable.

"Griffin hates art. He thinks it's a weird hobby. He prefers video games and football." Jeffrey shook his head.

"He doesn't strike me as the emotional type."

Allison smiled.

Allison's phone started to chirp from her purse.

"Hello….Yeah, I'm having lunch…..with Jeffrey." She paused while listening to the response. "Stop it, Griffin. That's mean." Jeffrey pretended to study his food.

"Yeah, we're at Chow's. Okay, that's fine. I love you, too." He winced at the last line.

Allison flicked off the phone. "That was Griffin. He's going to swing by and pick me up."

"Hmm."

"This was really nice. We should do it again." Allison smiled again. *So beautiful.* "Oh, I have to leave some money for the food."

"No, no." Jeffrey waved her off. "I insist. It's my treat."

Allison reluctantly put away her wallet. "Okay, but next time it's on me." There was a loud growl from outside as Griffin pulled up in his new Charger. He had bought the car a few weeks back with his largest commission check yet. It was bright yellow with black racing stripes. Jeffrey had to admit it put his Altima to shame.

Allison got up from the table and headed out the door. "See you back there."

He watched as she ran to the car and jumped in the passenger side. Griffin kissed her hard, giving her a little bit of extra tongue just for Jeffrey's benefit. Then he turned and pointed his fingers into a gun and shot it through the window at his nemesis. They both waved and Griffin drove off in a wail of rubber.

Jeffrey pulled his wallet out and threw down some bills. He got up from the table and headed back to work.

He never touched any of his food.

MICHAEL WHETZEL

(tick tick tick tick tick tick tick tick tick tick tick tick tick)

That night Jeffrey sat in front of his television. He flipped through the channels, stopping briefly at every one, not really seeing what was on the screen. He looked up at the clock hanging in the small kitchen. It was a little after 2 am.

Jeffrey got up and pulled the weights and medicine ball from the closet. He began to do bicep curls in the middle of the room. Dressed in only his underwear, sweat began to drip down his lower back. He dropped the weights and started mountain climbers. His breath came in strong huffs as he pushed his body to the limit.

Back off the floor, now it was jumping jacks. His head was pounding but in a good way. He could feel the blood pulse in his temples, almost in time with the sounds.

(tick tick tick tick tick)

He plopped back down to the floor and began pushups. On and on and on past 30, now 50, finally out of breath when he reached a hundred. He grabbed the towel from the floor and wiped the sweat from his face and chest.

Back to bicep curls. He began noticing changes in his physique about two weeks ago. His arms were becoming muscular and more defined. His chest was also bigger and he began to see the beginnings of a six pack around his stomach. It made him feel good, these physical changes. He was a skinny, gangly kid in high school which carried over to college. Besides gaining the "freshman fifteen" his first year, he was still the same kid from earlier. His skinny build stood awkward when he was next to girls and especially next to other guys. The guys were all bigger than him, all athletes, the type the girls found attractive.

Like Griffin.

Jeffery began to shadowbox, something he only started doing this week. He punched his way around the living room, throwing jabs and overhands at imaginary opponents. And the opponents were always the same.

Ulee's face floated up in front of Jeffrey. He dispatched it with two left jabs and an uppercut. Peirce followed and was taken care of the same way. Donovan came into view and Jeffrey unleashed two strong left strikes and an uppercut to his boss' chin. The big man slammed backwards and was replaced with Darryl.

Jeffrey quick jabbed Darryl twice above the eye bringing blood into the older man's vision. He stepped back and ducked in with two hard body blows and another round of jabs to the head. He was toying with Darryl, leading the man back and forth, directing him with his punches. And with each jab, with each crossover thrown:

"Tick."

An audible sound escaping from Jeffrey's lips. He was as unaware of the vocalization as before.

"Tick."

Jab.

"Tick."

Jab. Jab.

"Tick, tick."

Huge uppercut and Darryl was knocked out. Jeffrey flicked sweat from his face and went in for the last round.

Griffin danced his way in front of Jeffrey. This round was different. Griffin was harder than the others. He knew how to fight back and deflect Jeffrey's shots. Jeffrey pushed in.

Straight jabs to the face landed, but Griffin shrugged them off. Jeffrey ducked and weaved as Griffin answered with jabs of his own. Back and forth, they exchanged punches looking for an opening in the other's defenses.

"Tick, tick."

Jab.

Jeffrey cut to the right and landed a body shot to Griffin's kidneys. Griffin's guard came down for a split second and Jeffrey landed three rights to the body and followed with a left crossover to the face. Griffin staggered back and Jeffrey closed with a flurry of punches. One two, one two, the furious onslaught staggered the bigger man.

Jeffrey bent at his knees and brought up a stupendous right uppercut that floored Griffin.

"BOOM!"

Jeffrey's voice thundered throughout the small apartment. A neighbor began pounding on the ceiling from downstairs, yelling for the noise to stop. Jeffrey swayed in the middle of the room. His mind was fogging up and his eyes were stinging with sweat.

Slowly, his head cleared. Jeffrey brought his hands up and wiped his eyes clean. He was drenched with sweat, but his body felt cool in the late air.

"Boom," he whispered to no one.

The apartment was still and quiet in the early morning. After a few minutes, new understanding dawned in his thoughts. *The apartment was quiet. Why was it so quiet?*

The ticking had stopped.

Boom.

VI.

Sleep still did not come even after the noise had left. Jeffrey used the rest of the morning to shower and sit comfortably on the couch. He did not feel fatigue, only a numbness that pervaded his body from head to toe. The images on the television floated by his eyes, helping time pass as if in a slow moving dream. *Girls Gone Wild* ads, penis enlargement infomercials, and old episodes of *Andy Griffith* flickered on the screen.

The sun peeked over the horizon and the apartment was bathed in natural light. Jeffrey got ready for work. He looked in the bathroom mirror, shaving cream slathered across his face. The ticking was gone, but behind his eyes he could see a pulsation, a nervous energy forming. He could feel it moving around in his skull. His eyes were still hollow looking, but this morning they seemed very alive. *Predatory.*

He did not know where that thought came from and shook it away.

He dressed in his shirt and tie, and combed his hair in the mirror.

His stomach rumbled. He realized he was hungry. But not just simple hunger. He was ravenous.

Jeffrey walked to the fridge. It was pretty empty. The milk had gone bad a few weeks ago. And the only other thing on the shelves was a container of leftovers which he really did not want to open.

He glanced at the clock. *Plenty of time before work. I'll stop somewhere and load up with a big breakfast.*

He grabbed his car keys and headed for the door.

To his disappointment, Ulee and Pierce were not out this morning. It was a little odd since they rarely missed an opportunity to mess with Jeffrey. He looked around the apartment complex and saw no sign of them. Shrugging he walked to the car and punched the unlock button on the key chain. The locks clicked and Jeffrey grabbed the handle.

His hand clamped down on something squishy and wet. There was cloth material stuck to the underside of the handle and when Jeffrey pulled his hand away from the door, he noticed blood covering his fingers. The object fell from the door to the parking lot, hitting the asphalt with a tiny splat.

It was a tampon.

A used tampon.

Jeffrey looked at his fingers. He slowly turned around, staring down the surrounding apartment buildings. Nothing moved but a few birds chirping in the trees. But he could feel them. They were watching him right now. *Probably yucking it up real hard. Ulee and Pierce. My two best friends.*

Jeffrey took out the small white handkerchief he kept in his pocket. He wiped his hand off, staining the bright white material with crimson streaks. He threw the hanky to the ground and when it landed he said:

"Boom."

He got in the car and drove from the lot. He stopped at the same gas station from the day before and used the bathroom to wash his hands. His appetite had left him with the nastiness of the trick.

Jeffrey stared into the dirty mirror. The eyes were still very alive. And now his head was burning, his skin felt like it was on fire. He leaned against the cracked sink and breathed deeply. Soon the sensation passed. He slammed the bathroom door closed behind him and got back into his car.

It was cleaning day at work. Every Thursday, the storeroom was cleaned from top to bottom. All the electronics and appliances were wiped down and the floors vacuumed. It was a one man job and that one man was Jeffrey.

"Sorry chum," Darryl said the first time he told Jeffrey he had to clean. "You *are* the low man on the ladder."

Jeffrey did not mind the cleaning. It kept him from having to talk to anyone else (Griffin) and gave him an excuse to stray near the receptionist area where Allison was. It was hard to make any sales though. Most customers thought he was the janitor and never asked him for any kind of assistance. Darryl was always watching the salespeople like a hawk and was always getting on Jeffrey to increase his sales on Thursday. He would also turn around and tell Jeffrey that he had missed several spots of dust on top of the televisions and that he needed to also wipe down each individual knob on the stereo systems.

"Cleanliness is next to Godliness, Walls." Darryl would walk around pointing out the various places that Jeffrey had missed with the duster. They always seemed to be places no customer in their right mind would seek out.

He was dusting the washer and dryer displays, stealing glances at Allison as she answered the phone and filled paperwork. Every now and then she would look over at him and smile. He nodded and kept cleaning. He felt a tap on his shoulder. It was Griffin.

"Yo Walls, how's it hanging?" Griffin was all smiles this morning. He had secured Salesperson of the Month for the seventh time in a row. Jeffrey looked over the taller man. Griffin had his dark hair slicked back with mousse and his goatee sheened with wax.

Griffin smiled a million dollar smile. "You have fun taking my girl to lunch?"

Jeffrey continued dusting the top of the dryer he was

working on. "It wasn't anything serious."

"Oh, I know. I mean, nothing against you pal, but she's way out of your league. Just look at those tits. They're beautiful." Griffin winked at Jeffrey. "Believe me I know."

Jeffrey stopped dusting and watched as Griffin walked over to Allison. She was on the phone and Griffin lightly slapped her on the rear. She turned and playfully slapped his hand away. She looked over at Jeffrey, slightly embarrassed. Jeffrey wanted to throw up.

A second tap landed on his shoulder. He turned around and faced Darryl.

"Why don't you come back to the office, Walls? Donovan wants to talk to you." Jeffrey threw the dust rag into the wastebasket and started walking back to Donovan's office. He turned just in time to see Darryl wiping a finger over where Jeffrey had just dusted, look at it, and shake his head in disappointment before following his salesman to the back.

Donovan was signing paychecks when Jeffrey entered. Darryl closed the door and took his seat behind Jeffrey. Jeffrey sat down and looked at Donovan.

"How is everything this morning, Walls?" Donovan looked up from the checks. Even though it was cool in the office, there was sweat already collecting on his brow.

"Fine. I'm having a good day so far."

"I'm glad you are because I'm not." Donovan eased back into his chair. His bulk rode hard on the worn leather and he placed his hands behind his head. "I'm here signing checks this morning. And I'm sure you know, giving away your money can put someone in a really sour mood."

Jeffrey did not respond.

"Darryl says you haven't even tried to sell anything this morning." Donovan was frowning at Jeffrey now. "He says the store has been pretty full this morning. Griffin has already moved over $500 in stock. Even what's her face has sold something. What's going on?"

Jeffrey frowned back. "It's cleaning day. I have to clean the store and dust all the shelves. I get…" Jeffrey stopped.

"Go on, what is it?"

"Well, if it's not done right, I usually get reprimanded." He looked at Darryl out of the corner of his eye.

Darryl piped in. "Jeffrey's right. I expect a clean store every week. But I don't see why he cannot complete sales at the same time." Donovan nodded and smiled and Jeffrey watched as some unknown understanding passed between the two men.

"Well, Darryl's quite right. The store needs to be spic and span. And we need you to sell." Donovan leaned forward. He grabbed an envelope and tossed it in to Jeffrey's lap. "That's this week's paycheck. If you ask me, it's pretty skimpy. You don't want skimpy pay checks do you? Right?"

Jeffrey shifted in his chair and Donovan continued.

"Remember what we talked about yesterday, Walls? About the jungle? And what kind of animal you are going to be? I know you thought about it. Well, I want to know. I want to know what kind of animal you are."

Jeffrey began to knot the envelope he was holding with his hands. His brow furrowed ever so slightly. The other two men did not notice.

"Griffin's a tiger. I'm a lion. Darryl's the wise old bear. Hell, we even got a sexy little pussycat out there." Darryl snickered at this. "So what is my salesman, Walls, going to be?"

Jeffrey was worrying the envelope between his hands. The paper began to tear and rip.

"Well, I'm waiting. This is Go time, Walls."

Jeffrey still did not answer.

"Donovan is talking to you," Darryl said. "This is your time to finally show us what you got."

"C'mon, boy. Show me some moxie here." Donovan was waiting.

The envelope ripped in two and fell to the floor.

"Boom."

Jeffrey sat staring at the floor.

"Boom? What the hell's a boom?" Donovan looked confused. He glanced at Darryl, who only shrugged his shoulders back. Darryl rose from his seat and came to stand next to Jeffrey.

"Well, Boss," Darryl turned to Donovan, "I guess this is that college education coming out. Everything has to have some utter deep meaning to it. Maybe he can explain exactly what "Boom" means." Darryl looked down at Jeffrey.

Jeffrey looked up at Darryl.

"Why don't you ever shut the fuck up?"

The silence was overwhelming. Both managers only stared at Jeffrey, their mouths slightly agape.

"What did you just say?" Darryl asked.

"I said," Jeffrey continued, his voice rising strong and loud, "why don't you ever shut the fuck up, monkeyboy?"

Darryl stood up. "Now wait a minute, son, I can't just...."

Jeffrey continued. "Monkeyboy. Yeah, that makes more sense. Not a bear. No, bears are respected and actually somewhat liked. Monkeys, though, who the hell likes a monkey? All they do is throw shit and beat off all day. Yeah, that's better. You should be a monkey." He looked up at Darryl. "Then you can spew shit all day long."

"You are out of line, Walls! This is a huge write-up coming!" Donovan's face was turning red as he spat the words out.

Jeffrey settled back in his chair. He turned to Donovan.

"And lion? Really isn't that stretching it a bit, Boss? I mean lions are proud and majestic. You don't quite measure up if you ask me. You're more of an ass if you think about it. Kind of good for nothing, lying around taking big dumps. Like you do on your lunch break when you head back to the john with the newest Hustler. Everyone knows you're shitting and masturbating at the same time."

Jeffrey leaned forward. "Why are you masturbating every day, Boss? Things not working out with the missus. I guess not. Probably why Darryl is over at your house on *his* lunch break fucking your wife all the time."

Darryl turned beet red. He glanced nervously at Donovan, and began licking his lips.

"Now wait a minute…" Darryl was easing away from Donovan and reaching for Jeffrey.

"If you touch me, I'm going to break your face." Darryl froze.

"Get out." Donovan squeezed the words from his mouth. "Get out of here, you little smart ass. Before I call the cops."

"Get the fuck out of here!!!! Now!!!" Donovan rose from his chair, screaming.

Jeffrey got up and turned to the door. He looked back at his former bosses.

"Happily. But first I want to thank you. You're right. Everyone should cater after some sort of animal, that primal instinct that lies buried deep inside ourselves. But I don't know. I think I feel a bit different today. Not really animal-like."

"Today I feel like a hunter."

"Have a nice day, assholes."

Jeffrey slammed the door behind him.

When he walked out into the showroom, everyone was staring at him. All the other employees, customers, even the delivery person who re-filled the drink machine had paused in what he was doing. All had heard the commotion coming from Donovan's office.

Jeffrey nodded at the spectators and headed for the entrance. Allison was looking at him with concern. Griffin ran up to him, all smiles.

"Holy shit, Walls, what did you...." Jeffrey punched Griffin in the face. His fist connected straight with the middle of Griffin's skull and the taller man hit the floor like a sack of potatoes. Blood was squirting from Griffin's nose, which was now broken and smashed like a pancake.

"What the hell are you doing?" Griffin was gasping through watery eyes.

Jeffrey raised his foot and kicked Griffin between the legs. Twice. Griffin began to yowl with pain, holding his balls while trying to stop the blood from flowing down his face. Jeffrey stepped over the prone man and walked up to Allison.

"You deserve better. He's trash, a complete fuck-up. He doesn't know how to treat you right. You are the sweetest person I have ever met." Jeffrey turned and headed for the door. "You need to wake up and drop his dumb ass."

He was out the door before she could respond.

VII.

His hunger from earlier that morning now returned with a vengeance. He pulled the car into a small diner and picked a table far back in the corner. Jeffrey wondered if Hi-Tech would call the police. Then he found that he really didn't care if they did or not.

When the waitress came to take his order, he picked out three different entrees and four kinds of dessert. As he plowed into the food, he felt like he would never get full, would never be able to stem the tide of energy that had erupted from his stomach and head.

Boom indeed.

He ordered a milkshake and downed it with a large cheeseburger. Steak and eggs disappeared along with a Ceasar salad and meatloaf. He finished his lunch with a glass of sweet tea.

Sitting at the table, waiting for the waitress to bring back his change, Jeffrey looked out at where his car was parked.

My car. What did they keep saying? It's a really nice car, Jeffrey.

"A really nice car," he said out loud to himself.

Jeffrey got in his really nice car and drove home.

They were waiting for him when he pulled into his parking spot. Ulee was already clapping Pierce on the back, both of them wearing innocent smiles. Jeffrey turned the car off and sat looking at the duo through the windshield. Ulee took a few steps forward and lightly knocked on the hood.

"C'mon. Don't be mad. It was just a joke. A little gift from my girlfriend." Ulee was standing in front of the car, his hands held up in front of him. Pierce was snickering and lighting a cigarette.

Jeffrey got out of the car. Ulee began to walk towards him.

"Hey Walls. It's okay. That's nice car you got…." That was as far as he got. Jeffrey hit Ulee in the throat. Ulee immediately began to choke and cough. Jeffrey grabbed him behind the head with both hands and thrust a knee up into Ulee's chin. The man's head snapped back violently and Ulee bounced off the side of the car.

Pierce's mouth hung open, his cigarette dropping to the ground in front of him.

"Hey. Hey Walls…" Pierce stumbled towards Jeffrey.

Jeffrey snatched the side of Pierce's face and pulled. Every piercing on the right side of the punk's face came away with a nasty wet rip. Pierce screamed bloody murder and fell to the ground, grabbing at his face. Jeffrey kicked him in the stomach and turned his attention back towards Ulee.

Ulee was trying to backpedal away. Jeffrey grabbed him by the hair and pulled him to his feet. He guided Ulee to the front of the Altima.

"You like the car, Ulee?" Jeffrey hissed. "You like it so much I'm going to give it to you. Here you go." He slammed Ulee face first onto the hood. Ulee's head bounced up and Jeffrey slammed it back down again. Over and over he drove Ulee's head onto the metal exterior. A large dent began to form on top of the hood.

One last time Jeffrey slammed Ulee's head against the car. Ulee was bleeding from his nose and forehead. His eyes were turning glassy and began to roll back into his head. Jeffrey released him and the thug hit the ground.

Jeffrey leaned down and whispered into the beaten

man's ear. "You like my car so much, I'm going to feed it to you."

Jeffrey walked to the driver's side of the car. He lashed out with his foot and kicked the side mirror off the door. The mirror fell to the parking lot with a clatter. He reached over and snatched it up.

Ulee's eyes were beginning to clear as Jeffrey leaned over him. He pulled open Ulee's mouth and began to stuff the mirror between his jaws. Blood spurted as Ulee's lips were cut open with broken glass. Jeffrey pushed down harder and now he could hear teeth and plastic cracking apart.

Ulee began to make a strangled gurgling sound. He began to gag and choke on mirror and skin. Pierce sat up on one knee and watched in horror at what was unfolding before him.

As he shoved the mirror down Ulee's throat, Jeffrey turned to Pierce and smiled. "Every time I see Ulee, I'm going to feed him another piece of my car. And every time I see you, I'm just going to beat the living shit out of you." Pierce nodded emphatically.

"Please, you're going to kill him. Please. We'll never bother you again." Jeffrey gave the mirror one final shove. Blood shot out of Ulee's nose. He knelt beside Pierce. The side of the young man's face was a series of small bleeding holes. He reached up to one of the remaining ear pieces and yanked it out. Pierce screamed again and began to cry.

"You better not. You better never ever fuck with me again."

Jeffrey stared into the mirror. His face was new. Maybe it was the blood flecked across his cheeks and forehead, but the face looking back at him was of someone else. A new Jeffrey. A reborn Jeffrey. His hands were covered in blood as was the whole front of his shirt. He quickly stripped and turned the shower to scalding. The day rinsed itself away down the drain.

He exited the shower feeling refreshed. He quickly toweled off. Walking naked to the living room, he glanced out the window to where his car was parked. There was no sign of his victims from earlier. The broken mirror lay on the asphalt and there was a huge head-sized dent in the hood of the vehicle.

He looked around the room and immediately wanted to leave the apartment. He was wide awake; his skin and head thrumming with electricity.

Go out. Go out and explore your new world. He dressed in jeans and a black t-shirt and headed out the door.

He took the parkway to downtown, looking for a place to have a drink. The sun was easing slowly down below the horizon. Jeffrey had all the windows down and was blasting the radio as high as it would go. He didn't recognize the music. Something by Korn or Tool or some other band. All that mattered was it was loud and rocking and mirrored his energy buzz. He took exit 32 onto Glass Road and merged into traffic.

A few blocks passed and then blue lights flashed in the rearview mirror. Jeffrey glanced up and watched as the police car sidled in behind the Altima and pulled up on the rear bumper. *Took them long enough,* he thought. He figured Griffin called them. Ulee and Pierce weren't the policeman kind of person. *Maybe it was Donovan. Does it fucking matter?*

He pulled into the parking lot of a small dry cleaners

and waited for the officer to approach. The police car parked behind the Altima and the office sauntered up to the driver's side. Jeffrey turned the radio down halfway.

"How are you today, sir?" Jeffrey looked at his reflection, the new different Jeffrey reflection, in the officer's dark sunglasses.

"Do you know why I stopped you, young man?"

Because I beat the shit out of three people today. And I threatened to beat the shit out of my boss too.

Jeffrey glanced at the passing traffic. "No clue, officer."

"Were you aware that your driver's side mirror was missing?" The policeman pointed at the dangling wires and snapped plastic that recently held the mirror. It was less than ten inches from Jeffrey's face.

"Nope. I was not aware of that." He looked up at the officer, gauging him.

"State law requires that all motor vehicles must have a working driver's side mirror. Where is yours?"

Jeffrey yawned.

"Can I see your driver's license and registration please, young man?" Jeffrey brought out both and passed them to the officer. He watched in the rearview as the law strutted back to his cruiser. He turned the radio back up. Metallica. Old school Metallica. *Nice.*

The officer returned and handed the documents back over. "You need to get the mirror fixed ASAP."

"Can I ask you a question, sir?" Jeffrey turned the radio back down. The officer peered through his dark sunglasses and nodded.

"Did you see that guy two blocks back? The gangbanger looking dude standing in the median?"

The officer nodded. "I passed him when I was coming to pull you over."

"Yeah, ok. Do you know why that guy stands there? He stands there every day by the way."

The officer did not respond. He seemed unsure of where the conversation was going.

Jeffrey continued. "Well, the reason he stands there is because he sells ecstasy. He's the biggest ex dealer in the city."

The officer remained unmoving.

"Now I don't do drugs. But I know that he does sell them. Everyone I work with knows he sells them. And a lot of the people I associate with outside of work knows he sells them. I'm pretty sure almost the whole city knows that the thuggy looking dude on the median back there sells ex."

The officer began to shuffle a bit uncomfortably.

Jeffrey started to fix his hair in the working rearview mirror. "What I can't figure out is, if the whole population knows about the ecstasy dealer on the median back there, how in the world does the police department not know this?" He looked up at the officer, a very puzzled expression on his face.

The officer continued to stare down at Jeffrey. "It's not that simple. We are….aware of the suspect's activities."

"Oh you are. That's awesome. So are you going to arrest him right now? Cool, I'd like to just park and watch."

"Well, not right now."

"Not right now?" Jeffrey kept the puzzled expression on his face.

The officer was trying to choose his words carefully. "Well, see, the evidence is not as apparent with this particular suspect's activities."

"Not as apparent?"

"No."

"Not as apparent as what?"

"As...."

"....as a driver's side mirror?"

The officer frowned at Jeffrey and then stalked away. "Just get the damn thing fixed, asshole."

Jeffrey snickered and pulled out of the parking lot.

He spent the evening and most of the night at a small downtown bar called Guppies. He did not drink much before, but today was different. He wanted something to take the edge off today's events. He was on his third rum and coke and second platter of chicken wings (his hunger was growing and growing it seemed).

Jeffrey noticed the woman at the end of the bar watching him. He checked her out. Blonde, tall, really nice figure. She flashed him a smile. He nodded and returned his gaze to the television. He wiped his hands clean from the greasy wings.

The woman sat down on the stool next to him.

"Buy a girl a drink?" She smelled nice, like flowers. Up close she was even more attractive. Jeffrey looked up from his hands. He made a presentation of looking the woman over. Then he swallowed some of his drink.

"You want to talk to me?" he asked the girl. She looked at him, surprised. "You walked over here. Sat right down next to me. So I'm guessing you want to talk to me."

She nodded. "Yeah, I guess I do want to talk to you."

"Then you should be the one buying me a damn drink."

She laughed and ordered him another.

Later that night, in the darkness of the parking lot, she rode him in the backseat of his car. Sweating and heaving, he exploded in her. She shivered in the cool night air and he leaned his face into her large breasts.

"I love you, Allison."

"What?" She laughed and pushed him away from her tits. "What did you just call me?"

"What?" Jeffrey leaned against the rear seat and pinched one of her nipples. She laughed again.

"You called me Allison."

"No I didn't"

"Yes, you did. I just heard you. Who's Allison?"

Jeffrey closed his eyes and sighed. "I didn't say anything."

The blonde laughed and began to stroke him again. "It's okay. You can call me whatever you want. Go ahead, call me Allison."

He pushed her off. "No. Get the fuck off."

"What the hell are you doing?" she yelled as he opened the car door.

"Get the fuck out of here. It's time for you to go."

He pushed her from the car, her naked breasts bouncing. "You fucking asshole. You can't just kick me out right here."

Jeffrey got out and walked around to the driver's side.

"Watch me."

He got in and left her in the parking lot.

VIII.

The ticking had stopped but the sleeplessness was still present. The numbness from before had dissipated. Now it was replaced with a buzzing nervousness, and something else growling beneath the surface of the buzz. A shadow of some sort.

Jeffrey sat on his couch and stared at the television. He replayed the day's events in his mind. *Was that really me? Did I do all those crazy things?* Standing up to his bosses was one thing, but taking out Griffin in one punch? Busting up both Pierce and Ulee? He remembered all the blood.

I should be in jail right now.

He looked at his hands. The knuckles were busted open and scabbing over. He flexed the fingers and small bursts of pain spread through the hand. He had never bled like this before in his life, and had never caused anyone else to bleed like he had today.

He kind of liked it.

"Donovan is right. We are all animals," he whispered into the night air.

Jeffrey flicked through the channels. It was frustrating to see. A colored world of fake-titted celebrities, expensive desires, shallow problems, and bad news flowing outward into his living room every night.

He got up from the couch and picked up the TV. Raising it above his head, he slammed it down with a huge crash to the floor. The screen shattered and the dancing images disappeared. Jeffrey turned and hit the wall over and over again with his fists until blood peppered the white paint.

This is what is real. This is what it feels like to be alive. To be in control.

The neighbor from downstairs began banging on the floor, yelling for Jeffrey to stop making noise.

Jeffrey knelt on the carpet. He leaned forward and put his mouth as close to the floor as he could.

"FUCK YOU, MOTHERFUCKER!" he screamed to the mystery assailant. The banging immediately stopped.

He watched the sun rise from his seat at the small dinette set in his kitchen. By then he had made a decision to leave the city. He wanted to go out and find a path for this new person he had become.

He began packing some clothes into a duffel bag. He grabbed his keys and headed out the door. He was going to the bank to close out his accounts. He would figure out how to get more money when those funds ran out.

He threw his things in the trunk of the car and turned to get in. Ulee was walking towards him from the other side of the parking lot. He was holding a gun. Jeffrey leaned against the car and studied the man's face. It was a mass of bruises and cuts. Ulee's lips were super puffy and his nose was swollen immensely. When Ulee noticed Jeffrey watching him, he quickened his pace.

Jeffrey walked to the front of the car and yanked one of the wiper blades off. He turned just as Ulee was upon him and raising the gun. Jeffrey brought the wiper blade down on the gunman's wrist. The blade slapped hard across the skin and Ulee dropped the gun to the ground with a screech.

Jeffrey hit Ulee in the stomach. Ulee wheezed and leaned against Jeffrey. Jeffrey took measure of the wounded man and hit him in his swollen nose. Ulee fell to the lot, his eyes watering over and fresh blood pouring from his poor nostrils.

Jeffrey bent over and picked up the gun and the wiper blade. Then he began to rip the rubber blade off the wiper bracket. He ripped it all off completely and started tearing it into more manageable pieces. Then he bent over Ulee.

He pressed the gun to Ulee's temple. The man instantly

froze, his eyes growing large.

"Open your mouth." Ulee complied and Jeffrey stuffed the first handful of wiper into the hole.

"Start chewing." Ulee began to weep as he chewed on the foul tasting rubber.

"I'm leaving after today. You won't have to eat any more of my really great car. Well, except for the rest of this wiper. I'm going to take your gun though. And we'll call it even. Got it?" Ulee nodded furiously.

Jeffrey was true to his word. Ulee ate the whole wiper.

He drove to the bank. The gun was nestled in the glove compartment. Jeffrey had never fired a gun in his life. But he liked the feel of it in his hands. He wanted to fire it right now.

After closing his accounts and stuffing the envelope full of money into his duffel bag, Jeffrey drove down to the Flying Rabbit, a small shooting range.

"I just got this gun and want to learn everything about it," he told the young guy behind the counter. "And then I want to fire it."

The young man showed Jeffrey everything about the firearm. He was a good teacher and Jeffrey was a good student.

He was a good shot too.

He stopped at an outdoor specialty shop and bought shells and cleaning supplies for the gun. Then he pulled out onto LaGrange Avenue. He would ride through the city one final time and then hit the interstate. He was thinking he would head to the west coast. Take in California. Get a job as an orange picker or something for a while.

Jeffrey braked at a stoplight. There was a red Jeep stopped in front of him. A man sat behind the wheel and a woman on the passenger side. He could make out a baby seat in the back. *A nice little family,* he thought to himself. A brief image of his mother came to mind and he quickly pushed it away.

The man in the jeep leaned over and slapped the woman in the face. Jeffrey froze. *What the fuck?* The man was saying something to her now, nodding his head and pointing his finger in her face. He slapped her again and then pushed her head against the door frame. Jeffrey looked around the intersection. They were the only two cars in sight.

Jeffrey put the car in park and got out. He walked quickly up to the driver's side of the jeep and opened the door. The driver was very young, younger than Jeffrey. He had long bushy brown hair and was smoking a cigarette. The woman was a young skinny brunette. She was crying softly and turned around trying to calm the little boy in the car seat.

"What the hell you think you doing...." Jeffrey cut the man off by unlocking the seatbelt. He grabbed the driver by the hair and hauled him from the jeep. The young guy was too stunned to say anything.

Jeffrey threw him against the vehicle. The girl started screaming from inside. The man was cursing Jeffrey to no end.

"You like hitting defenseless women? You like beating people up? Why don't you hit on me, fuckface?" Jeffrey slapped the driver. The man tried to push Jeffrey away but he held on tightly to the guy's shirt. He punched a knee into the guy's midsection.

The driver was bent over gasping for breath, snot and

spit dripping from his face. Jeffrey grabbed the man's hand and leaned it against the door jam. He slammed the jeep door on the hand. There was a sickening crunch as all the fingers cracked under the pressure. The man screamed in agony and fell to the earth.

Jeffrey proceeded to kick the guy over and over again. In the face, the stomach, the arms and legs. He rained blows down on the man's prone body.

"How does that fucking feel? Huh? Not too good does it." He was livid. He couldn't believe this person could treat someone he should love so badly. This guy had no clue what he had.

Jeffrey kicked him again. Hands grabbed at his arm and he spun around to knock whoever it was down. It was the woman. She had run from the passenger side to stop him. She knelt over her spouse, crying and looking at Jeffrey accusingly through her bruised eyes.

"Please, he's had enough. Just leave us alone," she screamed at Jeffrey. The baby inside the jeep continued to wail. Jeffrey gaped at the battered woman.

He took a step towards her. She flinched backwards against the jeep.

"Take care of your baby."

He walked away from the couple and got back into the car. He thumbed the radio up and peeled off.

He never looked back.

IX.

Jeffrey pulled into a parking spot underneath a huge oak tree. He was at a small park near the city line. He had stopped before (after the jeep incident) and bought a pack of cigarettes. Since leaving the couple his hands began to shake and he wanted something to steady them with.

He pulled a smoke from the pack of Dunhills and lit it. He had never smoked before but his father had partaken for close to thirty-five years before they died in the car crash two years ago. The smoke felt rough sliding down his lungs, but there was a comforting mellowness to it. His hands started to calm down and he could feel the shadow gliding deep into his stomach.

God, what is wrong with me? I feel so crazy.

He glanced around the park. Several children were playing on the playground as their mothers watched them from the wooden benches scattered everywhere. It was a beautiful day. He finished his cigarette and leaned quietly against the hood of the car.

He remembered the night they had woken him in his dorm room. He had just completed his Design 101 midterm and was catching up on missed sleep. The knock jolted him from a deep slumber and he stumbled to answer it.

There was a police officer and the hall's resident advisor at the door. Jeffrey listened carefully as the officer told him about the accident. His parents were driving back from a dinner when a drunk driver ran a stoplight and T-boned their car in the intersection. His mother was killed instantly. His father was taken to the hospital but succumbed to his injuries during surgery.

Jeffrey blinked his eyes over and over again as the R.A. informed him he would be excused from school for the rest of the semester. She had called the school counselor. They would come and help Jeffrey pack and try to get him back home as soon as possible. He had nodded and thanked them for their help.

He sat on his bed, glancing at the last letter they had

written him, the one that said they were so proud of him and knew he would be a great architect someday.

A voice broke him from his memories.

"Jeffrey."

He glanced up and held his breath.

Allison was standing a few yards away. She was dressed in cutoffs and a tank top.

He pulled another cigarette from his pack and lit it. "What are you doing here?"

"Taking a walk in the park." She came closer and now he could smell her. She smelled like spring and summer mixed. "I live near here."

"Why aren't you at work?" He took a long drag and exhaled.

"I quit." She smiled. "Pretty much right after you did." She sat next to him on the car. "That was crazy, by the way." She looked at him but he couldn't meet her eyes.

"Sorry about Griffin," he said.

"Don't be. After you left, he was whining to everybody about how you suckered him and how he could take you one on one any day. It was kind of sad in a way. I think he got knocked off his pedestal a bit."

Jeffrey looked back towards the playground.

"You were right by the way."

"About what?"

"He was an asshole. And he didn't know how to treat me."

"Then why stay with him?" He looked at her now.

Now she was the one who could not meet his gaze. "It's just....sometimes things don't turn out the way you think they will, you know?"

He flicked the cigarette away. She leaned into him and rested her head on his shoulder.

"No. I guess they don't," he said.

X.

They left the park and stopped at Allison's apartment. Jeffrey had told her he was leaving.

"I want to go too. I need a change of scenery," she said. He nodded okay and they drove from her apartment out onto the interstate. There was an unspoken understanding between them now, a shift in their relationship.

Later that night, they pulled into a motel. Allison hopped into the shower as Jeffrey stood in the dark, smoking and looking out the window at the neon signs glowing across the way.

What is happening here? How is this going to end?

"Who says it has too?" He did not realize he was speaking out loud and did not hear Allison shut off the shower. He turned and she stood naked in the bathroom doorway. She stepped from the lit bathroom into the darkness and touched his hand.

"I feel like I'm going to explode," he said into her ear. "I've done some bad things and I am afraid I'll do more before it's all over with."

"Shh," she whispered. She kissed him softly and he rubbed her bare shoulders. "I don't care what you've done. And don't worry about the future. You are not alone anymore. Let's just think about the right now."

So they did.

Afterwards, lying in each other's arms they smiled and laughed. Jeffrey felt the shadow retreat a bit deeper. Allison grabbed one of his cigarettes. The ember glowed brightly in the dark hotel room.

"I didn't know you smoked," he said.

"There's a lot you don't know about me, Jeffrey Walls." She blew smoke into the dark room.

"Well, here we are. Two unemployed people with hardly any money and any prospects." Jeffrey scratched her back as she smoked. She continued: "What do you want to do? I mean besides heading out to the coast."

She looked at him in the darkness, could barely make out his features.

Jeffrey was looking towards where his jacket sat on the chair. The gun was in one of the side pockets.

"I want to rob banks," he said quietly.

Allison giggled and stubbed out her cigarette. She nestled down under the blankets and slid her arms around Jeffrey.

"You're kidding right?" She smiled in the dark.

There was no answer.

Jeffrey had fallen asleep.

PUNCHY

Punchy couldn't talk. He couldn't hear also. He had lost both those abilities seven years before, his last time in the ring. It was Svenson who did it. Gordy "Knockaround" Svenson who knocked around some wiring in Punchy's head, cutting it loose from its fleshy skull plugs. Synapses not sparking, pathways blocked or clotted or severed by violent jabs to the head that Svenson had thrust at Punchy's face.

This last fight had left Punchy lying spread-eagled on the mat, watching the little yellow birds dipping and diving across his blurred double vision. Later, he remembered a massive body of confusion running into the ring, leaning over him, blocking out the bright lights of bloody fame he was used to dancing in. The ring. The beautiful violent mastery of the squared circle. And this would be the last time he would ever be in it, lying down as if he was back in his bed at home. Or patiently waiting for his death shroud to envelop his sore body, and make the buzzing pain finally stop.

Back in the locker room, he tried to make out what his coach was saying to him. Sweat and blood dripped from his swollen face and mingled on the dirty green tiled floor. He watched Tony's mouth carefully; the lips forming each syllable, small specks of spittle flicking their own way to the cold floor. Punchy registered no voice. No sound vibrated his broken drums.

The water in the sink splashing silently into the drain. The reporters yelling questions from the hall, snapping eerie quiet light bulbs on their cameras. The heavy oak door to the room slamming shut into a noiseless vacuum. Nothing registered.

And then not speaking. He moved the muscles in his jaws, trying to form the words to tell Tony he couldn't hear him, couldn't hear anything. Punchy could only point desperately at his mouth and watch Tony's eyes grow larger as realization dawned on the old man's face.

"Nerve damage" the professional quacks diagnosed. Too many hits to the head, too much damage to the brain.

"Nerve damage" and a promising boxing career was done. At least he thought it was a promising career. A 21-5 record with 19 TKO's and the meeting with Svenson, the current #1 contender to the middleweight belt. The potential was huge until "nerve damage."

"Nerve damage" would turn Ricky "The Dynamite Kid" Jones into "Punchy" Jones.

And "Punchy" Jones was no boxer. He was told he couldn't box. The commission wouldn't let him. The commission said he was done. The commission didn't know shit.

Punchy folded the quilt neatly over the small cot. He downed the rest of his morning coffee and left the one room apartment. The apartment was located in the basement of the Liberty Hotel, one of the city's oldest buildings. The Liberty was still in fine working order and popular among tourists looking for somewhere swanky yet somewhat classy to spend a few days while catching the popular views.

The Liberty was classy because Punchy kept her that way. He had worked as the sole handyman for the hotel for the past five years. It was one of the few jobs he could actually find and keep. His disability check hardly afforded him enough for food each month, and this job helped bring in extra money and he got free room and board to boot. Besides, Punchy wanted to work. He needed to keep moving, keep active, always keep dancing.

Punchy flipped the light switch and the basement was bathed in bright florescent light. It was a large room, with one side dedicated to storage. Holiday decorations, stage costumes, and years of assorted bric-a-brac were stacked high against the walls. The other side of the basement belonged to Punchy. It was dedicated only to maintenance.

There was a large workbench that ran the middle of the space. On top was a huge assortment of tools and devices, all used to keep the aging parts of the old hotel running. The tools were arranged neatly and Punchy knew where everything was.

He walked past the bench to the main elevator. Next to the closed doors was a bulletin board. The board was empty much of the time, and only held safety notices for the hotel and the past building inspection. It was also were the shift managers updated what needed to be repaired every day.

Today the board held two service requests. The first was in room 245. The pipes under the bathroom sink were leaking. Without looking at the pipes, Punchy already knew they needed new O-rings. The rings in all the bathrooms were going as of late and he had spent much of the past month traveling to different rooms replacing them. It was an easy job and would take the better part of half an hour at most.

The second request was for room 532 on the top floor. The top floor housed large suites that were nicer than the basic rooms one could get at the hotel. Besides large living areas the suites also contained a full kitchen. These were usually rented by the week, by businessmen attending conferences or someone who had found work in the area but not a place to live quite yet.

The service request stated that the garbage disposal in the kitchen sink was clogged and stopped working. This would probably be a bigger job than the bathroom pipes. The disposal units were tough and it usually took something major to cause them to stop working. It could be a real messy task trying to clean them out.

Still, there were only two requests to start the day and if he was lucky nothing else would come in. If that happened, he could be finished by noon and knock off the rest of the day. He wanted to take in the flea market and see if he could find some more paperback westerns. Punchy read every night and his favorites were the classic Louis L'amour novels. The flea market was a haven for used paperbacks and he knew he could find some he had not enjoyed yet.

He ripped the service orders from the board and stuffed them in his shirt pocket. At the workbench he strapped on a worn leather tool belt and began filling it with the tools needed for today's jobs. He slurped down his second cup of coffee and punched the button for the elevator.

The doors opened and Punchy stepped in hitting the button and making the round 2 glow a bright yellow. He hitched up the belt and ran a hand over his smooth head. He was still in good shape for being out of the ring for so long. Every week he hit the gym and worked the heavy bag for hours, sweat pouring from his skin, finding seclusion in the silence in his head. No one ever bothered him at the gym. Sometimes he wondered if they knew who he was, who he had been. But most of the time, he worked out alone, watching the others drift by as if in a dream.

The elevator stopped on the first floor and the doors opened. A bellhop pushed a rack of luggage onto the car, followed by a short, chubby man and his chubby wife. They were talking incessantly, back and forth, the woman waving her hands in frustration. For once, Punchy was grateful he could not hear what they were saying.

The bellhop rolled his eyes at Punchy as he pushed the cart against the wall. Punchy nodded in return and settled further back into the elevator, giving the others ample room. At the second floor everyone got off. The bellhop led the arguing couple down the hall, the wife still waving her hands crazily about. Punchy grinned and turned the opposite way towards room 245.

Poor kid, he thought. *At least I don't have to deal with that kind of stuff every day.* He found he liked not having to interact with people. Despite the added challenges of being deaf and mute, there was the fact that Punchy just was not a people person. He never was. Even back in his heyday.

He knocked on the room door and waited for an answer. Nothing. He tried again and when there was no answer he took out his access card and swiped it through the door reader. The little light flickered green and he entered the room. His card gained him access to every room in the hotel, one of the perks of being the handyman.

The room was empty and Punchy was relieved no one was renting it. It became a challenge when guests were in the room. They always began talking really fast and it became awkward when they learned of his disabilities. They would nod slowly after reading the small note card Punchy carried with him and then look at him sadly. After that, they left him the hell alone. Which he was grateful for.

He went to the bathroom and pulled the leaky pipes. After about twenty minutes of work, he was finished and the pipes were sealed again. He cleaned up the excess water and left the room.

*****

There was someone standing at the door to room 532. Punchy rounded the corner and was surprised to see a man leaning beside the door. The man was dressed in a polo shirt and dress slacks and was reading a magazine. Punchy stood before the stranger and made some noise by arranging his tool belt.

The man looked up from his magazine and said something. After seven years of being deaf, Punchy had gotten skilled at reading lips, but the stranger was talking to fast and now seeing that Punchy wasn't responding to his words began to move towards the handyman.

Punchy reached into his back pocket and brought out the info card. He handed it to the man who looked at it warily and then read it:

Hello. My name is Punchy and I am the handyman for the Liberty Hotel. If I do not respond to your questions it is because I am a deaf mute. If you need to communicate with me, please talk slowly and I will be able to read your lips.

Thank you & have a nice day.

The man handed the card back to Punchy and then leaned in really close. This time Punchy understood what was being said:

"What the fuck do you want?"

The man's breath smelled of cigarettes and stale liquor. Punchy took a step back. *What was this guy's problem?* He brought out the service request and presented it to the man, who looked it over and then looked back at the handyman.

"Wait here."

The man went into the suite and closed the door. Punchy looked around the hall at the other rooms but no one else was up and about. The man came back out and waved Punchy in.

There were four other men in the suite. They were sitting around the oak coffee table in the living area. They had raided the suite's mini-bar, downing the brown liquid in the clear tumblers and then refilling them again. A large order of Chinese takeout sat on the table and the men stuffed their mouths with Lo Mein noodles and fried rice between sips from their tumblers.

Three of the men did not even look up as Punchy entered but the fourth did. This one was the oldest by far, maybe in his sixties, with slicked back grey hair. Punchy noticed him immediately, not because of his age, but for the exquisite gray three piece suit the man wore. The others were young, in their late 20s, and dressed much the same way as the man who guarded the door was: polo shirts and slacks or jeans.

The older man addressed the guard.

"Were you rude, Russell?" Punchy watched their lips move.

"Maybe," Russell replied, "It don't matter none anyways. He's retarded. He can't hear or talk."

Everyone chuckled at Russell's insult. Everyone except the older gentleman.

"That's not funny, assholes." The laughter quieted immediately. "Just because he is deaf mute does not make a man stupid." He glared at his younger accomplices, daring each one in turn to challenge him on this statement. When none did, he continued. "Every man has his weakness," the older man looked at Punchy, "and every man has his strengths."

"You came to fix the disposal?" the man asked. Punchy nodded. "Good. I apologize for my younger compatriots. They wouldn't know where to piss unless someone told them." Punchy remained still.

The man motioned to the kitchen. "Please, if you would, fix our garbage disposal." Punchy nodded again and headed for the kitchen. He began pulling tools from his belt and taking apart the disposal, all the while keeping one eye on the hotel's guests.

Eventually he learned all their names. The older gentleman was Weston. He was obviously the leader of the group as the others took their cues from him. The younger ones were: Russell, the doorman who was back outside the suite, Billy, who seemed to talk a lot even when no one listened, Crow, who was quiet and only talked when he needed to, and Hayden, who kept flicking a butterfly knife open and closed over and over again and did not seem particularly bright.

Most of the talk in the room centered around horse racing. It seemed Weston liked to bet on the horses and they were glancing at the forms, trying to pick the winners. No one paid any mind to Punchy which made it easier for him to eavesdrop while he worked at the counter. He was curious. Who the hell were these guys? They were not the usual travelers the hotel catered too. And what was up with having someone stand watch in the hall?

Billy stepped to the bar to pour Weston another drink. "Pop's Galore is the favorite in the fifth, boss. But the betting odds are on Groovy Gravy at 8-1." He handed the drink to Weston and plopped back down into one of the plush chairs.

Weston shook his head. "Vincent told me Gravy hasn't run good since early June. The inside is on Ricochet to win. That's the bet."

"What inside?"

"My inside," Weston answered, "and my inside is never wrong. Take Ricochet in the fifth, Stormy Roses in the sixth, and Sleeping In Sunday in the last. Call them in."

Billy dialed a number on his cell phone and went out to the balcony. Hayden continued flicking his knife. Punchy sat the disposal in the sink. He needed to take the top plate off to check the teeth and see what had stopped the disposal from working. The sink was a good place to work because usually water and nasty grime spilled out. He reached for an Allen wrench and started removing screws, all the while watching the living area.

Weston turned to Hayden. "Hayden."

The young man kept flicking the knife, twisting it and making it dance open and swing shut in a blur.

"Hayden."

Hayden was absorbed, looking at a spot on the wall while the knife twirled over and over.

Weston leaned forward. "HEYDEN!"

The loud voice made Hayden jump and the blade sliced open one of his fingers. "AAHH! What the hell, Weston? What did you do that for?"

Hayden glared at the old man who calmly returned the look.

"Something wrong?" Weston asked. Hayden slowly shook his head and grabbed one of the restaurant napkins to cover his finger. "Good. Did you order the girl some food?"

Hayden nodded. Weston turned to Crow. "Mr. Crow, will you make sure our guest has her lunch?"

Reddish water began to spill from the disposal as Punchy removed the plate. He watched the water pool into the sink and slowly disappear down the drain. For a brief second, the water returned him to the cold locker room and the drops of blood collecting in the sink as he rinsed his bruised face off. He shook away the memory quickly and continued his task. Punchy worked his fingers into the disposal and began to clean the teeth.

He watched as Crow grabbed two containers of Chinese and opened the door to the bedroom. There was a young woman sitting on the edge of the bed, crying silently. Crow towered over her and she looked at the floor. He sat the containers on the bed with a small pack of utensils. As he walked from the room, the girl looked out at Punchy. She saw him staring. Her lips moved and the handyman could barely make out what she was saying. But he knew.

Please.

Crow closed the bedroom door and returned to his seat on the sofa.

Punchy's fingers gripped something wet and solid in the disposal. He reached in and pulled out a mangled mess of grapefruit, coffee grounds, and something else: a twisted piece of plastic that turned out to be a driver's license.

Punchy turned the license around in his fingers. One half of it had been twisted up by the disposal but the other half, the part with the picture, was readable. It belonged to a woman and Punchy could see it wasn't the girl in the bedroom. Where the one on the bed had short blond hair and was college aged, the picture woman was a bit older with long black hair and wore glasses.

Punchy could make out the first name. Meredith. This license belonged to Meredith. She obviously was not in the suite. So where was she? And why was her license in the disposal? Punchy looked up to see Weston watching him.

"Everything okay, friend?" Weston asked, his lips moving in perfect fashion.

Punchy nodded and reached into the sink. He held up the mangled grapefruit mess. Weston nodded.

"Russell ate that shit," Billy quipped as he stepped back into the suite. "He screwed the damn thing up."

Weston nodded, still watching Punchy. "I'm sure it was very *accidental.*"

What the hell is this?

Deftly Punchy slid the license into his pocket and then threw the pulped fruit into the trash. He put the disposal together as quickly as possible. The men began talking about hiring a car for the afternoon, and who was going to stay at the suite. It turned out it was Billy's turn to hang around and the youth groused loudly about the bum deal.

"I don't know why we just can't get the money today. You said Vladimir wanted the girl pretty badly," Billy whined.

Weston turned to him seething. "Shut your stupid mouth, you useless little worm." Billy recoiled as if slapped hard in the face. Punchy acted like he did not see or understand this exchange. He slapped the disposal back under the sink and tightened the fittings. Weston was looking at him again.

He flipped the switch on the disposal and the machine churned to life. He could feel the heavy vibration through the counter and knew it would work fine now. As long as no one tried to dispose of any more licenses.

Quickly, Punchy cleaned his tools and stuck them back into the belt. Billy came to the kitchen and grabbed a juice box from the fridge, not giving the handyman a second glance. Punchy turned to the other men in the living area. Weston raised his eyebrows in anticipation and Punchy gave him the thumbs up.

The garbage disposal was good to go.

Weston waved him over. Slowly Punchy made his way into the living room as Weston stood. The older man was reaching into his inside jacket pocket. Punchy felt himself stiffen but forced himself to remain calm. Weston reached out and shook hands with Punchy.

"Thank you so much, good sir. The Liberty is everything we were told it would be." The old man was staring into Punchy's eyes, studying him. Punchy forced a grin and nodded his thanks. Then he turned and left the suite.

Russell stared at him in the hallway. Punchy watched from the corner of his eye as the guard mouthed the word *retard* but he pretended not to see. He walked around the corner to the elevator. Only then did he look at what Weston had palmed him during the handshake.

He looked down at a crisply folded $100 bill.

MICHAEL WHETZEL

*****

When Punchy returned to the basement, he took off the heavy tool belt and slammed it on the workbench. He leaned against the table, his brow furrowed in thought. He knew the girl was in some kind of trouble and that Weston and his crew were bad news. He just didn't know what to do.

Do I call the cops? But what if I am totally off here? What if I'm wrong? I could lose my job. And I was lucky to find this one. Somehow getting the cops involved seemed like a bad idea. It would be him against them, five against one and his one was serving with half a brain. No, they would be able to win out against him with the cops involved. He was sure of that.

I can't help her, he thought to himself. *I'm no good. Can't do anything. I'm just a handyman.*

He sighed deeply and his body suddenly seemed to grow very small in the dark basement. *I can't help her. I am a retard.* He had never felt so helpless in all his life. He knew something was not right, but couldn't figure out how to help. He shook his head.

The elevator doors opened and one of the maids hurried in. Punchy watched her as she marched up and handed him a slip of paper. The maid looked with distaste at the handyman and his surroundings. It was another service request. This one was an emergency in room 301. A pipe had burst in the bathroom. Another faulty O-ring. Punchy nodded at the maid and she hurried back onto the elevator.

When she was gone, he grabbed a small book of matches from one of the shelves and lit the $100 note. He threw it on the workbench and watch it burn down to ash, leaving a small black scorch mark on the rough wood.

He grabbed his tool kit and headed back upstairs.

The least he could do is turn down their money. No matter how much he needed it.

*****

It took three hours to complete the last job. The O-rings had gone out but the pipe was also old and rusted and he ended up replacing the whole works. It was a job he could usually finish in half the time but his mind kept slipping back to the suite upstairs and the crying girl.

Now he got off the elevator, wet and tired, and slowly getting pissed off to boot. He slammed the tool belt back onto the table and went to the small fridge sitting in the corner. He grabbed a bottle of water and chugged it, then went into the small apartment.

The girl was sitting on his bed.

Punchy felt his jaw drop and froze. The girl's eyes were red and swollen from crying and her bottom lip was fat and busted from where someone had slapped her. He closed the door behind him and knelt on the floor of the room before the cot.

She was talking now, too fast for him to make out what she was saying. He motioned for her to stop and grabbed the card from his pocket. He felt foolish as she read it and more tears slid down her cheeks. She gave the card back to him and he slid it back into his pocket.

"They're looking for me," she said. "Please. You have to help me. They kidnapped me. I think they're going to…to sell me to someone." She looked off into the corner. "They…they hurt me…" Punchy shushed her and nodded that he understood. "I ran down the stairs but they saw me. One of them was in the lobby and…and I'm just so scared."

Punchy patted the girl's knee and frowned.

Suddenly the girl's eyes grew large with fear and her mouth formed a sold O. He looked at her puzzled.

"The elevator. The doors just dinged open."

Punchy summed it all up quickly in his mind. She needed help. They were looking for her. They were here now.

He held one finger to his lips. *Stay quiet.* The girl showed she understood. Quickly the handyman turned and walked out of the apartment. He shut the door closed behind him.

Russell and Billy were searching the storage side of the basement. He watched them for a few seconds, kicking over decorations and calling out. He stepped around the corner and showed himself.

Russell noticed him immediately and motioned to Billy. They walked over to where Punchy stood. He watched their lips move.

"Hey Billy. It's the retard." Russell stepped forward and moved close to Punchy. "Hey there, big guy, have you seen a hot little piece of ass running around…" Punchy sent a sharp jab into Russell's face. He felt his fist connect with the man's nose, felt the crunch of the cartilage and the give of the bone as it slid back into Russell's head.

A small gurgle escaped from Russell's lips as blood exploded from his nose. He slumped quickly to the floor, dead.

Billy stood shocked. Then he began to move. He ran at Punchy and delivered a huge haymaker aimed at the bigger man's head. Billy put all he had into the punch and Punchy knew that this was a mistake. He moved back slightly, and the off balance blow glanced off the side of his head.

Punchy had hardly gotten the full brunt of the attack but it still hurt like hell. His cheek went numb, but Billy had too much momentum and began to pitch forward. Punchy landed two hard hits to the back of the man's head and Billy skidded along the floor.

Billy slowly got to his hands and knees, shaking the cobwebs from his head. He looked up at Punchy who began to dance and weave around the youth.

"You fucking nancy ass. You're dead." Billy got to his feet. Punchy sent two jabs to the side of the man's face. Billy's head rocked with each shot. He staggered forward and Punchy ducked down and swung upward with a massive uppercut.

Billy was knocked off his feet and his head bounced off the concrete floor. Punchy stood over him, fists raised, waiting for the man to move. He didn't.

Punchy stepped over the prone body and opened the apartment. The girl stood inside and he motioned for her to come out. She looked at the still bodies of her captors and turned back to Punchy. He pointed upstairs and she nodded. They moved to the elevator.

Once inside, Punchy hit the button for the first floor. He could feel the girl's eyes on him and he tried to look at everything else, the ceiling, the glowing button, the sealed doors. It had been quite a while since he was so close to a female before. He was nervous and the adrenaline from downstairs was beginning to wear off.

Now with the girl, they could call the police. They would go to the manager's office and report what had happened. If they could make it that far, he was sure the girl would be safe.

The doors slid open at the first floor lobby. Crow

stood before them. No one moved, too surprised to react.

The girl hit the button for the top floor but before the doors could close Crow leapt at Punchy. He hit the handyman twice and stars exploded in Punchy's vision.

The doors slid closed and the men began to grapple as the girl dodged to one side. Punchy hit Crow in the stomach but the assailant shrugged it off. Crow had both hands behind Punchy's neck and he pulled down and head butted the former boxer. Sharp pain radiated inside Punchy's skull. It was a familiar pain and his mind flashbacked to Svenson dancing before him, shocking him with those quick sharp jabs.

Crow jumped back and hit Punchy in the nose. Blood squirted and Punchy realized his nose was broken again. But he found himself strangely satisfied. Crow backed away and got ready to swing in again but stopped. Punchy was smiling at him.

Unlike the two punks downstairs, this kid could fight.

Punchy beckoned Crow to come on. Crow ducked in but was met with a hook to the side of the face he staggered against the side wall of the elevator. The doors slid open.

They were on the third floor. An old woman holding a small Yorkshire got ready to enter the car then stopped. She glanced at the two bloody men beating each other senseless.

The old lady screamed.

The girl moved to leave the elevator but Crow pushed her back into the corner. Punchy smacked him against the wall but Crow spun and Punchy found himself being flung through the elevator doors.

The doors slid closed on Punchy's body then re-opened again.

The old lady let out a second scream.

Punchy leapt back into the car and slammed into Crow. He unleashed a flurry of blows working inside of Crow's hands and punishing the body. Crow wheezed and tried to circle away. Punchy met him with another hook to the side of the face.

The girl punched the button to keep the doors open. She waited for a chance to escape but none came. The old woman was disappearing down the hallway, the dog slung over one shoulder watching the fight with interest.

Crow kicked out and his foot landed in Punchy's stomach. All of the air left his body and he staggered back. Crow punched him in the face and Punchy flew back through the open elevator doors and landed in the hallway.

He stared up through blurred vision and saw the girl looking helplessly down at him. Crow pushed her back against the corner and hit the elevator button. The doors closed.

*****

Punchy staggered to his feet. His head was ringing and his vision was fogging in and out. He spat a mouthful of blood onto the hallway carpet. Eyes peeked out from behind doors as the 3rd floor guests peered out at the beaten man.

Punchy wiped his eyes clear with one hand and headed for the stairs. He knocked the heavy door open and staggered up the two flights to the 5th floor hallway. He stumbled down the hall, heading for room 532.

He rounded to corner just in time to see Crow push the girl through the suite's doorway. Crow glanced back and saw Punchy coming. He called something into the suite and pulled the door closed.

Crow ran at Punchy with his hands up. He connected with a straight right. Punchy absorbed the blow. Another right followed by a left pushed Punchy back a few steps, but the boxer regained his composure quickly and pushed forward.

He ducked a hook from Crow and again started to work the body. Left right left right left right. Crow staggered back into the wall. Punchy sent two right jabs into the man's face, making his eyes water. Then followed with a left cross and a right uppercut. Crow rocked back against the wall.

Punchy threw another round of jabs. Crow's head ricocheted back and forth. Punchy kneed him in the stomach doubling the man over. He clasped both hands together and delivered a powerful ax handle blow across the back of Crow's neck.

Crow went down.

Punchy sucked deep lungfuls of air. Everything hurt. His knuckles were split open and bleeding heavily and bells rang in his head louder than ever.

He shook the fog away. It took a bit longer to clear this time.

He went to the suite door and kicked it in.

They were in the living room. Weston still sat as before, watching attentively as Punchy entered the room. The girl was nowhere to be seen. Punchy assumed she was in the bedroom.

Hayden stood by the windows. He flicked open the butterfly knife and pointed the blade at the new arrival.

"The handyman is here, Hayden," Weston spoke. "Do we have something that needs to be repaired?"

"No, boss." Hayden stepped from the windows and

now stood between Punchy and Weston.

"Shame," Weston replied. Punchy could barely make out what they were saying through his blurred vision. "What do you need if you are not here to fix something, sir?"

Punchy motioned to the bedroom.

Weston smiled. "Oh, you want the girl. Heh, I understand. She is a delightful young thing. The boys were telling me earlier how lovely she was." He leaned forward. "How juicy." Punchy glared at the man.

"Unfortunately, she is not mine to give." Weston picked up his drink and took a sip. "She has just been paid for. Just within the past hour. Otherwise, we could have worked out a deal. But it seems she is destined to go on a little trip. To fulfill a special destiny."

Hayden flicked the knife closed, then back open again. Weston leaned back in the chair.

"So you should just leave. We will let bygones be bygones. I'll forgive the trespasses made on my other associates. They were......expendable."

Punchy stepped forward and Hayden stiffened. The blade glinted under the suite's lights. He pointed at the bedroom door again, staring daggers at Weston.

"Not going to leave, huh? Okay. Suit yourself." Weston straightened one of the cuffs on his perfect suit. "Kill him, Hayden."

Hayden struck out with the knife and Punchy ducked back into the hallway. Hayden sliced outwards and this time the blade nicked Punchy's arm. He grimaced at the visceral stinging that now radiated there. He swung a hook at Hayden's head which connected solidly. The goon stumbled back and then approached slowly with the blade held out in front.

Punchy turned and Hayden followed with the blade. The handyman dodged back into the kitchen area. He swung the fridge door open as Hayden lunged again and the knife bounced off the plastic frame of the door. Punchy threw two jabs at Hayden's head but he was too far away to connect.

Hayden sliced at Punchy again and the boxer ducked backwards. He reached in and grabbed Hayden's wrist and twisted. There was a cracking sound and Hayden yowled in pain, dropping the blade to the floor.

Hayden kneed Punchy in the gut as they fell grappling. Punchy took the blow and answered with an elbow to Hayden's temple. They rolled back into the hallway, a few feet from the knife.

Punchy rolled on top of Hayden just as the young man reached out and grabbed the blade. As Hayden thrust the knife up at Punchy's face, the handyman stuck his arm inside of Hayden's elbow causing the goon's arm to bend quickly the other way. With his other hand he caught the knife hand and thrust downward hard, putting all his weight behind the attack. The blade lodged into Hayden's forehead with a THUNK.

Punchy rose to his knees and pulled the knife from Hayden's head. Bits of blood and brain flicked from the blade and landed on the hallway carpet.

He stood up and turned to face Weston. Instantly, pain shot through his stomach and back. He fell against the wall and slid slowly into the living area. He looked down and saw blood flowing from a small round hole.

Weston was standing now, still pointing the handgun at Punchy. He was talking but Punchy could not make out what he was saying. His vision blurred and he slumped down to the floor, leaning against the wall. Blackness faded in and out across his eyes. His pants were soaked and he realized it was from blood.

One second Weston was standing there and then he was gone. Time seemed to have stopped and Punchy became vitally aware of something else, a familiar sensation that had long been dormant.

"Shut up, you little bitch. You might be sold but that doesn't mean I can't knock the shit out of you."

Punchy could hear again.

He forced his eyes open and saw Weston pulling the girl through the bedroom door. She was screaming and calling for help. Weston punched her.

"Shut up!" He threw the girl down and she landed before Punchy. She looked at him pleadingly, and he could hear her gasping for help as Weston approached.

Punchy could hear again. Somewhere something had re-fused some synapses or cleared out some broken cogs and sound infiltrated his mind. He could hear Weston's expensive dress shoes as they moved across the carpet. He heard the whoosh of the air conditioner working to cool down the suite and the hum of the refrigerator coming from the kitchen. He heard people yelling in the surrounding apartments. And he heard something else far of in the distance: sirens.

"Get up. We got to move now, whore." Weston bent down to haul the girl from her knees. A sudden movement caught his attention and he turned. Punchy socked him square in the face.

Weston lurched backwards dropping the gun and hitting one of the sofas. He rebounded off the furniture and lurched forward, right into a wicked left cross. Weston flipped over the couch. Punchy stooped and picked up the butterfly knife.

He turned to the girl who was slowly getting to her feet. She looked at him as she cried and reached her hand out to him. He could hear her gentle sobs.

Punchy tilted his head slightly, a simple acknowledgement. She returned the nod. He watched her run from the suite. He turned his attention back to Weston.

The old man was struggling back to his feet. There was a cut above his right eye, and snot and spit dribbled down his face.

"You cocksucker," Weston sputtered. "You're going to die, handyman. Dead man." Punchy socked him again with his left. Weston rolled across the coffee table. A tooth rattled off the table's surface. He still gripped the knife in his right hand.

"Stop. Please," Weston begged, "I got money. Women. Whatever you want." Weston patted Punchy's arm as the boxer bent down and twisted the old man's tie in his hand. "You can be rich. I swear."

Punchy jerked the old man up by his tie and drug him to side of the room. He pushed Weston back against the wall and grabbed one of the old man's hands, laying it flat against the white surface. Weston screamed as Punchy plunged the blade through the hand impaling Weston to the wall.

Punchy stepped back as the man flailed wildly with his free hand.

"Fucking," Weston sputtered. "Stupid……fucking…..die….you retard…." He tried to remove the blade from the wall but it was stuck too deep.

Punchy spit blood and bile from his mouth. He wiped his lips with the back of his hand. His stomach was on fire and he was a plastered crimson mess of a person.

"Fu-fu-fuck y-y-youuuuuu," he answered Weston.
Punchy worked his heavy bag like never before.

*****

Officer Raab surveyed the mess in the suite. Two dead men. One from a gunshot wound to the stomach, the other beaten to a pulp. He shook his head. The Liberty was too classy a place for this business.

Stinson joined him in the living room. "Damn, what a mess."

Raab nodded. "How's the girl?"

"She's still in shock but she will be fine. Amanda King. 19 years old. Reported missing four days ago." Stinson flipped his notebook closed. "She's damn lucky. They're questioning her now. Trying to get the story figured out."

"What about the others?" Raab bent down in front of the beaten man. His face looked like grape jelly.

"One dead in the basement," Stinson replied. "The other goon is alive but barely. The one outside in the hallway is still ticking too. I'm sure they all got priors and are probably wanted by someone somewhere."

Stinson knelt down next to Raab. "This one is the handyman?"

"That's what they're telling me," Raab answered.

"Huh."

"What?" Raab looked over at Stinson.

Stinson pointed at the body in front of him. "I know this guy."

"What?"

"Yeah. This is The Dynamite Kid, Ricky Jones."

"The boxer?"

Stinson nodded. "Yeah, he was a hell of a fighter.

Before he lost his hearing or something. I saw him knock out Junior Wells in three rounds. Ate that schmuck up, I tell you."

Raab stood back up and Stinson joined him. "Damn. I remember him. I saw him fight Doc Collins. He had this superfast jab that no one saw coming."

"It's a damn shame," Stinson nodded. "Too bad he never amounted to anything."

Raab nodded and headed for the door. He needed a cigarette.

BANDWIDTH

"I HAVE TO GO OUTSIDE, Bill."

Wayne depressed the large button on the side of the mic and waited for an answer. His eyes worked their way across the map that hung above the small table and ham radio set. The map was covered with red marks, highlighting the infected areas. The blacked out areas were the ones that were already lost. Wayne looked at the title of the map: Eastern United States. It was all covered in red or black, had been for the past 16 months.

Wonder what the map of the west coast would look like? he thought to himself. *Wonder what the mid-west looks like? Hell, how about Canada? Japan? Africa? Or the whole damn lot of EDA NATO territories?*

He turned the volume up a bit on the radio, waiting for an answer from Bill.

Wonder if there are any stupid penguins left in the stupid Arctic?

Wayne leaned forward and pressed the open button on the mic. He heard the small backlash of static as the frequency cleared and his signal crossed miles of open space to connect with Bill's receiver on the other end.

All that way in only a matter of seconds. No one can cover ground like that anymore. Never again. Not now.

Why would you want to? Karen's face flashed into his mind as if to answer the thought and he quickly pushed it away again, becoming mindful that he was still pressing the button and had not said anything.

"Did you hear me, Bill? I said I got to go outside." He let the mic go and waited. Still nothing. He looked at the awkward buttons below the radio's dials. The radio was an antique for sure, but it was the only way to communicate right now. The main communication relay towers for the base, for the state, maybe even the whole country were apparently not working for some reason.

Wayne glanced back at the map and figured he knew pretty well why they weren't working.

He tapped his fingers on the smooth tabletop, waiting for the speaker to come alive.

"Shit," he muttered to the small concrete room. If Bill's radio was broken or screwed up some way, that was it. He would be all alone for good.

Wayne pushed down the panic and ran his hands through his graying black hair. He had cut it a few days earlier with a pair of scissors, bagging up the trimmings and flushing them into the vacuum lock. It felt great to have a fresh cut, felt cooler and cleaner.

He leaned forward to press the button again, trying to keep the panic at bay but feeling it tighten around his throat.

Suddenly, the receiver squelched and Bill's steady voice chimed back.

"Damn, Wayne. You sure?"

"Yeah. I only have rations left for two more days. And

that is after cutting back almost two weeks ago."

"Damn."

"Yeah." Wayne settled more comfortably into the leather roll chair. The chair was the nicest thing in the old bomb shelter. The table, radio, and shelves full of rations and water bottles were all from the turn of the century. The chair was too, but it was comfortable and durable. And after 16 months had pretty much conformed to Wayne's backside.

Bill came back on. "That sucks, man. I'm sorry. I know what…well, I just know, okay?"

"Yeah." Wayne glanced at the map again. "The supply depot sits about sixty yards from the door. At least it was there before. It's my only chance at food. If I have to go any further, percentage drops. Drops fast."

"You got ammo?"

Wayne glanced at the Pulsar Kick rifle leaning at the foot of the ladder. The Bolt Skin hand gun hung from one of the shelves, still in its holster. He had about 200 rounds for the rifle and another 30-40 for the Bolt. "I got plenty. If anything, I'll take some of the bastards with me."

"Your power supply is still good?"

Wayne looked over at the dial set attached to one of the concrete walls. The needles were stuck at ¾.

"Yep. I got power reserves for another 2 years if need be."

"You can say one thing about the damn Republic. They built a good power structure. Even if they did kill the whole fucking planet. Assholes."

Wayne chuckled. *Yeah, they sure did that.*

"Bill, I'm going to try and get some rest. I need to do some thinking. I really need to sit down and try and remember the layout of the base. Maybe I'll diagram it or something. Shit, I don't know."

"No, No. You do what you got to do. I'll try and think of something too. Some way to make it easier or another way to....well, shit, I don't know. I just don't have anything else to do, you know?"

"Yeah, I know what you mean. I'll talk to you in a bit." Wayne signed off and flipped the power switch. The radio whistled softly and died away.

He got up from the chair and stretched his 5'10" frame. He wasn't skinny but always had a gangly type of build. His back ached a bit from sitting for so long, and his left foot had fallen asleep. He began to jog in place, easing blood back into his extremities and working the tight muscles in his body.

Got to relax. Got to stay calm. You still have time. You still have time. He repeated the thought over and over again. It was his mantra now, for however long that was. *You still have time.*

He sidled over to the small cot and sat down. Unlacing the heavy leather boots, Wayne glanced around the small shelter. It wasn't very big, roughly 30 feet square on either side. It was one of a handful of shelters built into the foundation of the checkpoint barracks. There were four others that he knew of, located in the various spots of the small base. He was pretty sure they were all empty save for this one. He was pretty sure he was the only survivor of that first wave of infected.

Small wonder I never lost my head in this tiny bit of a place. But small places never bothered Wayne. He was a Front Gunner. They were used to being holed up in all kinds of tight spots, staying out of sight, waiting for the right moment to ambush enemy squadrons. Or give covering fire to those trying to escape infected areas. But that was a long time ago. Almost two years since seeing any action and being transferred to checkpoint duty.

They were all so thankful to finally be off the front lines, and working in a civilian setting. Thompson, Myers, Cutter, and himself. The Four Amigos they always joked together. Now Thompson, Myers, and Cutter were either dead or had joined the ranks of crazy. Which was probably worse than death. He was here. Lucky enough to remember the bunker. Lucky enough to get here in time. Lucky enough to survive.

"Luck's run out, soldier. Looks like the end of the line." His voice died against the concrete walls. The small Day Glo light bulbs (they were supposed to simulate real day light, but Wayne thought they were for shit), wavered a bit in their fittings.

His boots thumped to the floor and he lay back on the cot. His stomach was growling but he ignored it's rumblings. It was not time to eat yet, not for quite a while.

Two days. Two days to figure it out.

"So do it already," he said, his voice steady.

Wayne pushed one arm up under the pillow and closed his eyes. *Visualize the barracks. Where are we? Where would you start?*

He would go up the ladder. The Bolt would be strapped on one calf, his right. He would carry the rifle. The Bolt would only be used once the rifle was out of rounds. He could carry five additional clips in his pack. They would be the only thing inside the bag. He would need the room for supplies.

Up the ladder, through the door lock up into the side main lock. The bunker was located on one of the small extended wings out from the main barracks. *Okay, the main lock will be secure. If I go right I'll be back to the...no, that's wrong. I go left and I enter the main barracks. Right takes me out. Outside to the center lot.*

There was no way in hell he was going back through the main barracks. The last time he passed through there he was running for his life. That was where they had caught Myers. He shuddered remembering how the main mess hall had filled with the sounds of twisted laughter from infected. The laughter mingled with the screams and gurgles of the dying and tortured played hell on his dreams for months afterwards.

Wayne opened his eyes and pushed the vision of the cafeteria massacre away. *Focus.* He closed them again and continued his journey.

Go right. There is the door lock. There was no way the doors on either side of the bunker entrance would be broken. They were too heavy and air sealed. A combination code was punched in to open them and he highly doubted any of the attackers would have it. As far as any of the survivors who would have turned into infected, well, they never seemed to recollect any previous memories of their old life.

Only that urge. The urge to maim. And torture. And laugh. Always laughing when they caught the scent of a potential victim.

I'll exit the door lock. Straight outside to the lot. There will be some parked vehicles. Maybe some patrol "rats" or a Buggy. They'll make good cover. I'll have to go slow, be patient once outside. And aware. Very, very fucking aware.

Across the center lot would be the supply warehouse. It was split into two different caches. Weapons and armor were on the north side. But this side, the south end, which he would be facing once he left the door, housed the food rations. There would be water, vitamin packs, protein meals, everything he would need for another few months right there.

And then what? You get the supplies you need and you are right back here. Right back to your little hole in the ground. And a few weeks later, you got the same problem again.

"But I'll still be alive. And as long as I'm alive, I'll have a chance, goddamn it."

He sat back up on the cot and rubbed his hands across his temples. *And what happens when....if you die? Bill is alone then.* But he couldn't think about Bill. That was not his problem. His problem was figuring out how to make it past the next 48 hours. Bill would have to fend for himself. And hope one day he wasn't in the same predicament.

Wayne hopped from the cot and started doing pushups. He exercised every day. He was limited in space and movement within the bunker, but made sure he stayed active to keep his strength up. He counted off the pushups in his head, breathing deeply in and out. Soon he was covered with a thin sheen of sweat.

He stood up and began doing squats with his hands clasped behind his neck. Soon his shirt was drenched and he stopped and walked slowly back and forth from the desk to the far wall where the ladder was located. He stood at the bottom rungs and looked up at the darkened circular door above.

Nothing. No noise came from the other side of the door. Which was not surprising. The hatchway was at least six inches thick. He pondered the door for a few minutes trying to envision what the other side was like. Would the air taste different? Will he be blinded by all the natural light? He was sure after being cooped up for so long that the outside was going to be shocking to his senses at first.

You'll wait at the main lock after going up. At least until you have adjusted to being outside.

He left the hatch and peeled his sweaty clothes off. At the other end of the bunker, next to the table with the radio was a small fresher closet. He leapt in and let the cool sprits of water melt the sweat from his body. Then a blanket of warm air enveloped him, drying the dampness and leaving him feeling somewhat refreshed, but still very hungry.

He grabbed a change of clothes from the drawers and sat at the small eating nook. He began to diagram the base. Even though the supply barracks were only sixty yards away, he would need to have emergency plans and backup plans to those. He would need to remember the layout of the whole base. *Why there is no map of the base down here is beyond me,* he thought to himself.

The base itself was not large, and the supply warehouses were located on this side of the base. The first one, the one he was aiming for, held the food on one end and the ammo dump on the other end. The second warehouse held parts for the vehicles and tech upgrades for the communications depot and maintenance offices.

Wayne was under the mess hall and main offices. And on the opposite side of the base sat the medical unit and flight pad. There were two checkpoint gates on the north and south ends of the base and a large concrete wall surrounded the area.

The last time Wayne had seen the checkpoints they were being swarmed with infected and the soldiers manning each station had been trampled underfoot and then torn apart.

If this side of the supply warehouse was blocked, he would have to circle all the way around to the ammo side and enter from there. This was something he did not want to do, but it would be the only way he could enter the building if the first set of doors would not open.

He looked at the finished drawing, feeling satisfied with what he saw.

"That's pretty good," he said aloud.

He looked at the clock. Time for dinner. Reaching over to the nearly empty ration closet, he brought out one lonely pack of protein drops. Cherry flavored.

"All the advanced tech the Republic has sponsored and we still have only cherry flavored protein drops to look forward too." He opened the small pack and wolfed down the drops. Despite the bland taste, he was starving and finished the pack in seconds. He looked longingly at the remaining rations.

No. Make it last.

Wayne marched over to the radio and sat in the chair. He hit the power switch. Every time he switched the set on he scanned the network, looking for other survivors. The only one he had ever found was Bill.

The radio squelched as it worked the band, looking for another live broadcast frequency. It stopped on only one, Bill's.

"Hey Bill, you busy?"

This time Bill answered quickly. "Nope, just having fun staring at the walls. I'd cut my arm off for a television."

Wayne laughed.

"You figure out your plan?" Bill asked.

"I figured out all I'm going to be able to. I'm not going to know anything until I leave the building." Wayne fidgeted with one of the dials, trying to bring the signal in clearer.

"It's weird."

"What's that?"

Bill paused a bit before continuing. "I mean, I know going out is the last thing in the world either of us wants to do. But I have to say, it's exciting. I mean, aren't you curious?"

Wayne thought about it. "Yeah. I think I know what you're talking about. Just the idea of being somewhere instead of this bunker *is* exciting. And who knows, maybe there is nothing up there. Maybe something happened and all the infected keeled over and died."

"Exactly. The unknown. There's a sense of adventure in it."

"Even though I'm probably going to die." Wayne leaned back into the chair. "It could be even worse. The whole damn building could have fallen down on top of the bunker. I just don't know."

Bill did not respond.

"Sorry. I didn't mean to be such a negative ass about it." Wayne waited.

"No. you're right. Best to be a realist about such things. We're military men. We don't subscribe to false hope. We go head first and find the truth of things."

Wayne nodded. "I am going to change one thing."

Bill waited.

"There's no sense in dicking around and driving myself crazy at the same time. I'm heading out in the morning. First thing."

Now the silence stretched for quite a bit between the two.

Bill was the first to speak. "I'll be here. I'll be waiting for your full report, Sergeant. Good luck."

"Thanks." Wayne cut the power.

*****

That night Wayne slept pretty soundly. He swallowed four sleeping pills to help him rest and it seemed to work. This time there were no dreams of Karen, or Myers, or Cutter screaming for his mom or horrible laughing coming from bloody shadows with long reaching fingers.

He eased out from the cot as the timer sounded on his watch. Slowly he blinked sleep from his eyes and then started to get ready.

After a quick trip to the fresher, he grabbed his corded cams from the drawers and put them on. Next he put on the heavy boots and then the padded fingerless gloves that were standard issue for army regulars.

Glancing in the mirror, he caught sight of his dog tags rattling against his chest. He pulled them off and looked at the metallic plate.

WAYNE LAWRENCE COLLINS
SER# 67007739

Lawrence. He hated the name Lawrence.

He laid the tags on the pillow of his cot.

Let them be a memorial.

In case I don't come back.

A small headstone for Wayne Lawrence Collins and his big bag of shit luck.

He went over to one of the side racks and pulled the gray Kevlar vest from its hanger. He snapped it in place and then strapped the Bolt pistol to his leg. Next came the sturdy back pack and over that he slung the rifle.

The last thing he grabbed from the rack was his helmet. It was one of the newer designs. Padded Kevlar over PlastiKing, the new plastic polymer the Republic scientists came up with. It was extremely strong and very lightweight, making the helmet feel like a ball cap sitting on top of his head.

Wayne checked the load on the Pulsar. It was good. Safety on. *Until I reach the outer lock anyways.*

He looked at himself in the mirror. It was the first time in sixteen months he had worn his gear. He looked like a soldier, a highly trained soldier, and he felt like a badass.

"Time's up, Wayne," he spoke to himself. "You need to go out and make you some more. Because time is up."

He huffed air in deep breaths, calming himself down and relaxing the tension in his shoulders and stomach. He slapped his helmet hard and headed up the ladder.

At the hatch, he twisted the round wheel that opened the door. There was a whirring sound as the locks pulled back from the frame and then a thump as the hatch gave way.

Wayne pushed the hatch open and crawled from the bunker. He slammed the door closed again and listened for the locks to seal in place. Once satisfied with what he heard, he turned to his surroundings.

It was the first time he had stepped out of the bunker in over a year.

To his right was the main door to the outside. He clicked the safety off of the rifle and peeked through the small window. The morning sun was already high in the sky and the base was bright with daylight. He could see a couple of rats parked right outside. He took one final glance and turned back to the opposite door set behind him.

This one led into the main barracks. The cafeteria was straight down the highway. Along with the dead.

He peered into this window but could make nothing out in the darkened gloom of the hall.

Wayne turned back to the main door and looked at the

keypad. This one took a five digit number.

He couldn't remember it. He recalled some of the digits, but not the whole sequence.

He punched in a code.

45342

The pad buzzed. The code was wrong.

45322

Buzz.

45344

Buzz.

43342

Buzz.

"Dammit!" Wayne smacked his helmet against the door. *What was it? He had entered it a hundred times over and over again. What was the damn code?*

43322

Buzz.

45321

Buzz.

He paused. This was something his hands had done every day for years. He lifted his fingers from the pad and let his hand waver over the board. The muscles would remember. Instinct could take over if he just focused and remained calm.

45326

Buzz.

45313

Beep.

The code was accepted and the door locks flipped open.

Wayne smiled. He checked the rifle again and looked at the Bolt strapped to his leg.

Now or never. He took one glance back at the hatch and

pushed the door open.

The daylight was jarring. After spending so much time in the false light of the bunker, the sunlight was intense.

Wayne blinked his eyes quickly. He stood in the doorway, not moving, just letting his eyes adjust. After a bit, they began to settle and he took in the morning air.

It was amazing. He filled his lungs with as much of it as possible. After breathing the re-generated air in the bunker, the fresh oxygen was almost causing Wayne to feel delirious.

Slow down. Slow your breathing and maintain or you're going to freak out.

Wayne inhaled slowly and kept still. He was focusing on his heartbeat, trying to keep it calm. After a few minutes, he felt better.

He studied the side lot. There were three rats parked on the side of the building. They resembled small thick-coated HumVees. The first two appeared empty. The driver's side door on the third was pulled open and a body lay half inside the vehicle. The head was missing and a trail of gore left the neck and disappeared around the corner of the building.

Okay. Not going that way. Wayne checked the interior of the first rat. It was empty. He went to the second, making sure to be as quiet as possible and always looking for movement in the surrounding buildings. The second rat was empty but Wayne saw a familiar green pack lodged up on the dashboard, under the windshield.

"Jackpot," he whispered. He grabbed the bag and checked the contents. Incendiary pegs. Ten of them. They were the size of a lipstick but carried a nice sized charge. Click the button on top and you had just enough time to pitch it before it exploded. He stashed the pegs into his pack, putting one of the small cylinders into the side pocket of his vest. *Just in case.*

Wayne stood at the rear of the rat and looked across the way to the supply warehouse. It was a straight shot, blocked only by the occasional corpse. He tried not to look at these, but his eyes kept focusing on the blood-matted hair or the dried out expressions on the faces of the soldiers. Wayne shook his head, driving the images from his mind. He ran across the lot, bent forward, always looking for movement.

*****

The door to the ration depot was locked. This door did not require a punch code as it was usually open to soldiers and personnel throughout the day. Only now someone had locked it from the inside. He examined the small keyhole. Picking it was not going to work. He would need to shoot it open or use one of the incendiary pegs, and that was going to be trouble. The noise would bring unwanted company.

He leaned back against the door and racked his brain. *Do I blow the lock and hope they are far enough away that I can get in and out? Or do I go around to the ammo side and come in from that direction? What if that door there is locked too? What it there are infected waiting over there? What if? What if?*

"Hell," he said into the bright morning sun. He let out a deep breath. He wanted nothing more than to go back into the bunker and talk to Bill. At least there he had someone to support him, to help him focus his thinking as his unseen friend had done for the past several months.

So focus on that. Getting back to Bill. Getting back there alive and being able to continue on. Wayne cleared his thoughts and turned back to the lot.

Something moved next to the barracks.

Wayne brought the rifle to his shoulder and sighted at the location. He stopped breathing and waited. It moved again. A small fluttering motion.

He exhaled ever so slowly and put more pressure on the trigger. He had to be sure. If it was nothing and he fired, they would come. From wherever they were hiding. They would overwhelm him in seconds.

A small plastic bag whirled out from around the corner of the building. A slight breeze had caught it and lifted it into the air. Wayne kept the bag in his sights then moved the rifle back to the original spot.

Nothing else moved. Just the bag, dipping and diving its way across the base.

He relaxed, the tension in his shoulders flowing outwards.

I'll go around. Maybe the base is empty. Maybe after killing everyone, they got bored and found somewhere else to shit on.

He eased over to the corner of the building and peeked around the side. A large troop transport lay overturned in the front lot. The truck was what they called a Deuce 12 and looked to have caught fire sometime during the initial attack. Next to that was another rat, this one also burned out. Dried out corpses were strewn around the vehicles in haphazard fashion, some missing limbs, others with screams of anguish frozen on their faces.

He turned the corner and came to a side door. This led into a small office that oversaw special orders and supply requests. He had been in it once before, a long time ago. He used the barrel of the rifle to ease open the door.

The room was a mess. A woman lay naked, bloody, and quite dead across the desk. Another body, this one a man, was piled in the corner. He was missing his arms and lower jaw. The smell was overpowering.

Wayne covered his mouth with one hand and held down the bile that was threatening to exit his body.

Goddamn animals. Filthy animals. To hell with them all.

He eased the door closed again and hurried past it. Several of the side windows were shattered but the openings were blocked with thick iron bars. They would not provide a way in. Still, Wayne tried to see into the interior of the building but after a few feet the darkness ate everything.

He scuttled to the opposite end of the warehouse. There was another small parking lot here; this one empty except for the lone corpse tied to the chain link fence that ran across the base. It was another soldier, the body stripped and maimed beyond recognition.

Wayne glanced quickly at it and headed for the warehouse door.

There was a slight shift in his peripheral vision. He turned around and looked back at the corner of the building where he had come from.

There was a shadow moving on the ground. Someone was approaching from that side of the building. Wayne knelt and took aim a few feet above the ground.

He waited stealing glances between the growing silhouette and where he was pointing the rifle.

A man came around the corner. Blood oozed from the corners of his eyes and from his nostrils, a sure sign of infection. The man hitched along as if willing his legs to move was proving a challenge. He wore army fatigues, a fellow soldier, but even through the heavy material Wayne could see how skinny this host had become.

They're starving. Maybe they're dying out. Maybe the situation has changed. He sighted along the rifle and stiffened his trigger finger.

The infected caught sight of him. His mouth broke into a grin. The soldier was missing all of his teeth, and his gums were a blotched canvas of blood and gore. He began to laugh, a soft chuckle as he looked at Wayne.

"Shit," Wayne said under his breath. The laugh was another sign of infection. All of the infected would begin to laugh uncontrollably, whether running after their victims or in the process of torturing them. It was unsettling to hear. Especially when you had an attacking horde trying to get to you. It scared the hell out of Wayne. It scared the hell out of everyone.

The infected man's laugh grew louder and Wayne grimaced as the sound echoed throughout the lot. The soldier charged. Wayne fired.

The report of the rifle was deafening.

The bullet ripped through the man's head and chunks of bone and brain splashed the pavement. The soldier fell, twitching violently and then was still.

That was one thing about the bastards. The scientists said they were still alive. The infection made them crazy and uncontrollable and left them laughing like hyenas, but you could kill them with traditional means. Shoot them, burn them, stab them in the heart and the infected would fall.

Wayne did not move, still aiming the rifle at where he had fired, and listened.

Silence. Nothing happened.

Please. Please let that be it. Sweat began to pour down his forehead. The sunlight glistened on the thick sheen of moisture and Wayne ignored the running drops that began to spill from under his helmet.

Then the base came alive.

Laughter floated from the still surroundings. Dark evil laughter. It seemed to come from behind Wayne, from above him, from the very ground he stood on.

The rifle began to shake. And Wayne realized his hands were trembling.

Now the laughter was deafening. Wayne gritted his teeth and turned back towards the door. He ran in a dead sprint, his helmet flying from his head and the backpack bouncing against his shoulder blades like a cowboy riding the prize bull at the rodeo.

On the other side of the chain link fence sat the med hall. The doors exploded open and a mass of infected bodies pushed through the entrance. Men, women, children all laughing and spitting blood and mucus from their open maws and seeing Wayne, began howling into the sky.

The horde attacked the fence and it began to shudder and twist under the heavy impact of the bodies.

Behind him, Wayne could hear other doors belonging to other buildings bursting open and empting their hellish contents into the asphalt parking lots.

Wayne looked at his pursuers. And now he saw how they had survived for so long, saw why so many had flocked to the base, had made it *their* base. They were feeding off of themselves.

Infected bodies missing skin from their faces laughed guffaws of insanity at the fleeing soldier. Infected missing arms and fingers and noses pushed against the metal links of the fence. A few of the attackers still carried the remainders of their meals while others kept reaching for their accomplices and trying to tear another bite from their moving bodies.

Wayne was ten yards from the door when the fence collapsed.

He heard the weak metal give way and fired a round of bullets into the oncoming rush before hitting the door.

If this door is locked, I am dead.

He kicked at the closed door and screamed as it gave way and swung inward.

Wayne hurried into the main office and ran for the interior double doors. He needed to be on the other side of these doors when the infected hit the building. He knew what the next room housed.

An arsenal.

Wayne hit the unlock button on the keypad and heard the click of the tumblers give way. The door whooshed open and he dived inwards as the sound of howling laughter burst through the front entrance.

He dodged to the right and punched the lock button, closing the doors. His hand hurt from where he had dislocated two of his knuckles jamming the button so hard. Daylight poured through the iron bars of the windows and Wayne slid between two racks of Pulse rifles and ammo. He quickly shrugged off the pack and slid the incendiary pegs onto the floor.

He reached up and grabbed two more rifles and stacked them next to him. Then he grabbed three boxes of clips and put those next to the rifles. He checked the load on his current gun and aimed at the doors.

Something huge slammed against the thick metal. The doors sagged against the frame and Wayne gripped the rifle even tighter.

There is no way that door holds them. There are too many. The doors to the warehouses were weaker than the ones on the main barracks. These entrances were always under heavy guard and Republic higher ups doubted that anyone would dare steal from their providers. The punishment would be too severe. So in place of the heavy air locks the barracks had, these door were thinner and under normal reinforcement.

The doors began to sag inwards and Wayne could hear the heavy metal of the locks begin to squeal in protest.

Any second now.

The doors began opening and a few inches of space appeared between them. Wayne watched as bloody hands reached inside, reached for him. He saw an eye looking at him and watched as bloody lips turned upwards into a terrible smile.

Wayne fired as the gap grew larger. He needed to kill as many as possible before the doors opened all the way. The dead bodies would start piling up and slow the ones behind.

The supply room echoed with the sound of gunfire, screams, and laughter. He fired into the gap and watched bodies bounce away as the doors pushed wider. There was a loud crunch as they finally broke apart and the horrors tried to pour into the room all at once. Wayne smashed the trigger down as round after round tore into the bodies.

Infected fell to the ground, large holes blown through their heads and torsos. The rest piled over the dead, trying to get at Wayne. Some fell to their hands and knees looking to pull flesh from the already dead, so hungry that they became oblivious to the gunfire. Wayne shot them with ease, adding to the growing pile.

The second rifle fired its last rounds and clicked off. Wayne ejected the clip and grabbed a new one. Now he began picking his targets instead of firing crazily into the crowd. The entranceway was littered with bodies and blood rolled across the floor towards him.

But the infected continued to break through and a second wave now joined the first. The walls on either side were beginning to give. The sound of laughter filled his ears and began to saw against his nerves.

The walls holding the door finally gave way.

He grabbed two of the pegs and clicked the buttons on top. He threw them at the door then dived for the floor. The explosion rocked the building.

The laughter was replaced with ringing. Wayne rolled over, groggy from the force of the blast. A large cloud of dust billowed across the room and his face and hands were littered with small cuts from flying debris.

Get up. Get up, damn you, they're coming.

He swung to his knees and looked for the rifle. Already more of the sick filled the gaping hole in the armory. Wayne's hand closed on the gun and he brought it up pulling the trigger while sliding across the floor towards his backpack.

He grabbed another peg, this time smashing the button against his thigh while he fired into the oncoming mass. He threw the peg high, watching it arc over the frontline of infected and into the small office area.

Wayne ducked as the explosion lifted infected and concrete into the air.

He mowed down the front runners. He swung his pack on quickly and stuffed the rest of the pegs into his front pocket. He grabbed the rifle and headed for the rear of the armory. Something hit his shoulder and knocked him down.

Wayne rolled onto his back. A woman crawled over his stomach and pushed down on his neck. She smiled and blood dribbled from her lips onto Wayne's cheek.

"Fuck!" He had dropped the rifle when he fell. He used one arm to push the woman back off of him while the other reached for the Bolt handgun strapped to his leg. He pulled the gun and stuck the barrel into her mouth. The woman giggled and Wayne fired.

He covered his face with both arms as the back of the woman's head exploded. Gore rained down onto the floor and Wayne made sure none fell into his mouth or eyes. He would have to be careful to keep from touching his face with his hands.

He pushed the woman off of him and staggered to his feet. A man rushed from the darkness and Wayne shot him down. Another from his left and Wayne turned and fired. A small infected boy fell to the ground.

He fired the rest of the clip into the crowd and ran for the rear door.

The door gave way as he thumbed the lock. He was now in the small access hallway between the two storage areas. The door exited onto a small metal platform and a flight of stairs led down to the hallway. At the end of the hall was the entrance to the supply depot.

Wayne closed the armory door and secured it. He reached into his pocket for the pegs. On the side of each cylinder was a second button. He lodged one peg into the door handle and looked above him. The supports for this part of the building ran across the low ceiling. He stuck three more pegs on top of the beams, pushing the small button on the side of each one and on the one against the door. He ran down the stairs.

The door began to shudder and sounds of glee echoed from the other side.

Wayne backed down the hall. He pulled another incendiary peg from his vest pocket. When he had pushed the side buttons on the other devices, it had activated a small transmitter within each one. Once he clicked the detonator on this one, they would all go off together. He had five seconds.

The door began to buckle. Wayne clicked the button and threw the peg at the foot of the stairs. He turned and ran down the hallway trying to reach the door.

He was lifted from his feet and thrown against the wall. He bounced off and cowered in the corner as the explosion collapsed the ceiling onto the small platform. The noise was tremendous. The stairs were buried underneath a mountain of debris.

Wayne sat stunned for a few minutes. He was shaking from fear and adrenaline. Carefully he looked up. Sunlight poured down from where the ceiling had been. The small room was gone now, buried under rubble. He could not see the door. It was buried also.

But the walls had held, as he guessed they would. The Republic built their buildings strong and because of that he managed to collapse the ceiling without losing the whole warehouse. He had sealed himself off from the infected, but could still hear them laughing and moaning from within the armory.

Lucky the whole damn armory hadn't gone off. The walls held. That's what counted. He was safe for now.

Wayne stood up and checked his body. He was sore as hell but luckily nothing was broken. He wiped the blood and gore from his face with the back of his sleeve, being careful not to rub anything into his eyes. He would be able to find water in this part of the building and would wash up as soon as possible.

But now he needed to get moving. He had bought himself some time and he needed to take advantage of it.

RAW FEED STORIES

He opened the door and entered the main supply depot.

Pulling the door shut, Wayne spun around.

He stared down the barrel of a rifle, the tip almost touching him between the eyes. Wayne looked down the gun at the man holding it. Bloodshot eyes glared back at him.

"D-D-Don't you fucking move!"

*****

The city was quiet. Its sidewalks empty, its streets full of corpses and stalled vehicles. The city had slept for over a year. Nothing stirred. Nothing moved.

The explosion ripped through the quiet serenity of the forgotten metropolis. The huge ball of fire and smoke mushroomed over the skyline, the noise sending a signal in the afternoon stillness.

The city came alive. Its hotels and fancy chain stores, broken apartments and dark subways, voided a large bloody mass of murderous infected into its main streets.

The noise had awakened them from funny dreams of mass murder and rape and torture. The noise had distracted them from scavenging for food from bloated corpses and former friends. The noise was an event. It signaled life.

The infected hated life.

They turned to the blast and began to walk, stagger, and run towards the fireball.

Thousands upon thousands.

A great exodus had begun.

They were all heading for the base.

*****

Wayne dropped his handgun to the floor.

"Don't move," the man repeated. He was shorter than Wayne and older, his hairline receding pretty aggressively back away from his tall forehead. The barrel of the rifle was shaking slightly. His nervousness showed.

"Okay. It's okay. I'm not here to hurt you." Wayne tried to remain calm.

"Who are you? Where did you come from?" The gun shook even more. The man licked his lips and thrust the rifle at Wayne again.

"Whoa! Calm down. My name is Wayne. I was stationed here. I've been in one of the underground bunkers here."

The stranger's eyes widened in surprise. "You've been here all along? Here on the base? How?"

"The bunker has all kinds of supplies. It's outfitted with everything. It's got power and all. But I ran out of food. I had to come up." Wayne pointed to the storage facility behind the gunman. "I knew there was food here."

"What was all that gunfire? The explosion?"

"The infected are out there." Wayne watched as the stranger glanced towards the windows of the warehouse. It was his chance. In one swift move, he pushed the rifle barrel up and smacked the man across the forearm with his fist, dislodging his grip from the gun. Wayne turned the rifle around on the man as he fell to the floor.

"Please. Please don't kill me. I'm sorry." The man climbed to his knees, pleading.

"Stop it. I'm not going to hurt you." The stranger stopped begging and looked up at the soldier. "You're the first person I've seen in over a year. I'm not going to hurt you." Wayne lowered the rifle. "What's your name?"

The older man wiped his face clean with his sleeve and leaned back against the wall.

"My name is Alan."

"How long have you been here?"

"About six months." Alan glanced nervously out the barred window next to him. "Are they really out there?"

Wayne nodded. "Yeah, they've pretty much taken over the base. How did you manage to stay alive for so long?"

Alan pointed to the front of the warehouse. "There's a small basement. It's out of the way and pretty secure. I stay there. I sneak up here to get food and such. Whatever I need. I figured help would eventually come." Alan looked at Wayne excitedly. "It's coming, right? You're a soldier. You would know. Help is coming?"

Wayne stood unmoving. Alan read the expression on his face and his body sagged.

"Oh my God, it really is the end of the world, isn't it?"

Wayne changed the subject. "You stay in a basement? Can we go there? I think we need to find a place to hole up a bit until things calm down. And I need to wash this stuff from my hands and face."

Alan nodded. He helped Wayne grab some food and water from the shelves and led him to the front part of the warehouse. Wayne stopped and peeked through the double doors to the office. From there he could see through the front door to the outside. The sun was beginning to fall from the sky, and smoke billowed across the lot from the explosion.

But he could see the main door to the barracks. And on the other side of that was the entrance to the bunker. Sixty yards away.

He ducked behind the door as infected appeared from around the corner. He knew he had put a large dent in the number of attackers but there was still a large group on the base. He snuck a peek and watched them milling around, blood and now guts dripping from their faces. *They've been feeding on their dead*, he thought. *Better them than me.*

He joined Alan at the top of the stairs and they walked down into the dark. Alan snapped on a small LED flashlight and pointed it at a large unmarked metal door. He pulled the metal handle and the door opened onto the basement.

He closed the door behind them and Wayne covered his eyes as the fluorescent lights cut on. They were built into opposite walls of the basement and were almost painful to look at.

"Come back here next to the storage racks. The light doesn't shine directly there and you won't be blinded." Alan led the way over to some tall racks that held assorted office supplies. Replacement bulbs, reams of copier paper, stacks of batteries and more littered the shelves. The basement itself was small, only a little bigger than the bunker. It was darker, even with the annoying lights, and smelled musty. There were several small pipes protruding from one wall, their ends open to the room.

On the floor was a makeshift bed made from several blankets. A few ratty paperbacks lay next to the bed along with some packets of food and a couple of bottles of water.

"It's not much," Alan turned to Wayne, "but it's kept me alive for a quite a bit." He leaned the rifle against one of the racks and grabbed a bottle of water.

Wayne pointed at the small pipes. "What about those?"

"Near as I can figure, it was some sort of pneumatic mailing system they had here once. You remember anything like that?"

Wayne shook his head.

"We had one in my office building. Pretty neat setup. Throw your message in a cylinder and it would zoom off to the desired destination." Alan patted one of the pipes. "The best thing is you can hear things from around the base. Sound carries through these and they run all over the place."

"Really?" Wayne looked into one of the pipes. Nothing but darkness stared back at him.

"When I first found this place, I could hear all kinds of stuff. Bodies moving. Furniture getting pushed around. Sometimes screams. And of course, laughing. That damn laughing. That was the worse. I didn't sleep for days. Just sat here, listening to that, that…..insanity."

Wayne leaned back against the wall and checked the load on the Bolt. Six shots left. That was it. He still had two pegs in his bag. His rifles were lost in the explosion.

"How many rounds in that rifle?"

Alan shrugged. "Full clip. I found it in one of those jeeps outside. I grabbed it and ran in here before anything could see me. I've never fired it."

*Need more ammo. It's not far to the bunker but if we get pinned down by infected…..*Wayne let the thought trail off.

He wished he could talk with Bill. Bill always seemed to be able to figure things out. His base had the same basic layout as Wayne's. Bill would be able to piece together a better plan to get across.

Wayne looked up. Alan was asking him something. "What?"

"I said are you going back to the bunker? I mean, you came up to re-supply, right?"

"Yeah." Wayne nodded more firmly. "Yes. I am going back to the bunker."

Alan stood in front of the soldier. "Will you let me come with you?"

Wayne stared at the man. The *alive* man. The first one he had seen in so long. He did not speak for several minutes.

"Yes. Yes, you can come with me, Alan." Alan smiled in gratitude. "It will be cramped. But I can't leave you. We can help each other. And Bill, he'll be happy to talk to someone else too."

"Bill? Who's Bill?"

Wayne explained about the ham radio and the other survivor.

"Oh crap. So there are others out there?" Alan snapped his fingers. "Of course, there are. There have to be. We survived, didn't we? You say he's at another army base."

Wayne nodded.

"Holy shit. That's one hell of a coincidence." Alan leaned back against the wall, still smiling.

"Believe me, I know. Damn lucky he answered my call. I would have gone insane down there, all by myself."

"But if the radio is working, then you can contact others, right?" Alan started to show his excitement. "There have to be others out there."

"Not exactly. We both scan the channels daily, looking for any other working frequency. Sometimes we get blips, but we can't get anything to come in. We're lucky these bases even have these radios. Most of them were destroyed when the Republic green lit the new communication satellites." Wayne took a seat on the floor. He was tired and starting to feel the effects of the day. He grabbed one of the water bottles and began washing his hands and face.

"But then something happened, the satellites failed," he continued. "The rumors were that the infected had overtaken PSD Technical and destroyed the whole thing. You remember the day every cell phone and face box stopped working? The only things we could rely on were the older devices. They issued talkies to all of us here. Good for a mile tops. In one fell swoop, we all regressed thirty years."

"Citizen's band. Unbelievable." Alan grabbed a ration pack and opened it. He offered some to Wayne, who took a pack of protein mix. They took a few minutes to eat.

"Where is Bill? How far away?"

"He's at Louisville. About eighty miles east." The mix tasted terrible, like eating wet ground up metal.

"I didn't know there was a base in Louisville."

"It's there." Wayne looked over the basement and turned back to Alan. "We're going to leave early in the morning. We grab as much stuff as we can carry and we cross over to the barracks." Alan nodded. "By then, hopefully they will have settled down again. Maybe they'll go back into the buildings to escape the heat."

As if in answer to his assumption, sounds emanated from one of the pipes. They ran over to listen to what was happening.

It was a struggle of some kind. There were the sounds of things being knocked down, snarling and fighting. More noise as others joined the fray and then loud yelps of pain.

Now they could hear the sounds of flesh tearing and then the chomping of jaws and smacking of lips. This was followed by about five minutes of giggling.

Alan shivered in the cold room.

"They're eating each other," Alan broke the stillness of the room.

"That's how they've stayed alive for so long." Wayne saw the other man tense up. "We'll take shifts tonight.

Keep a watch and listen. Then we head upstairs before sunrise. Get our supplies and run for the bunker."

Alan nodded slowly, his eyes fixated on the pipe as the giggling turned to laughing.

*****

Alan woke to whispering. He wasn't sure how long he had slept. The room was dark. The fluorescent lights were turned off earlier. It was hard to make out anything.

He heard the whispering again. *The pipes,* he thought. And then he realized the sounds were not coming from the far wall. They were closer.

His eyes began adjusting to the dark and he could see the shadow of a man sitting in the corner.

Wayne. It was Wayne whispering in the dark.

Alan lay still, trying to pick up what the man was saying.

Wayne was talking very low and Alan could barely make it out. He heard "Go over it again." And then some details about the plan to get across to the bunker. Wayne was going over each step, saying it softly into the darkness. Alan smiled. *Soldiers,* he thought. *Always very methodical.*

But then he stopped. He heard "Bill" mentioned a few times. Then "Karen." But he couldn't make out any of the other words. Alan sat up on the cot.

"Wayne?" he called softly into the dark.

The whispering stopped. After a few seconds, Alan could see the soldier stand in the corner.

"I'm sorry. I know you were going over everything for in the morning," Alan found one of his water bottles and took a sip. "Who's Karen?"

"She was a nurse here at the base."

RAW FEED STORIES

"Oh. Your girlfriend?"

Wayne shuffled some in the darkness. "No, but we were close. I was hoping she would become my girlfriend. But then, well, you know."

Alan nodded. "I understand. Was she pretty?"

Wayne chuckled. "She was a knockout. Beautiful eyes. Nice personality. And I'm not just saying that to be a gentleman. She had a genuinely nice personality. And the best smile I ever saw."

Alan nodded in agreement. "I'm sure it was. What happened to her?"

Wayne paused again. "She died."

"I'm sorry. I'm sorry that happened to you." Alan got up from the cot. "It's probably time for my watch. Why don't you get some rest?" They switched places in the darkness.

"Here," Wayne pushed a small watch into Alan's hand. "When the alarm goes off, wake me. Keep listening for movement. There hasn't been a sound for quite a long time. And that's a good thing." He settled down onto the cot.

"What about you?" Wayne asked.

"What about me?"

"Were you married?"

Alan chuckled. "Only to my job. Just never found the right girl. And I liked my work. I was building a nice nest egg. Hoping to buy a house before….well, before all this happened."

They did not speak again and Alan could hear the heavy breathing that marked Wayne's sleep. No sound carried from the mail pipes. He sat and thought about the bunker. The bunker was special. You could hold out for a long time if you had the necessary supplies. And everything was right here. Right across the lot. You just had to be careful. And the radio. That was important. Eventually there would be others, accessing the band the same way. They could rebuild a new communications network, try to get re-organized.

There was still hope.

This nightmare could still end.

*****

Alan woke Wayne at the correct hour and they gathered their supplies together in Wayne's pack. They went back upstairs, trying to be as quiet as possible. It was still dark outside and Wayne made them stop at the top of the stairs to let their eyes adjust.

"We can't use the flashlight now. Too risky." Alan nodded in agreement. They were looking for another pack to carry more supplies in. There were a few lockers attached to the wall on the far side of the warehouse. Wayne hurried over and began searching them. He pulled a large messenger bag from one and emptied the contents onto the floor.

Another locker contained a small gym bag. Wayne emptied that one too.

"I'll take the guns and be the lookout. Do you think you can carry these plus my back pack?" Wayne looked at the smaller man. *Was he strong enough?*

Alan nodded. "Yeah, I can do it."

"We're going to fill them up as much as possible. And we'll have to move fast."

"It's not far. You just keep them away from us," Alan replied. They took the bags back to the food racks and began filling them. Wayne grabbed the messenger bag.

This one would be for water only.

It's not enough, he thought. *Food and water for two people. This won't last a month.*

He paused, looking over at his new companion, watching him pour over the rations and stuffing them into the packs. *You can't leave him. If Bill found out you left someone behind, he would never talk to you again.* Wayne started packing as much water as he could carry.

They could do this. Could make the runs back and forth between the two buildings. He was here now. He was sure there was a key in the office for the depot door. They could run quickly here, use both the bunker and the basement as a base of operations. There were talkies in the rats outside. If someone had to wait out the infected by themselves in either place, they would still be able to communicate with the other.

Wayne smiled. He was damn lucky to find Alan.

Now he had someone to fight beside him. Someone who could help carry the burden of surviving in this hellish place.

And who knows. Maybe Bill found others while I was gone.

Once the packs were filled, Wayne snuck through the double doors into the office. He sidled up to the front door and peeked out the window.

Oh my god. Where did they all come from?

The lot was filled with infected. They milled around the rats and in front of the barrack doors. Even in the darkness, he could see the large group meandering around.

There are even more than yesterday.

He ducked back behind the window.

"Hell," he muttered into the darkness. They would need to bring them around to the other side of the building. A distraction somehow. He would have to figure that out later. Right now he needed to find the key for the door.

He began searching the desk in the office. The drawers were filled with paperwork and pens and paperclips. But no key. He pulled the last drawer open. One of the Bolt handguns sat in the bottom of it.

He picked up the pistol and stuck it in his waistband. *We'll need that for sure.*

He turned to the bulletin board behind the desk. Hanging from a small chain was the key to the depot. Wayne pulled it over his head, feeling the small key lay against his skin. He snuck back to Alan and filled him in on the growing number of infected.

Alan shook his head in disbelief. "What are we going to do? How can we make it through them?"

"Look, there's more, yeah. But not that many more. If we can distract them some way we can get across. Then wait a few days for them to settle back down and we'll be fine." He relayed the plan he had come up with regarding using the basement and bunker to hide in. "I have the key to the depot now. We'll be able to come straight in from this side and get whatever we need. We just need to make it to the bunker."

"How?"

Wayne pulled the last two pegs from his jacket pocket. "With these." He explained how he could set the timer on one and activate it with the other.

"We'll toss this one out the window into the side parking lot. The last one I'll throw from the window near the office. Both explosions will be on the side of the building and far enough away to not damage anything. Once they start heading for the noise, we book it to the barracks."

RAW FEED STORIES

Alan nodded. *That will work. The infected were drawn to two things: blood and commotion. Explosions were a hell of a commotion*, he thought to himself.

"One more thing," Wayne said. "I'll be covering you with the guns. Which means you have to open the door lock at the bunker. You have to memorize the code."

45313. Over and over again, Wayne had Alan say the code until the man had committed it to memory.

"I've got this," Alan said.

"You punch in the code and open the door. Once I'm inside, close it and it will lock automatically. They'll go for the door but we'll be down the hatch by then. And that door is the strongest on the base." Wayne pulled the Bolt from his back and handed it to Alan. "Found this. You keep this one. Just in case."

Alan slipped the gun into his pants pocket. They loaded him up with the packs. Wayne's pack was strapped onto Alan's back. The messenger bag was over one shoulder and the duffel bag was slung across the other.

"Damn, it's heavy. But I'll manage."

Wayne smiled and patted Alan on the cheek. "We can do this, partner." He went to one of the rear windows as Alan took a position near the double doors. The glass had been shattered some time ago and Wayne stared out between the iron bars. Blood soaked infected walked around the parking lot outside. He could see them clearly now. The sun was coming up and morning was here.

Wayne slipped the first peg from his pocket and pushed the small button on the side. Watching the pacing maniacs carefully, he tossed the peg through the bars and watched as it rolled slowly across the parking lot.

Good. That's perfect. The explosion would not harm the warehouse.

He ran back to the front of the depot and stood next to Alan. He looked out this window and again saw the infected walking this side lot too. He took the second peg from his pocket and held it in his hands.

"When the explosions hit, we go." Alan looked at the peg in Wayne's hands.

"Let's do it."

Wayne hit the small button on the side of the cylinder and then clicked the button on top. He hurled the explosive through the bars as far out into the lot as he could throw it. They huddled against the wall.

The building shook from the dual explosions. Dust rained down from the ceiling and Alan started coughing.

"NOW!" Wayne yelled and pushed through the double doors. He hefted the rifle and opened the front door. Already the infected were moving to investigate the scenes of the explosions. But not all of them.

Wayne burst out of the front door and waited for Alan to follow. The smaller man grunted his way past and headed for the barracks. The slower moving infected turned towards the newfound victims. They cackled laughter as they gave chase.

Wayne turned and fired the first couple of rounds into the first two attackers. They dropped quickly. He could see the majority of the infected on either side of the building, disappearing into the smoke from the pegs.

Alan lifted the packs and ran, huddled over, for the access door. A huge gust of wind blew through the lot, pushing him back a few steps. He gathered himself and pushed on. He had a clear line of sight to the door now and focused on getting there.

The wind blew the heavy black smoke up above the rooftops and Wayne glanced at the infected horde. They were beginning to turn at the sounds of the gunfire. And now there was something else: past the two explosions and the gathering group he could see the rest of the base. It was filled with infected. The whole base, and beyond, was a swirling, moving mass of bodies.

"Oh my God," Wayne muttered. There were thousands of them. They swarmed over everything and all of them turned at the sound of the gunshots.

"Alan! Get that fucking door open now!" Wayne screamed. He turned towards the barracks. A woman jumped in front of him, snarling and clenching her teeth. Wayne fired one shot into her head. As she fell, he fired two more shots into a man running up behind her.

They were beginning to close in.

Wayne lifted the rifle and squeezed short bursts into the crowd of crazies. He glanced over and saw Alan throwing the bags into the barracks. He had remembered the code. *Good boy. I'm coming as fast as I can.*

Wayne fired round after round into the living flesh running after him. He maneuvered his way between Alan and the infected. The rifle clicked empty and Wayne pulled the Bolt. There were not many rounds left in this one.

He fired into an open mouth. Blood sprayed from the headshot and covered the other infected nearby. They opened their mouths, catching brain bits and gore on their tongues. As the fresh blood hit the group, they went into a frenzy attacking and biting each other.

Something grabbed Wayne's leg. He looked down to see a little girl looking back up at him. She smiled and opened her mouth to bite his thigh. Wayne turned away as he fired the Bolt into the top of her head.

The lot was close to full as the army of living zombies began to push their way towards the soldier.

Wayne turned back to the barracks. The door was closed again.

"Alan!" He ran towards the bunker but three more infected intercepted him. Wayne fired the gun at them, knocking them to the ground. They were quickly replaced by others.

He fired over and over again until the clip finally emptied, waiting for the door to reopen.

"Alan!" Wayne began to cry as he felt the crush of the bodies crest over him. He was grabbed in a million places and then pulled apart in a million places. The pain was an electric current rolling across his body.

"ALAAAANNNNNNNNNNNN!"

Alan knelt inside the heavy access door. He waited patiently as Wayne's screams pierced the air. And then they stopped.

"I'm sorry, Wayne."

He stayed that way for quite some time. Every now and then he could hear the infected push against the door and their laughter radiating through the walls of the building. He looked over at the bunker's entrance.

Slowly he snapped the outer locks and pulled open the hatch. He dropped the bags down into the opening and then climbed down the ladder into the bunker.

*****

Alan surveyed his surroundings. It was quite nice, especially compared to the dank basement. He sat down on the cot and held his head in his hands. *I made it. I'm here and I'm alive and I have food and a radio.*

The radio.

Alan looked over at the far wall. There was a small desk

and chair sitting against it, and above those tacked to the wall was a map. Under the map, sitting on the desk was the radio.

It was beautiful.

Alan moved over to the desk. He looked at the map, studying it. Someone had taken red crayon and colored in most of the surrounding area. There were arrows drawn every which way and he could not make sense out of any of it. Writing peppered the wall next to the map. It was the word KAREN over and over. Again written in crayon. And below that: BILL : FREQUENCY 102.4

He studied the radio. It was in great condition.

What do I say? How do I explain it to this guy Bill?

He bit his lip, thinking over what to tell the stranger on the other end of the line.

Finally Alan sat down and thumbed the power switch.

Nothing happened.

He clicked the switch on and off again. Still nothing.

Alan pressed the large black button on the mic. The radio sat dead. He pushed the chair away from the desk and scrambled underneath the table. There were no cords or plugs anywhere. There wasn't even a power outlet.

"What the hell?" Something caught his eye. Lying next to one of the back legs of the desk was a pill bottle. He grabbed it and brought it out into the light. It was empty and the lid was missing.

Alan read the label:

Thorazine 1 dose tablet

Prescribed by NP Karen McDonald

Another empty pill bottle sat on one of the shelves beside the fresher. He picked it up. This one was for Xanax, again prescribed by nurse practitioner Karen McDonald.

Alan threw the bottles across the bunker.

Maybe it just needs fresh batteries. He picked up the radio and his eyes grew wide with surprise.

The radio was extremely light. He turned it around. The entire backside of the receiver was missing and the body was hollowed out. Inside the casing was a small white sticker that proclaimed: Training model #238650 CB

The radio did not work.

It had never worked.

Alan dropped the radio back to the desk and slumped into the chair.

16 months alone in this bunker. What would that do to a man? Would he snap? Would he begin to have delusions? Alan eyed the small pill bottles in the corner. *What if he was already suffering from some sort of mental deficiency?*

"Son of a bitch."

Alan's voice ricocheted off the concrete walls.

*****

The sun dropped from behind the horizon and darkness fell. The infected, now covering every corner of the base and the surrounding area, began to circle slowly in place as they were apt to do when it grew dark. Some still feasted on the fallen bodies of their dead comrades.

One of the infected paced in front of the barracks door. He was missing an arm starting below the elbow. Blood dribbled from the wound but the man paid no heed to it. He felt no pain and was not aware of the missing limb.

The infected man shuffled past the others, sometimes knocking into a fellow victim. Growls were greeted with snarls and every now and then a vicious fight broke out among the group, usually ending in someone's death.

The man ignored the pushing bodies around him and scoured the ground for a late night snack. There was a huge red splotch below his feet and he could feel the wet stain of blood and guts on the asphalt.

Something glittered in the moonlight. It was stuck in the gore at the infected man's feet. He knelt down and picked up the small silvery object.

It was a key, although the man did not recognize it as a key. He had long forgotten what such things were and what they were used for. It was the enticing color of the thing that drew the man to it.

He swallowed the key, hoping it was something good to eat, disappointed when it wasn't.

He searched the pile of guts again looking for something to eat and finding nothing, moved on across the base.

Soon the man began to giggle uncontrollably. The others around him joined in and the sound of their growing laughter rose up into the air, carried on its own frequency, communicating the chaos of a brave new world.

CUBE³

Part 1

Ammo barked and the sound echoed through the forest.

Curtis stopped and listened for the direction the noise was coming from. He hefted the small .22 and turned right, following the distinctive howls of the beagle. His feet landed smoothly on the thick layer of leaves and moss, a telltale sign of late Fall. He ducked low hanging branches and dodged grasping thickets, closing in on the dog's position.

Curtis pushed the battered ball cap back across his head. Even in the cool evening air, he was already working up a sweat.

Ammo howled again.

He must have a coon cornered, he thought. And then another surfaced. *Or maybe a wildcat.* He picked up his pace, hefting the rifle across one shoulder, and pushed his way deeper in the forest. If it was a wildcat, better he get there before the young dog did something foolish and ended up hurt.

Curtis made his way up Grayson Ridge. The ground began to climb at this point and he steadied himself by grabbing onto nearby trees and large rocks that dotted the ridge. Ammo was somewhere near the top, over to the right of where Curtis was now. The dog's barks continued to disrupt the relative quiet of the woods. Whatever Ammo was into, it had him pretty excited.

Curtis thrust his lean frame up the hillside and dug his boots into the soft soil. He had climbed this ridge many times before and was as familiar with the terrain as he was in his own living room. Curtis loved the woods. It was his comfort place, his soul food. He would spend days exploring the back country, Ammo in tow, hiking and camping or fishing and hunting the beautiful Blue Ridge Mountains. He was a Virginia boy, born and raised, God willing he would die one too.

Today he had decided to take Ammo on a squirrel hunt. The flop-eared beagle began to pace the cab of Curtis' small truck eagerly as they pulled into the familiar dirt gravel parking lot off of State Road 322. The dog jumped from the truck as soon as Curtis opened the door and tore off into the woods, baying and barking and yapping joyously. Ammo liked the woods too.

But now the dog was into something. And it did not sound like any squirrel to Curtis.

He paused midway up the slope and looked towards the top of the ridge. Ahead he counted four squirrels leaping through the leaves and zipping up the tall maples that covered the hill.

"Squirrels are over here, stupid mutt," he muttered under his breath. He pondered taking a shot at one of them but thought better of it. Ammo sounded pretty excited and that usually meant mischief. He needed to see what the dog was into. The last time the beagle was this loud he had happened on a mother skunk and her young. The smell was tremendous and it took almost two weeks and a dozen baths to finally get the dog back to normal.

It better not be another skunk. I'll leave his little butt here and he can walk home. He knew in his heart he would never do that. The dog meant too much to him. Ammo had been a gift from his grandfather two years ago on his 18th birthday. It was the last of many gifts from his pappy, as the old man finally passed in April. Since then Curtis had moved out of his parent's house, and rented a small cabin near the outskirts of the George Washington National Forest. When he wasn't in the woods, he was doing farm work for a local produce vendor. Curtis would help plant, harvest, and even sell the goods at the local outdoor market.

In the summer he hitched a trailer to the back of his pickup and sold homemade ice cream at the markets and other special events. All in all he was able to live comfortably in his simple life. He never thought of joining most of his peers in college, even though his grades were more than adequate, and the thought of what he considered a "real" job with a big company or factory filled him with dread.

Curtis stopped and looked back up the ridge.

Ammo had stopped barking.

He waited a few minutes to see if the dog would pick back up again but nothing followed.

"AMMO!" he called. It was unusual for him to go quiet so suddenly. *Something must be wrong.*

He started to run up the ridge, now holding the gun in

front of him with both hands. Sweat soaked the brim of his hat and large wet patches formed under his arms.

"AMMO! Here boy!"

He tried to keep one eye on the brush ahead, expecting the dog to bounce out and join him, but it was hard to do that and try and watch his footing too. Curtis dug in hard with his feet and pushed his way to the top. The ground began to level out and he began to make better headway through the brush.

Finally he was on flat ground and the undergrowth began to clear away some. He cleared his throat and spat on the wet ground.

"AMMO!" he yelled. "You rotten ass mutt." Curtis followed the ridge towards where he figured the dog's racket had originated from.

Soon he heard Ammo's familiar whine, punctuated with deep guttural growls. It was as if the dog was trying to be scared and angry all at once, something Curtis had never heard the animal do before. He gripped the gun tightly in his hands and eased his way along the ridge.

Ammo was a few yards down the other side of the mountain. His backside was facing Curtis; his tale sticking straight up in the air.

"Ammo! Get over here!" The dog ignored his master's command. Curtis' concern grew. The beagle was usually very obedient. He looked the area over, scanning for signs of other animals or a sign Ammo had been in a skirmish with something. Nothing moved long the ground or in the trees, and the area on this side of the hill was undisturbed.

Curtis sidled up to the dog. Ammo was digging furiously in the soft earth. He had been working for some time as he had dug a hole roughly three feet in diameter.

"Stop it," Curtis told the dog. Ammo was filthy. Mud

and dirt caked the front half of his body and large clumps of earth clung to his head as he stuffed it deeper into the hole.

"Ammo, come here." Curtis grabbed the dog by the collar and began to pull him back from his digging. "You're filthy!" The dog fought hard against Curtis and with a snap, broke from his owner's grip. Curtis stumbled backwards, surprised and a little pissed.

He laid the rifle on the ground and grabbed the dog's collar with both hands. Using almost all his strength he wrestled the dog from the wet earth. Ammo began to fight, growling and barking at the hole he had made.

"Stop it! Behave, you stupid dog!" He could not believe how much Ammo was fighting him. With one hand still on his collar, Curtis wrapped his other arm around the dog's body and lifted him from the ground. Ammo continued to growl and bark, twisting to and fro trying to escape.

Curtis walked a few yards down the slope and dumped the dog into the brush. Hard. The dog cried out in surprise. He spun around flinging leaves and sticks up into the air. Curtis stomped his feet and yelled loudly.

Ammo stopped.

Curtis pointed a finger at the dog.

"Stop." Ammo quietly sat down on the ground. His head, usually a mixture of the white/brown/black coloring found in these types of beagles, was now completely covered in dirt. Ammo looked at his master with glassy eyes.

"What the hell is wrong with you dog?" Curtis watched as the beagle turned his head and studied the man. "Stay!"

Curtis picked up his gun and went back to the hole. Behind him Ammo began to whine. Curtis turned and looked at the dog. The animal was shivering slightly, his head still turned watching Curtis.

"Stay, Ammo." The dog barked and then quieted down.

Curtis studied the hole. It was quite impressive. The ground was extremely soft this time of the year and the dog had easily broken through the top soil. Ammo had managed to dig a good foot into the ridge. He turned to scold the dog further and then stopped.

There was something at the bottom of the hole.

He knelt down in the thick leaves and studied the earth at the bottom of the hole. Sticking up from the brown clay dirt was a corner of…..well, something. Curtis reached down and wiped the surface as clean as he could with his fingers.

The corner was made of some sort of metal and was a silvery white in color. Whatever it belonged to was still stuck pretty good in the dirt. Curtis turned and looked back at the dog.

Ammo laid his head flat and thumped his tail against the ground.

"Is this what has you all crazy? Some old tuna can or tobacco tin?" He turned his attention back to the hole. "Sometimes I wonder about you, mutt."

He reached down into the dirt and started digging the object up. Where Ammo was all chaos and mud flying everywhere, Curtis slowly started at the corner of the mystery and followed the edges. The object began to take shape as he removed more and more dirt from around its sides. Now he could see the first couple of inches of the thing and could tell it was definitely square. He kept digging.

After a few minutes he had unearthed the final product: a small cube.

It was still covered in muck and clay. He tried to wipe most of it off with the sleeve of his shirt but only smeared it across the cube's sides.

He held it up, looking all around the small object. It was perfectly square, roughly 4 inches wide on each side. It was very light to hold. Curtis did not believe it was hollow; there was no evidence of a seam or hinges of any type. It was metal, but he could not quite identify what type. Tin, maybe? But it would need to be a re-enforced type of tin for the cube to keep its shape so perfectly buried in the ground like it was.

It was a curious thing.

He held it out to Ammo.

"Here it is. Now what are you going to do?" The beagle whined low in the back of his throat and licked his lips. Curtis watched the dog for a second, not understanding its curious behavior.

He took out a small red bandanna he kept in the pocket of his jeans and safely tucked the cube away in it. Then he dropped the whole works into his front shirt pocket. The package bulged from its resting place but Curtis took no notice of it. He glanced up at the falling sun and sighed.

No squirrels today.

"Come on, Ammo. I'm starved. Let's go to Pocket Aces and get some burgers." That would cheer the pooch up. Ammo loved Pocket Ace burgers and fries and barked at the mere mention of the place. But not this time. Curtis watched as the dog slowly followed him back down the ridge towards the truck, staying well behind his master.

They walked in silence and Curtis watched the trees for squirrels but they had all retired for the day. They exited the woods and headed for the beaten up red pickup Curtis had owned ever since he first started driving. Curtis opened the passenger door and waited for Ammo to jump in. The dog kept pacing back and forth next to the truck.

"Come on. Let's go." Curtis reached down and plucked the animal from the ground and sat him on the seat. He walked over to the driver's side and got in, placing the rifle behind the bench seat. By the time he started the truck, Ammo was curled up on the floorboard whining softly at Curtis.

Curtis reached over and patted the dog on the head lovingly. Ammo licked his lips and thumped his tale.

"Relax. We're going to get some good food, okay?"

Ammo stayed on the floor the whole way to the restaurant.

*****

Pocket Aces was packed as it usually was during dinner hours. Curtis pulled the pickup into the drive-thru and waited for a family of five to finish ordering. He watched the people inside sitting at their tables eating thick hamburgers and greasy fries. Children ran around wearing their red Pocket Aces cardboard hats and spitting straw wrappers at each other. The family in front of him pulled up to the window and Curtis drove forward and leaned towards the black ominous speaker.

"I'd like three doubles and a large order of fries."

"Would you like anything to drink with that?" the speaker squawked back at him.

"Yeah. How about a medium strawberry shake?" He turned to the dog and was happy to see Ammo had jumped up on the seat, anticipating food.

"Your total will be the cube root of 27," the speaker

squawked again.

Curtis turned back to the black box, confused. "What was that?"

"Transparency....***SKIZZ***.....***BUZZ***.... the formation of parallel universes within a....***SKIZZ***....set linear time line." The speaker filled with white noise and then cut off. Curtis stared at the box for a second. He shrugged and pulled up to the window.

A pimply faced teenager met him at the glass and opened the small door.

"That will be $12.35, please," the boy said vacantly. Curtis grabbed his wallet from the windshield visor and handed over some bills.

"What was all that you were saying on the box?" he asked as he waited for his change.

"What?"

"You started saying something about time and something else and then the speaker kept filling with static." Curtis placed his wallet back under the visor. "I didn't get all of it."

The teen looked puzzled for several seconds and then understanding dawned on his face.

"You know what, that receiver on the speaker picks up the local radio stations sometimes." the boy handed over a large bag of food. "It's kind of crazy sometimes."

Curtis nodded. That made sense. He pulled out into the road. As he drove, he opened one of the burgers and threw it onto the floor. Ammo dived down and began eating voraciously. Curtis helped himself to the other two. All the climbing up and down the ridge had given him a pretty nice appetite. He finished the burgers off and started in on the fries, throwing a handful to Ammo who greeted them with gusto. French fries were one of his favorites.

They pulled onto Blackberry Lane and drove up the pot marked dirt road. Blackberry Lane was a mile and half of rough road. It ended at a State D.O.T. barracks, which housed some of the smaller work trucks and road repair gear. The barracks and the cabin that Curtis was renting were the only active lots on the lane. The county had tried for years to get some investors to develop more residential units in the area, but to no avail. It was too far from the highway and even further from the city limits.

Curtis pulled the truck up to the cabin and cut the engine. Ammo jumped out his side and ran for the front door. The cabin was small, just roomy enough for a man and his dog. It had one bedroom with a small bath, a kitchen, and a dining nook. Most of the interior was taken up by the main living area. There was also a small workshop connected to the rear and accessible on the other side of the kitchen.

Ammo ran into the living area and plopped down on the floor in front of the small fireplace.

"No! The first thing you are getting is hosed off." Curtis went through the back door and filled a large metal tub with water from an outside faucet. The sun was just starting to set as he pulled Ammo from the house by his collar.

The dog hated baths. He tolerated them with a sad, defeated look which made Curtis smile. He lifted the dog up and plopped him into the tub. Ammo immediately began making dough eyes at the man.

"Nope, don't give me that. Serves you right for digging in mud and making a mess." Curtis began washing the beagle down. He started rinsing Ammo off with the hose when the dog gave a mighty leap and promptly exited the tub. He ran a few steps away and shook the excess water from his body. Then shaking his tail, he turned back to his master.

But Curtis was not paying any attention to Ammo. When Ammo had leapt from the tub he had knocked the small wrapped package from Curtis' front pocket. His master was now staring down at the cube, which had come unwrapped from the hanky and clanged on the bottom of the metal tub.

Curtis reached into the dirty water and picked up the small square. He gave it a quick shake in the tub, rinsing away all the dirt and mud. Satisfied that it was clean, he lifted the small form up and stared at.

It was a perfect cube, solid, with sharp edges and corners. Even in the fading sunlight, he could see the cube was a brilliant white color. He held the cube in the palm of his hand and hefted it, feeling the weight of the thing. It was not very heavy at all and fit solidly in the flat of his outstretched hand.

Ammo sat still watching his master. A small whine escaped from deep in his throat.

Curtis wiped the cube dry with the tail of his shirt. He carried it inside and walked back through the kitchen and out into the workshop. Ammo followed keeping his eyes on the small white square in his master's hand.

The workshop was small but impeccably neat. On one side was an assortment of lawn tools including a small push mower and weed eater. Along another wall ran a sturdy, very clean workbench. The wall itself was covered with pegboard and assorted tools were neatly organized on the board.

Curtis stood at the bench and clicked the large desk

lamp he had connected to one corner. He studied the cube underneath the bright light, looking for any hint of a seam or other way to open his newfound treasure. The surface was smooth and whole as far as he could tell.

He sat the cube on the table. His cell phone chirped from the kitchen. Ammo barked at the steady ringing and Curtis shushed him with a wave of his hand. He had an idea who it might be.

He grabbed the phone from the dining table.

"Hello," he answered watching Ammo watch him.

"Hey. I was wondering if you were home," said the gentle young female voice on the other end.

"We just got back from the woods. Ammo was a mess and I had to give him a bath. How was your day?"

"It was good. Work was blah, but nothing terrible happened." The young girl paused. "So I was actually making spaghetti for dinner tonight and wondered if the two of you might want to come over and share."

Curtis turned to Ammo, who was anxiously looking at him. "Do you want to go over to Annie's for spaghetti, butthead?"

The dog barked, loud and clear, and Annie laughed over the phone.

"We'll be there within the hour," Curtis said and turned the phone off. He went to the bedroom to shower and change clothes. Ammo took up his seat in front of the fireplace, waiting until it was time to leave and wishing it was cold enough for a fire.

*****

Curtis knocked on Annie's door and she greeted him and Ammo with a warm smile. She was the same age as

Curtis and nearly a head shorter with short brown hair and a plethora of freckles covering her cheeks.

"It's the troublemakers!" she said as she bent down and rubbed Ammo behind the ears just the way he liked.

They were friends. And Curtis thought they were more than friends. Even though neither one of them had ever brought it up with the other. They acted like more than friends; not that they were intimate with each other but there seemed to be an unspoken agreement between the two of them. Curtis knew that they were *close* friends. This seemed to make them more than just friends which brought him right around to where he was before: confused.

Either way, he really enjoyed Annie's company and figured she enjoyed his, or he wouldn't be here right now getting ready to eat dinner. He just wished he was more experienced at this type of thing. Instead he always seemed to be sitting on the couch next to her watching TV and wishing he had the courage to hold her hand. Or tell her how he really felt which was that really and truly he was pretty sure he had fallen in love with her.

"I heard you were a terrible dog today, Ammo," Annie cooed at the pooch, who loved her attention just as much as Curtis did.

She went over to the stove and began draining the noodles while Curtis set the table.

"Were you up on the ridge today?" she asked giving the sauce a stir.

"Yep. And then Fido over there decided to dig up the whole hillside." Curtis placed the knives and forks down, trying to remember the proper way they went and then settling on what looked neater instead. "He found something buried in the mud. You should have seen him.

He was filthy."

"What did he find?" Annie asked.

"Huh?"

"What did you find buried on the ridge?" Annie served up generous portions of noodles on both their plates and then turned and spooned some into a bowl for Ammo. The dog thumped his tail greedily.

"Oh," Curtis began to reply and stopped. He wanted to tell Annie all about the cube and how unique it seemed but found that when he tried to bring the words forward they wouldn't come. After a few seconds of struggling, and Annie looking at him with anticipation, he finally gave up. "It was nothing. Just an old snuff tin."

She nodded and they began to eat the spaghetti but now Curtis was concerned. Why couldn't he tell her about the cube? What was that all about?

His train of thought was interrupted by Annie asking him something.

"I'm sorry. What?"

"I'm going to make some hot tea. Did you want to stay longer and have some?" She turned from the stove and looked at him with her soft brown eyes.

"Yeah. That would be good."

She winked at him and smiled. "Good."

He loaded the dishwasher while she made tea. Ammo lay on the chair in the living room, his belly stuffed. He closed his eyes and snored loudly.

Annie sat across from him at the table. He poured tea from a nice ceramic pot into their mugs. She slid a small tray of sugar cubes over to him.

"I got cubes this time. I know you like yours sweet."

He nodded and dropped one into his cup. He picked up a second and paused staring at the shape.

A cube. Just like the one he found in the woods.

Annie looked at Curtis, who was staring at the sugar cube he held between his two fingers.

"Curtis?" she asked. "Curtis? Why are you staring at that thing like that?"

He made no move that he heard her, only continued to stare at the small square of sugar.

Just when she was beginning to really worry and made a move to get up and come to his side of the table, he finally spoke.

"Dark energy exists throughout the universe, pushing out all the matter. It pushes and spreads everything out thinly. Soon all that will be left is empty space. And from empty space more dark energy flows creating sub-universes. They exist in parallel. Multiple tangents. Each one a different side of a different universe. It is the law of inflation."

Curtis dropped the cube into his cup and it dissolved rapidly. He blinked quickly and looked up at Annie.

Annie was wide-eyed in surprise. "Where did you learn that?"

"Learn what?" he replied, confusion blanketing his face.

"All that stuff you just said. About dark energy and the universe growing and all that." She grinned at him. "Have you been watching PBS, Curtis? Are you trying to impress me?"

He shook his head. "What did I say? I can't even remember what I said."

"I'm sure I can't even remember all you said. Sheesh. I'm just a simple little country girl. All that big universe stuff is beyond me."

Curtis smiled. "You're more than a simple little country

girl. Well, your cooking might be kind of simple."

"Hey jerk," she squealed, throwing her napkin in his face. Then she smiled and sipped her tea. "Drink your tea before it gets cold. Jerk."

They drank their tea and talked about making plans for the weekend. Annie wanted to check out the flea market over at the county fairgrounds. Curtis said that would be fine. He tried to enjoy the rest of his evening with Annie, but a headache began to throb across his temples and he said he needed to leave early.

She walked him to the door and he called for Ammo. The dog shuffled out to the truck.

"Thanks for having me over," Curtis said.

"Anytime. You know that," Annie responded. "You are always welcome here." They stood in the doorway and smiled at each other. She placed her hand on his arm and called out to Ammo.

"Be good, sweetie pie!" she called to the dog. He barked at her and ran around in a circle.

Curtis bowed his head. "Good night."

He opened the truck door and waited for Ammo to jump in and then back out of the driveway. He looked in the rearview mirror and watched Annie watch him drive away.

Ammo was staring at him from the passenger seat. He turned and looked at the dog.

"What?"

Ammo yawned and curled up on the old upholstery.

Curtis drove home and went straight to bed.

His headache seemed to get worse the closer he got to home.

MICHAEL WHETZEL

*****

The alarm blared at 6 am and Curtis rolled over and turned it off. He was in the middle of a dream when the blaring clock interrupted and now his mind was quickly losing the details. It was something about a library.

Yes. He vaguely remembered it now. He had been walking in a library, a huge vast room filled with shelves and shelves of books. He remembered books floating down from their assigned perches and opening before him. He would quickly scan each book as the pages fluttered past in a whirlwind of activity.

And he remembered everything he read. He was reading hundreds of books and memorizing all the information that flowed from them. He was like a balloon filling up rapidly with air; only the air was knowledge streaming into him from all the different subjects.

Curtis felt the dream go and he lost the last details of it. He usually didn't dream much, and if he did it almost always had something to do with hunting or the woods. Ammo was always present, only in dreamland he could talk and always seemed to have something sassy to say to his master.

Curtis went into the bathroom and showered. He was supposed to be at the farm around 8 to start work. He flipped the coffee maker on and dumped some food into Ammo's dish. The dog walked lazily in from the living room and watched Curtis jumping around the kitchen.

"Good morning, Ammo," Curtis said. "How did you sleep?"

The beagle opened his mouth in a mighty yawn and then started to nibble on his food. Curtis buttered some toast and ate it quickly. He checked the weather outside and then grabbed his coffee and entered the workshop. He needed some tools to work on the old sprayer out at the farm.

He stopped in the doorway. Ammo came up behind him and began to bay at the door. The dog yelped and jumped quickly out of the way as the coffee mug dropped from Curtis' hand. It hit the floor and shattered, splashing its hot contents across the concrete floor of the shop. Ammo started to bark. Loud, piercing barks that filled the small house.

Curtis walked into the shop and stood before the workbench where the cube sat. It was still there but now it was a lot bigger than before. Where he could hold the small object in the palm of one hand yesterday, it would now take both arms wrapped around the whole thing to carry it around.

He looked at the peg board, his bottom jaw hanging open. Every one of his hand tools was gone. His screwdrivers, socket set, all his wrenches, even his cordless drill set had disappeared. He placed his hands on the bench and studied everything carefully.

The metal pegs that held all the tools were gone. The small pile of hinges that were stacked against the wall was gone. The jars that held assorted nails and screws were gone, as were the jars themselves. His small Craftsman vice that he had attached to the side of the workbench had disappeared. It was all gone.

"What? What happened?"

Ammo quieted down and sat at the door of the shop, watching.

Someone broke in, Curtis thought. *They broke in and stole all my things. Took all my tools. I don't believe it.* And he didn't believe it. He had left the cabin locked up as he always did.

It was his habit to double check the doors. All the windows were secured. He never opened them. They had been locked ever since he moved in.

Curtis went to the door that led outside from the shop. It opened on the small backyard behind the cabin. But now it was locked; had been for quite a while. The small window in the door was fine, no signs of tampering or breaking. He turned to the corner that held his yard tools and for the second time that morning, stood astonished.

His lawnmower was gone. Well, not all the way gone though. The motor and the tall handle on the push mower had disappeared but the metal base and wheels were still there. Curtis leaned forward and looked at the floor.

There was a small trail of metal bits and pieces leading from the mower base to the workbench. He recognized several of the bits as components for the inside of the mower motor. It looked as if someone had turned the motor inside out and then sprinkled a small trail of parts to the workbench. His eyes flowed over the small trail where it ended on the floor at the base of the bench. He looked straight up from the end of the trail to where the cube sat.

It glowed a stark white in the early morning light. Curtis went to the cube. This side of the large box was smooth as the top. He leaned over and studied the other sides. These had rough looking patches disrupting the flat surface. He ran his hand over the patches. It felt like something was hiding just below the surface, trying to poke out from the flat edge of unknown metal. He leaned over to the other side and suddenly stopped.

This opposite side was still flat and would have looked normal if not for the 7 to 8 inches of mower cord sticking from the surface. The cord ended in the triangular, black, plastic pull handle lying on the wooden surface of the bench. Curtis leaned in, examining the spot where the cord disappeared into the metal surface. He could not decipher any type of hole or entrance that the cord was entering by. Instead it looked as if the cord met the cube and then changed into the cube. He reached up to click the table lamp on, cursed under his breath when he realized that too was now gone, and turned back to the cube.

He watched as, with the barest of movements, ever so slightly, a few centimeters of cord was pulled into the cube.

Curtis yelled and fell backwards onto the mower base. His feet kicked out and knocked over the weed eater and large leaf rake. Ammo brayed loudly and ran into the living room, diving under the couch. Curtis sat back on his rear, steadying himself with his hands and stared at the cube. His front pants pocket began to chirp as his cell phone started to ring.

He sat that way for a few seconds, trying to comprehend what he had just seen. Finally he realized his phone was ringing and grabbed it quickly.

"Yeah," he answered. His voice sounded far away. He stared dreamily at the cube.

"Good morning, sunshine." It was Philip, his employer at the farm.

"Yeah," Curtis continued.

"Hey, the parts did not come in for the sprayer. They won't be in until Wednesday. So we have to wait on that job. I've already got everything ready for the market tomorrow so I'm calling to tell you that it's a free day if you want."

"Yeah," Curtis responded.

"I'll have you do the market in the morning and then we'll work the south field until sundown." Philip coughed into the phone.

"Yeah," Curtis said.

"So enjoy the free time. There won't be many more starting next month, with summer coming in and such. I won't see you tomorrow when you come for the truck. I got a meeting and then have to take the kids to the dentist..." Philip yammered on for quite a while. He was a bit of a talker.

"Yeah," Curtis stared at the cube.

"So have a good day." Philip finished.

"Yeah," Curtis slowly lowered the phone. "Yeah, right." He clicked the phone off and looked at Ammo, who had come out from under the couch.

Ammo flipped his head to the ceiling and howled a long, loud cry of confusion.

"Yeah," Curtis nodded at the dog.

What in the world is going on?

*****

Curtis sat at the dining nook and stared at the small scratches that covered the old table. He was sure the cube had eaten all his tools and most of his lawnmower. What was puzzling was the why and the how of the situation. He turned to Ammo who sat on the floor looking earnestly at his master.

"You dug it up, you should deal with it." Ammo thumped his tail on the floor in response and tilted his head to one side. "Why did you dig it up anyway? You won't even go near the thing now." Ammo tilted his head the other direction. "Why do you do any of the things you do? You lick your own butt, for goodness sake." The beagle barked and wagged his tail.

Curtis drummed his fingers on the table. The cube was absorbing all the metal and plastic within close proximity. But the cord from the mower wasn't all metal or plastic. It was made of rope, or fibers, but it was absorbed too. However the workbench and peg board and surrounding walls were not touched. They were made of wood.

"What's the difference?" Curtis asked out loud. Wood was organic, not like metal or plastic. But wasn't the cord considered organic too? He figured the rope fibers had to originate from some sort of wood or plant. That would be organic too, right? Or maybe it was not organic enough for some reason.

Curtis' head was beginning to throb.

The cube made him nervous. It was a bit scary not really knowing what exactly it was or what it was used for. But he was also very curious about the strange object. It was something new and even though it was a bit scary, he did not feel like he was in danger.

He couldn't explain it but he felt safe, here in the cabin, so close to the cube.

Curtis slammed his hand down on the table. Ammo jumped up, startled, and whined at his master.

"We shall find our answers," he paused for dramatic effect, "with scientific experimentation."

Ammo barked.

Curtis moved to one of the kitchen drawers. *Wood was organic and metal was not.* He brought out a small carving knife. The blade was stainless steel and the handle was wood. He went to the counter and grabbed an apple and carried everything into the workshop.

A couple of hours had passed since Philip's phone call. In that time the mower cord had disappeared and most of the small parts on the floor were gone. The large mower base had rolled from its resting place a few feet closer to the bench. Behind the remains of the mower, he noticed that his weed eater had moved about a foot across the floor.

It was like some sort of weird magnet, he thought to himself.

He sat the knife and apple next to the cube. It was bigger than before. Now it was as wide as the workbench from front to back. Pretty soon it would either fall off or collapse the bench. He wrapped his arms around the block and lifted. It did not budge.

So the weight has increased also. Makes sense if the size is increasing. He studied the sides again, feeling their rough surfaces. They were changing, different from before, as the cube swallowed more and more of its surroundings.

Curtis placed the knife and the apple on top of the cube. He centered them neatly next to each other and stepped back. Immediately he noticed the color of the cube had grown brighter. But only for a split second.

He watched the two objects he had introduced for several minutes. Nothing changed.

I guess it takes some time. He went back into the kitchen and refilled Ammo's bowl.

He went back to the bathroom and grabbed a bottle of aspirin from the medicine cabinet. His headache was returning. He swallowed three of the chalky white capsules and grabbed the sides of the sink. He could hear Ammo barking from the next room but dizziness had swarmed over his body.

Curtis' arms and legs tingled and his vision blurred. He stumbled back to the bed and plopped down on the cool comforter.

Ammo plodded in from the hallway and jumped up next to Curtis. He was not allowed up on the bed but

Curtis was too weak to object. Ammo curled comfortably next to the man and started to snore softly. Curtis passed out too.

As soon as his consciousness shifted down, he found himself in another dream. This time instead of the massive library, there was only blackness. Curtis looked down and saw his arms and legs, floating in the inky black as if he was floating in dark water. He pulled his arms in to his chest and then thrust them outward, swimming through the black.

There was the sensation of moving, of traveling through a secret veil. Up ahead, something glittered and then the something turned into many somethings, all glittering in the dark blackness. He knew right away that they were stars and they were very, very far away. He shifted his weight and floated in the dark.

Dark matter. He did not know where the thought came from, only that it was projected into his sub-conscious and that it was correct. He was moving through dark matter. He turned to his right and his eyes grew wide.

There was a sharp piercing bolt of red light that flashed in front of him. Right after the flash, millions of shapes and gases and more dark matter exploded from a small spot in the black darkness. The new shapes raced outwards and, arriving at the spot he watched from, passed through him and continued racing to their mystery destinations.

This is a universe, he thought in his dream. *This is a universe being born.*

He watched the birth of the young galaxy, feeling its life pains vibrate through his skin and shimmer across his body. Many of the shapes and gases joined together and formed planetoids. Stars erupted into being, their bright luminescence blinding Curtis, causing him to raise an arm and cover his eyes. Comets whirled and moons collided, reforming into larger moons, and more stars winked into solid existence.

And through it all, a young farm boy from Virginia bore silent witness.

Until it stopped and everything became very still. Comets paused in their dramatic arc. Planets stopped their revolutions. Stars stopped blinking. A huge shadow cast across the small universe and gripped Curtis in dark blackness again. He turned to look at this newest arrival.

It dwarfed the growing galaxy, an immense structure of steel and metal. Curtis looked far to the right and far to the left, and then deep down and way up to study its entire shape. He recognized it quickly. It was an engine, a great and massive engine, much like the one found on Philip's tractor or his broken lawnmower. This engine was sleeker in its design but still easily recognizable, even though he had never seen one like it before.

The great engine ramped up its power. A large hum vibrated from the massive body, throwing Curtis backwards. He pin wheeled across deep space, unable to control his fall through the emptiness. As the planets and stars raced past his peripheral vision, Curtis woke up.

He bolted upright in bed, waking Ammo and causing the dog to jump to the floor and hightail it under the couch. Next to his bed, on the nightstand, was a small notebook and pencil kept to record phone messages. Curtis grabbed these up and turned to a blank page.

His mind took over and he began sketching rough schematics onto the paper. He was oblivious to where he was, the barking of his dog, the setting sun of late evening, or the bright light emanating from the crack under the workshop door. The only thing Curtis saw was the drawing in his mind and the need to get it down on this small sheet of paper.

Once he was finished, he dropped the notebook onto the night stand and fell back onto the comforter. He passed out again, but this time slept soundly through the rest of the day and into morning.

*****

When he woke, his head felt lighter than it had all week. Curtis lifted himself from the mattress, surprised to find he was still wearing his clothes from the day before. He wiped the sleep from his eyes and stretched way up high.

He hopped from the bed and hit the shower. The hot water felt amazing and he found himself singing a small bit of an old country tune. He could not remember the name of it. It must have been something he picked up at Annie's. He dried and quickly dressed.

"Ammo!" he called from the bedroom, combing his hair quickly. "Let's get some breakfast. We got to get out to the farm by eight."

He listened for the clack of the dog's toenails on the hardwood. Usually Ammo raced in barking up a storm in anticipation of a meal. "Hey, Ammo. What are you doing?" The last time the beagle was quiet like this he had chewed one of the cushions off of the couch and then hid in shame.

Curtis walked to the kitchen and found the dog. Ammo was standing stock still, staring at the workshop door. Curtis stopped. Suddenly, everything came roaring back and he began to sway from the explosion of information. The cube, the missing tools and parts, the amazing dream from last night.

How could I have forgotten all of that? He pushed his way past the dog and opened the door.

The cube was sitting on the floor now, its weight having broken the workbench sometime last night. It was now roughly 4 feet square. Its sides were completely smooth and Curtis turned to his lawn tools. They were all gone including the weed eater, the large tree clippers, and the heads of his rake, shovel, and ax.

When the workbench collapsed, the cube had fallen from the table and landed in the middle of the small work room. Curtis walked around the large object. The thing seemed even brighter in color than before and he thought he felt a small hum emanating from the box. But all these things were secondary to what was happening on top of the cube. He stared at the objects he had brought in the day before, his science experiments.

The handle of the kitchen knife stood on its end as if someone had stabbed the blade down into the interior of the cube. Curtis grabbed the handle. It came apart from the cube easily enough and the blade was gone. Again the mysterious object had assimilated the metal and left the wood behind.

"Wood is in a state of flux. It is both inorganic and organic. Transitioning is not complete on the molecular scale." He had no clue where the thought originated from; nor did he really understand it completely. There was something about the wood that was different from the other organic compounds. He dropped the wooden handle to the floor and turned and stared at the apples.

There were three of them now, setting neatly next to each other in a straight line.

Curtis knelt down and poked one of them tentatively

with a finger. It rolled slightly and nudged one of its kin. He could not tell which one was the original apple. They were all perfect copies of each other, right down to the small dents in the outer peel. He picked them all up and carried them into the kitchen.

At the counter he grabbed another knife and sliced each apple open. He took turns smelling each one and then, pausing only for a second, he took a small bite out of all three.

They tasted like apples. They smelled like apples. They were all apples.

He sat in the dining nook. It was amazing. The cube was an amazing find. It ate things and it made copies of other things. Curtis laughed.

He immediately thought of Annie. She would love this. He reached for his cell phone and pulled up her work number to call her. But he couldn't do it. He physically was unable to press SEND and make the call.

Curtis looked at the phone. He wanted to make the call, wanted to share this find with his best friend, but his thumb would not budge. He looked through the doorway into the workshop. A bright light pulsed from the interior of the cube.

No one can know. He shook his head trying to loosen the fuzzy feeling of the strange voice in his head. *No one can know. Not yet.*

"Okay." His voice was loud in the quiet kitchen. Ammo plodded out from underneath the couch at the sound of Curtis' voice.

And then he remembered the diagram he drew last night.

MICHAEL WHETZEL

*****

Curtis was late for work but Philip paid no attention. He was too busy helping unload the new pull-behind sprayer from its flatbed trailer.

"Forget fixing the old one. By the time we get it up and going, it'll be winter." The farmer turned and smiled at Curtis. "I got a good deal on this one."

Curtis nodded and looked over at the old sprayer he had spent most of the fall trying to fix. As Philip played with the new sprayer settings most of the morning, Curtis set to work picking beans.

He walked up and down the rows, snapping the small green pods from their branches and filling the large metal bucket he carried with him. He hummed while he worked. In his mind he planned out the rest of the day and what he would do that night. Annie would call. He was sure of it. He would take a break then and maybe join her for dinner or a trip into town. And then he would get back to work. He would ask Philip for the day off tomorrow. He had already thought up a make believe doctor's appointment and even though he did not like lying to Philip, figured that was the best way to get off.

He never mentioned the cube to his boss and he would not tell Annie about it tonight. He didn't know why but he knew for now it was important to keep it a secret.

And what if it is dangerous? He snapped peas and plunked them into the pail. *What if that thing is radioactive or killing your brain waves or something?* He stopped picking and stood up and stretched out the stiff muscles of his back. Curtis surveyed the lush green fields and turned his gaze to the crisp blue sky.

"It's not dangerous," he talked to himself. "I know

that. It's something else. Something new. And if I do everything I am supposed to it will….it will…." He looked back over the farm.

It will show me everything.

At the end of the day, he asked Philip about the sprayer.

"I don't know what you want with it, but go ahead. It saves me the trouble of getting rid of it." Phillip wiped his brow. "Since you're not working tomorrow, is it okay if we go late on Wednesday? We've got to get some more crops in this week."

Curtis agreed and then backed his truck up to the sprayer and hooked it up. He pulled off with a wave at his boss and drove seven miles to Buck's Outfitters. He bought a brand new variable speed chainsaw, a large 100 foot tarp, and some tie downs. He threw all this on the back of the truck and drove home slowly, mindful of the large machinery swaying back and forth across the road.

At home, he pulled into the drive and around to the back of the house. He unhooked the sprayer in the backyard and pulled the truck out onto the shoulder of the road. *Better safe than sorry,* he thought to himself.

Ammo pounced on him as soon as he entered the cabin.

"Good grief. Calm down, mutt." Curtis smiled at the dog and gave him a nice rubdown behind his ears. Ammo barked and wagged his tail crazily. He rolled over onto his back and Curtis rubbed his belly. The dog followed him into the kitchen but stopped short of the workshop entrance.

Curtis carefully walked across the threshold. He flipped the light switch but nothing happened. Then he recognized why. In the late afternoon sunlight, he could see that the electrical outlets were gone from the walls. Long lengths of electrical wire reached from the dark holes and disappeared into the cube. The light fixture was gone from the ceiling and more wire draped down and ran into the top of the cube. The cube itself was a little larger than it had been this morning. There was something else he noticed too; the edges and corners had become rounder and softer.

He went to the rear wall and knocked on the wood paneling. There was no outside entrance to the yard from the workshop. He picked up the chainsaw and yanked the cord, starting the loud motor. He revved the small engine over and over again. Then began cutting into the wall. He worked for about an hour, cutting and stripping and breaking until he had a huge square hole in the rear wall of the workshop.

Ammo sprinted from the kitchen and darted past the cube out into the yard.

"Hey!" Curtis yelled at the dog. Ammo turned and looked back. "Don't go too far. And don't get dirty!" The dog barked and ran into the woods.

Curtis went to the truck and grabbed some wire clippers from the dash. He came back and clipped all the electrical wires entering the cube and then laid the clippers on top. He wouldn't need them anymore. He walked behind the cube and began to push it through the hole. Even with its larger size, it was still extremely light to handle.

He guided the object through the wall and slid it across the grass to where the sprayer sat. He pushed the cube flush with one side of the sprayer and stopped. The new tarp was unwrapped and Curtis unfolded it and pulled it over the cube and sprayer all at once. Then he tied the whole thing down tightly.

Once he was done, his cell phone started to ring.

"Hey," Annie said on the other end. "How about dinner again tonight? I picked up some taco fixings and also rented a movie."

"Sound good. I'm starving." Curtis stared at the large lumpy shape hiding under the blue tarp. He doubted anyone would see anything even if it was left uncovered. The cabin was too far from the main road, but he wanted to make sure it wasn't discovered. "Let me get cleaned up and we'll be right over."

He called for Ammo and the beagle came bounding from the woods. They walked through the large hole in the workshop and got ready for Annie's.

Annie was her radiant self when she answered the door. Ammo walked slowly past her and took up a spot near the bottom of the staircase. He had become unusually quiet on the ride over.

"What have you been doing?" Annie asked, looking Curtis up and down. "You look different."

"What do you mean?" he replied. He glanced down at himself. He was wearing his usual flannel shirt and clean carpenter jeans. "I just showered."

"No," she said, standing aside to let him in. "It's your eyes. They look different. They look radiant."

Curtis snorted. "Wow, you really know how to woo a guy." Annie slapped him on the shoulder. "Radiant? Good golly, I don't think I've ever been called radiant before." This time she punched him in the shoulder.

Dinner was salad, Spanish rice, and chicken tacos. It was delicious. As they cleaned up, they talked about the new housing development that was going up on the north side of town and the loss of farmland that would house it.

It was always sad to see good cropland being plowed under for something else besides crops.

Annie frowned. "What's wrong with Ammo? He didn't even touch his dinner." She reached down for the plate they had loaded with tacos for the dog and dumped it into the trash bin. "He loves tacos."

Curtis looked around the kitchen. Ammo was nowhere in sight. He walked into the living room and found the dog curled up on one of Annie's plush chairs. The beagle watched his master approach but made no sign to greet him. Curtis looked down at Ammo's face. His eyes seemed watery and sad.

A small whine escaped the dog's throat.

"What's the matter, boy?" Curtis knelt beside his dog and rubbed his ears. Ammo thumped his tail weakly in response. He whined again.

"Is he okay?" Annie knelt next to Curtis and petted the dog's soft head. "He looks a little sick."

Curtis immediately thought of the cube. Was it doing this to his beloved friend? Was Ammo sick because of the strange object he had hidden behind his house?

Ammo thumped his tail a bit harder and reached up and licked Curtis on the face. But his eyes still seemed full of pain and his throat continued to make little whining noises.

"I don't know what's wrong with him," Curtis answered. He picked up Ammo and carried him to the couch. Annie sat next to them and they petted and held the dog together. "He may have eaten something bad he found out behind the cabin." *Or he may be becoming slowly poisoned by the thing we have out behind the cabin.*

He looked at Annie and wanted to tell her everything. It was on the tip of his tongue. But it wouldn't come out.

Just like the cell phone earlier this morning, he could not get his muscles to do what he wanted. He hugged his dog closer to him.

"Maybe I should get him home and let him rest a bit. If he's not better in the morning, I'll take him to the vet." He lifted the beagle into his arms and headed for the door. Annie followed.

"I'm sorry to run out on you like this. I know you wanted to watch a movie tonight." He turned in the doorway. "Maybe I can make it up to you another night."

Annie smiled brightly and Curtis felt his heartbeat quicken. She reached up with one finger and touched his cheek lightly. "I'm going to hold you to that, Curtis Yankey." Her touch was electrifying.

Annie gave Ammo a quick hug. She watched them pull out and waved as they disappeared around the bend.

It was dark out when they finally made it home. Ammo sat quietly next to Curtis in the pickup, watching the passing roadway lit quickly by the truck's headlights. Curtis pulled into the driveway and immediately stomped on the brakes.

Sometime during the evening the tarp had become assimilated by the cube. The tarp and ties were gone, which did not really matter since the object they were meant to hide had grown too large for them anyways. The cube had grown even more since he had left.

But it wasn't a cube anymore. At least not completely. Curtis could still see the shape of the square within this larger shape. He could see some of the corners and a couple of edges on one side. But that was it. This newest incarnation now stood even with the cabin and was bigger than the pickup. The sprayer was completely gone too, no trace of its existence anywhere in the surrounding area. In the glare of the headlights, Curtis saw more wires running from the cabin to the white mass.

The lights won't work now, I bet. Too many wires have been pulled out.

He looked to his right and saw that much of the metal roofing that surfaced the workshop part of the cabin was gone too.

He backed the truck out and parked it onto the shoulder. He carried Ammo into the cabin and sat the dog on the couch while he went to find a flashlight. He tried one of the switches in the kitchen but just as he thought, nothing happened. He located a large flashlight and went to his bedroom closet to find the two battery powered lanterns he used when camping.

Curtis carried the lanterns out into the living room, casting the large room in a soft glow. He grabbed a comforter from the front closet and covered Ammo with it. The dog snuggled down and instantly fell asleep. Curtis watched his pet for a few minutes, hoping his dog was going to be okay. Then he went out back.

He stood next to the "cube," looking up at the top edge. It seemed to be in the middle stages of transitioning from the box shape to a more fluid amorphous shape. Curtis placed a hand on the side of the blob. It was still a metallic material and still smooth to the touch. Now he could definitely feel a deep hum emanating from the cube. He glanced up to where the electrical wires disappeared into the surface of the object. In the darkness, Curtis could barely see small pinpricks of white light shining out from where each wire broke the surface. He took a few steps back and watched his new treasure. He thought he could actually feel the thing still growing and reaching higher and higher towards the sky.

RAW FEED STORIES

It's hungry. It's growing and changing and it needs more and more to reach the end point. Curtis looked towards the cabin, biting his lower lip in thought. He went through the hole in the workshop and into the kitchen. Using one of the lanterns for light, he began emptying the refrigerator.

First the fridge, then the stove, he thought to himself. *After that I can look at the furniture. I don't need a bed to sleep in. Couch, chairs, they can all go.*

He worked most of the night before passing out on the floor next to the couch. He fell asleep while slowly petting his dog on the head. Ammo sighed and slept too.

*****

Curtis woke to a wet sloppy tongue as Ammo licked his face. He nudged the dog away and opened his eyes. Ammo sat next to him, tail wagging.

"Feeling better boy?" he asked. "You look like you feel better." Ammo leaned back in and resumed licking Curtis. "Ah! Okay, I love you too." He pushed the dog away.

Curtis stretched out on the hard living room floor, listening to his muscles creak and groan from last night's work. He had emptied the fridge and hauled it outside next to the cube. It was followed by the stove, microwave, most of his dishes and silverware, and the kitchen sink. He topped it all off with one of the living room chairs and his extra bath towels. He also found two old tires that came off the pickup last summer. These he tossed high up on top of the morphing metallic body.

It had been a long night.

He glanced at his watch. It was almost noon. He tried to roll over and get up but there was a small weight on his legs. He glanced down. Ammo was curled up on his shins, sleeping.

Curtis turned to his right. Ammo still sat looking at him, his tail sliding back and forth across the cabin floor. He looked back to his legs. Ammo raised his head and began wagging his tail, the short appendage striking Curtis' bare feet.

Curtis blinked his eyes quickly. His mouth began to feel dry and he realized his jaw was hanging open. He looked back and forth between the two dogs.

"Ammo?" he asked hesitantly. The first Ammo barked shrilly. The second one answered with his own bark. Curtis scrambled to his feet and stared at the two dogs. Both of the beagles looked up at him, tails wagging, eyes happy. He watched as they both turned their head to one side simultaneously.

Toenails clicked on the cabin's hardwood floor as another Ammo walked in from the bedroom, yawning and then sat next to the other two Ammos.

Curtis screamed. All three dogs jumped up and howled in response. They jumped and ran around their master, disturbed by his distressful behavior. As soon as all three animals began brushing against his legs, Curtis bolted through the front door and out into the road.

The asphalt was hot against his bare feet as he paced back and forth. All three Ammos sat on the small front porch, licking their privates.

"Three dogs?" he muttered to himself. "There are three dogs and it's because of the cube. Only it isn't a cube anymore. It's turning into something else. And there are three dogs because there were three apples. But Ammo was never left with the cube unless....unless it is from prolonged exposure to the cube. Then that would make sense and that is why I have three dogs licking their butts on my porch." He stopped. *Organic material is copied. Why? Why three copies? Oh my God, what am I going to do? How do I explain three Ammos? Annie is going to flip. How will I ever be able to keep this up? I can't hide all of this forever. I can't---*

Curtis slowly turned back to the cabin. The dogs jumped down from the porch and began sniffing around the front yard. Slowly, Curtis raised his eyes higher and higher until he could see the top of the cube. It now towered over the cabin.

Curtis stumbled back into the front yard. The object was now about two stories tall. It was skinnier than before and now Curtis could begin to see a shape starting to emerge from the white matter. He recognized the shape right away, could not believe what he was seeing.

"Is that what I think it is?" All three Ammos barked a response.

He ran to the backyard and stared up at the tall tower. Now he could feel the gentle hum of the cube vibrate through his body, through the ground he stood on. The small vibrations running across his skin like gentle ripples on a pond.

The rear windows of the cabin were shattered. But no glass lay on the ground. All the electrical wiring and metal roofing on the rear of the house was gone. The garden hose he kept to one side was slowly making its way into the bottom of the structure. The cabin and surrounding area was slowly being stripped bare.

Curtis searched across the yard, looking for more material to add to the growing monstrosity. The beagles ran back and forth, chasing each other and wrestling in the afternoon sun. He looked past the playing dogs and stared at something else that caught his eye.

Last spring, he had planted a small peach tree in the

rear yard. So far it had grown a bit every year and had become a nice sized sapling. The small tree was still there, but now it was flanked on either side by two copies, each the same height and same color. *Carbon copies,* he thought.

He shook his head and looked back at the dogs. Which one was the original? He stared and stared, looking for any noticeable difference between the three of them and finding nothing. Heavy in thought, he turned back to the thing that had taken over his back yard, had taken over his life.

"I need more supplies," he said. "Because if that is turning into what I think it is, I need a lot more metal, more plastic, more everything."

Curtis raced back into the house. He grabbed the sofa and dragged it through the workshop and plopped it next to the cube. Then he raced back inside. For the next few hours, he stripped the interior of the house. The metal twin set that was a gift from his parents joined the sofa. The other two plush living room chairs and the small lamps were added to the pile. He broke apart the bathroom sink and pried up the enamel coated tub. They joined the sacrificial pile growing next to the cube.

Curtis turned from the pile and looked at his truck.

"No," he stopped himself, "I still need that."

He furrowed his brow, trying to think up where he could get materials. Suddenly, he snapped his fingers, remembering what was housed up the road.

"Ammo, let's go!" All three dogs bounded from the back yard and hopped into the cab. Curtis looked over the crowded space and shook his head. He gunned the engine and tore up the lane, heading for the end of his road.

He glanced in the rearview mirror, watching the destroyed cabin and the growing rocket ship sitting next to it disappear through the trees.

*****

Curtis drove the half mile to the end of Blackberry Lane. He pulled the old pickup truck up to the locked chain link gate and got out. The dogs jumped down and began sniffing the ground and chasing each other. Curtis walked to the gate.

The Department of Transportation shed stood against the back fence. There was a small yellow Ford Ranger parked under the roof. Next to the truck were some smaller push machines covered with heavy tarps. But all of these were ignored by Curtis. He focused on the large object parked on the opposite end of the shed, next to the small office. It was a huge steam roller, resembling a dirty, prehistoric hulk from a bygone era.

Curtis went back to his truck and pulled a set of large bolt cutters from behind the seat. He snapped the lock on the gate and tossed the chains on the back of the truck. He pushed the gate open wide and then pulled the truck up to the office. The dogs followed, tails bobbing in the air.

Curtis tried the office door. Locked. That was not surprising. He looked through the small window. There was a desk and chair, and on the wall behind the desk hung a small metal box. He figured that was where the state guys kept the keys to whatever they parked out here.

Curtis looked around the empty lot and then smashed the window with the bolt cutters. The dogs barked at the sound of shattered glass. Then, they stopped and sat next to each other, watching the young man open the door.

He went straight to the lock box and opened it. There were the keys for the pickup hanging on a small hook and right next to them were the steamroller keys. They were smaller than the truck keys. He grabbed the black fob and headed for the door. He figured it would be a few days, maybe even a few weeks, before they noticed the equipment was missing.

Curtis pulled himself up on the small seat of the roller and pushed the key into the ignition. He twisted it and the machine's engine whined several times. *Who knows how long it's been since this thing was started?* He tried again, and then again, until suddenly the engine turned with a throaty growl and black smoke belched from the exhaust pipe. Curtis studied the group of levers on the dash next to the steering wheel. The roller had no traditional gas or brake pedals. He began slowly pushing levers, feeling the engine engage and the roller's weight shift underneath him until finally he had worked out how to get the heavy equipment moving.

He pushed one of the levers and the steam roller leapt forward. He guided the machine past his pickup truck and through the open gate. The dogs walked behind the roller, keeping pace with Curtis for a bit before running into the woods to explore. The machine was not fast by any means, and it took him a good twenty minutes to cover the ½ mile distance on the gravel road back to the cabin.

As he pulled within sight of his home, he stared at the ship towering above everything behind the small house. It was not complete, but the shape of the thing was there. There was a tall central cylinder which formed the heart of the object. The cylinder ended in a rounded point giving it a large rocket shape. Two smaller cylinders were forming on adjacent sides of the central core. These, Curtis could tell, were the main thrusters.

Curtis watched as steam began to rise from the very

bottom of the structure. Almost everything he had stripped from the cabin was fully assimilated into the ship. He could make out one side of the sofa and part of the tub sticking from one wall. But everything else was finished. All of it gone in a span of what, an hour? The cube was speeding up its process.

Curtis slowly pulled the roller into the driveway and around the cabin. He gently pulled up to the wall of the ship, watching the large front roller spin until it barely touched the gleaming white surface. He leaned forward to shut the engine off and noticed the roller was not completely flush all the way across with the ship. Curtis pulled the lever back to reverse the machine. The engine whined but the roller did not budge.

He turned back to the front of the machine. He squinted at where the metal roller touched the ship. Already the whiteness of the strange surface was reaching out to cover the metal barrel of the steam roller. It was already being assimilated. Curtis cut the engine and jumped down from his seat.

The Ammos ran from the front of the house and bayed at the sky. They were hungry. Curtis went into the cabin to find them some food. The kitchen was now a mess. Food and frozen goods sat defrosting in the afternoon sunlight. Empty space marked the places where the stove, fridge, and sink used to be.

Curtis opened all the now soft ground beef and dumped it onto the floor. The dogs raced in and greedily began gulping down the meat. Curtis went back outside and started walking up the road. He needed to bring the state truck down and then begin tearing the chain link fence apart.

Hopefully that will do it, he thought to himself. He was

not sure, but he had the feeling the cube was almost finished morphing itself into the ship. It would be done soon.

And then what? What happens after that? Deep in his gut he already knew the answer to his question. He wondered if he had the nerve to actually do it. *Can I actually hop in a rocket ship and leave this place?*

He thought about Annie and his parents. He thought about Philip and the farm he loved working on. He thought about the woods, and the beautiful valley, and sitting on the front porch watching Ammo chase fireflies. And then he thought of Annie again. Her bright red hair burning like fire on a cold night and her sweet face and smile, so kind and pure, all came crashing into his mind. And then he thought of her soft fingers grazing his cheek the other night and Curtis abruptly stopped in the middle of the road.

Crickets chirped in the lush underbrush. Somewhere, something ran through the soft thicket of leaves on one side of the road; a rabbit, or rodent of some kind. A thrush danced among the trees, whistling and singing. A cool breeze swept across the road. And Curtis stood still taking it all in.

"It's too late," he said softly. "It's too late to turn back. I've got to see it through."

I'm sorry, Annie. I'm sorry for never being brave enough to make a move and for what might have been.

Then Curtis pushed all these thoughts away, burying them deep. He continued walking towards the supply shed. He was running out of daylight.

RAW FEED STORIES

*****

He worked the rest of the day and into the night, stopping only for water. He never felt hungry or tired, only focused on finding enough inorganic material to feed the ship. As the moon began to climb into the dark sky, he finally finished. There was a great amount of steam billowing from the engines and a mighty hum filled the night air. He looked up into the darkness, unable to see the top of the ship, but he felt it there. And he realized it had stopped growing.

It was finished.

It was ready.

Curtis felt the day finally catch up to him. Fatigue ran up and down his arms and legs and his head began to pound. He walked back into the cabin and passed all three dogs sleeping on the bare floor of the living room. He went back to the bedroom, wanting to climb into the shower, and at the last second remembered he had torn the bathtub out earlier.

Sweaty and exhausted, he stretched his last blanket across the space where his bed used to sit. The mattress had been given to the ship along with the pillows and the comforter and the wooden box frame was now piled into the closet. Curtis slumped to the floor and passed into a deep sleep.

He was floating again. A large planet loomed in front of him. It was massive in shape, colored deep shades of green and red. Asteroid rings wrapped around the outer rim of the planet and on its surface ion storms rolled their way across Curtis' vision.

A shadow formed on one end of the planet and slowly engulfed the large body. Curtis turned himself around to face wherever the source of the growing darkness originated from. It was the engine again. It moved before the young man, dwarfing the planet and its surrounding stars. Behind the planet three suns gleamed together brightly, their rays reflecting off the bronze surface of the great motor.

The engine hummed and Curtis felt electricity flow through his body again. The engine was the Great Engine, the Engine of Life and the Maker of Worlds. Curtis felt these thoughts dance into his sub-conscious and he sighed a heavy sigh in his sleep, lying on the floor.

The Great Engine revved to life and Curtis felt himself pushed through the dark energy of space. He swam behind a moon and from this vantage point, watched as the engine began to slowly move forward. Everything was beginning to move outwards from the power of the great motor and Curtis could feel the moon he was floating behind moving closer to his position. The engine revved louder, and in a split second, it was gone. He could only catch a quick flash of movement as the marvel accelerated and disappeared across the cosmos.

The small moon floated closer and closer. Soon Curtis felt his feet touch the soft surface and with a puff of moon dust, he stood on the small rock. The three suns continued to shine brightly and as he watched they began to pull the stars into themselves and swallow them up. The large planet he was admiring pulled away from him and darted for the suns. Curtis watched in amazement as the planet crashed into the nearest of the fireballs, exploding and burning into a billion particles. The sun turned black for a brief second and then glared even brighter before settling back to its original luminescence.

This is the end. The end of a universe. For every birth, a death.

RAW FEED STORIES

For every existence, a final doorway.

Curtis shifted while asleep on the floor. He kicked out his legs and mumbled something. The dogs slowly plodded into the bedroom and lay down next to their master. They fell back asleep and in their dreams they chased falling stars and burning suns and all three shivered involuntarily at the same time as they slept.

When Curtis woke, it was late morning and he realized he was late for work. He slowly rose from the floor, his head beating horribly and his chest heavy with fatigue. He walked into the kitchen needing something to ease his dry mouth and throat. A jug of warm orange juice sat on the wooden table of the dining nook. Curtis gulped the warm juice down quickly, cringing at the sour tart taste. When he finished, he tossed the jug to the side and leaned against the kitchen counter. The ache in his head was easing bit by bit.

Where are the dogs?

He glanced around the cabin but there was no sign of the beagles. He thought about calling them but his throat still felt raw and unusable.

He turned and looked out the hole in the wall that used to hold the kitchen window. Here he had a view of the bottom side of one of the engines before it disappeared out of sight above the roof. He watched as a ball bounced from behind the engine, and rolled across the yard. Immediately all three dogs bounded into view and gave chase. The dogs met at the ball and began wrestling each other in an effort to capture the toy first. Curtis smiled.

What could be better than good old Ammo? How about 3 good old Ammos?

He walked out through the workshop and ducked under the hole in the wall. It seemed so long ago that he had cut the wall apart in order to get the cube into the backyard. He stretched his arms skyward, letting the kinks in his shoulder muscles pop and loosen. He paused that way, arms outstretched, mid-yawn, and stared at the man standing in his backyard.

It took him a few seconds to realize he was staring at himself. And that he was staring back at him.

Curtis fainted.

When he came to, the sound of his cell phone filled his ears. The chirping phone was a rhythmic pulse in his fore conscious and felt a bit relaxing. He kept his eyes closed and listened to the phone. But something was off.

Even with his eyes closed, he was still seeing things. Actually he was seeing himself, lying on the ground on his back. Curtis opened his eyes and found himself staring into his own face. He blinked, trying to flick the image away, wondering if he had a concussion. The face looking down at him smiled.

A sensation filled Curtis' head. He reached one hand up shakily and rubbed his temples. He felt something shift in his mind, a sudden spurt to the right or left, and now he could not only see from his point of view, but from the perspective of the copy staring down at him. They were sharing each other's perspective while still maintaining their own.

"Are you okay?" Curtis asked him. That is, Curtis 2 was doing the asking.

Curtis slowly nodded. Curtis 2 nodded also, reaching down and plucking the phone from Curtis' shirt pocket. He flipped the phone open, silencing its chirping ring, and started to talk.

"Hey, Philip, I know I'm late. The truck is giving me a hard time this morning." Curtis 2 walked away to the other side of the yard. "No, I'll be there soon. I just got it going and am grabbing my things right now. So I don't need a ride. I'm sorry about all this." A pause. "Okay, I'll meet you over at the west field."

Curtis 2 flicked the phone closed and headed for the house. "I'm going to work. You look like you may need to lie down or something. Take the day."

Curtis nodded. He watched one of the Ammos peel off from the others and follow his copy into the cabin. A few seconds later he heard the sound of the truck starting and pulling away. Slowly he climbed to his feet and brushed off his pants.

"Hello." He turned at the sound of his voice. There, with the other two Ammos seated at his feet, was the third Curtis.

"H-H-Hey," Curtis answered. He walked over to the dogs and bent down to pet them, trying not to look at this new Curtis. But in his head, he felt the shift again. And now there were three points-of-view in his mind. They were like televisions all lined up side by side; only his consciousness was the biggest T.V. But if he concentrated just a bit he could turn to the other sets and make those the more pronounced picture.

He could see the road leading up to the farm disappearing quickly as Curtis 2 raced to work.

He could see himself petting the dogs as Curtis 3 studied him.

He kept looking at the Ammos. They licked his hands and wagged their tails.

"Crazy, isn't it?" Curtis 3 asked. Curtis looked up at the new arrival. It was amazing. He was looking into a physical mirror image. Even the small scar on his cheek from a motorcycle wreck years earlier was there. The scruffy beginnings of a beard, the way one eyebrow was a little more pointed than the other. Even the cuts on his hands from tearing apart the cabin were there.

But the clothes were off somehow. They were the same clothes he had on himself, but fainter in their colors. The jeans were now heavily washed out and the flannel shirt was faded profoundly. *Why is that?* He wondered.

"Because inorganic compounds are more difficult to copy. It's not the nature of the cube. It was made for assimilation and shifting only." Curtis stared at Curtis 3, nodding at 3's explanation. He did not why or how, but he knew that this was correct. He turned and stared at the beautiful rocket ship.

It towered high into the clouds, its brilliant white color glowing in the sunlight. There were no markings on the side of it, nor could Curtis see any kind of door or entrance. It was seamless from top to bottom.

He turned back to Curtis 3. "What should we do today?"

Curtis 3 looked back at the wrecked cabin. He tilted his chin at the large hole in the wall. "We should fix our home." He looked at the ship and then back to Curtis. "I don't feel like it is time to leave quite yet. And even then….." He trailed off, an unfinished thought that Curtis barely got.

We're not all going.

They went inside to clean up. Curtis sent Curtis 2 a mental checklist of items they would need to fix some of the things in the cabin. Curtis 2 would stop on the way home and also grab food. There were now several hungry mouths to feed and most of the food from the fridge had gone bad.

As the Ammos napped in the living room, Curtis and

his doppelganger worked on repairing the plumbing in the bathroom and sealing most of the holes in the walls. When Curtis 2 came home with supplies, all three of them got busy fixing the large hole in the workshop. They were finished by late evening. Tomorrow, they would sand and paint.

They settled down to a meal of canned soup, cheese, and crackers. The dining nook was crowded now, but Curtis found he did not mind at all. The dogs ate chow from a large bowl on the kitchen floor, also content in their own company. The men finished their dinner and dumped the paper bowls and plates into the trash, then settled back into the nook.

Curtis stared at his two copies. They returned the look.

"What does this mean?" he asked. He wasn't asking anyone in particular, but just wanted to voice the question. He understood that the cube would answer some things, like the faded clothes or the assimilation. But this was the chief question, the big one that had been on his lips since all of this had begun.

"I think it is an opportunity," Curtis 3 answered. Curtis 2 nodded.

"And what about that?" Curtis turned and looked through the window at the ship. "What does that have to do with us?"

Curtis 2 cleared his throat. "That is an opportunity too. I think we are given a chance to do something. To....choose."

"Choose what?" Curtis 3 asked. He turned back to Curtis, one eyebrow raised.

Choose a path. The thought popped quickly into his head. He looked up at his guests and saw that it had come to them too.

"The ship is one path," Curtis answered, "that we can journey on. With three of us, we have the possibility of three…different paths."

Silence followed this. It was a few minutes before someone spoke up.

"Lives. That's what it really means, right?" Curtis 2 said. "We're talking about parallel lives here. And we all three get to experience the others' choices."

Curtis turned to his copy. "I think that is exactly what it is." He leaned back against the wall, chewing on his bottom lip. "The ship is one path. This life here, I guess that is another path. But the third one? I don't know."

Curtis 3 shrugged. They glanced at each other but no one had any ideas.

"Maybe it's just a free pass. One life to do whatever you want with," Curtis 3 finally answered. "But I think the real question is: Who goes on the ship?"

The two copies turned and looked to Curtis. He was the main, the original; it really depended on what he wanted to do.

"I guess whatever path each of us is on, that experience is more real for that Curtis," he said. "We would share the consciousness of the others, but it would be faded a bit, I think." *Just like the clothes. Nothing beats the original.* The others nodded, understanding.

"I want to go on that ship," Curtis said. Curtis 2 stood and slapped him on the shoulder and Curtis 3 smiled.

"It's going to be a hell of an adventure," Curtis 3 laughed.

"I would like to stay here," Curtis 2 said. "I would like to see this life to the end. Continue working the farm. Maybe buy my own farm someday. That would be a grand adventure too."

Curtis looked at the last clone. 3 shrugged. "That's okay with me. I'm still not sure what I should be doing. But I'm ready for whatever."

"I think I know what I want you to do," Curtis nodded at the last clone.

*****

Curtis walked into the bank and waited for a teller to become free. It was the second time this morning he had come here. The teller finished with the next person in line and greeted Curtis with a smile.

"Back already?" she said in her pleasant voice. He had already withdrawn a few thousand dollars from his savings earlier and bought a used car. He had spent the past two hours at the DMV, getting the registration and licensing lined up. A quick call to his insurance agency and the car was ready for the road.

But now he needed some seed money.

"Yeah, I'm back," he said, a bit nervously. "I need to make another withdrawal."

He slid the paper slip across the counter and waited as the teller began counting the money. Another thousand dollars gone from his savings. *It's worth it though. This will get him started. And I've been so good with my money. Still got enough to get through and start saving again. Or at least #2 can start saving again.*

Curtis took the money and nodded at the teller. He slipped out of the bank and hopped into the driver's side of the truck. Curtis 3 sat in the passenger side, wearing a large parka with the hood pulled up, a hat, and sunglasses. His entire head and upper body was covered up.

"I feel stupid," he said to his partner. "And it's really

hot in this stuff."

"Better you are hot then everyone freaks out because there are two of us running around today."

"You mean three of us," Curtis 3 corrected. Curtis did not even want to think about that. He was silently praying that his other clone, and Philip, stayed out at the farm and did not have any spur-of-the-moment needs in town today. That could lead to a very awkward scenario.

Curtis drove the truck down a side street. There was a small parking deck here and he pulled the pickup into the dark interior. He parked beside an older model Chevy Lumina, the car he had bought that morning. Two Ammos were bouncing around in the rear seat, happy to see their owners.

They got out of the truck and Curtis 3 grabbed a large rucksack from the bed. They had bought some new clothes and toiletries for the journey. Curtis opened the rear door of the car and while they loaded the supplies, one of the Ammos jumped out and sat next to the truck.

"Are you the original Ammo?" Curtis addressed the dog. The dog thumped his tail in reply. "The original butthead dog?" Ammo barked and Curtis rubbed his friend's ears. It was weird how the dogs easily split themselves up between the three copies. He figured they knew who belonged to whom. He sure couldn't tell the difference.

Curtis 3 slammed the door shut and turned to the two of them. "I guess this is it."

"Where will you go first?" Curtis asked.

"I think I'll head up north. See how I can help with the Sandy cleanup."

Curtis handed over the wad of money. "This is to get you started. I'll have 2 send in money monthly to the spending account. It won't be much though. You'll have to do what you can for the rest." 3 nodded.

"Don't worry."

Curtis leaned in the back window of the car and patted the other Ammo's head. "Take care of him." The dog barked happily.

The men embraced in a strong hug of farewell. And then Curtis 3 got into the car and pulled out of the parking lot. Curtis watched him drive off. He turned to Ammo.

"Well, that's one down." The dog barked loudly, the sound echoing over and over again in the dark parking lot.

Curtis drove back to the cabin. In his mind, he could see 3 driving along the highway heading north and 2 digging up potatoes out in the field. But his main focus was on the rocket ship and the trip before him. He had not packed anything or bought food for the trip. Somehow he knew he would not need these things. Knew that everything would be provided for him.

He pulled into the driveway and walked back to the yard. Ammo followed closely.

"We should fix the yard where the steam roller tore everything up." He grabbed a shovel and began flipping over the ripped grass. Soon he was deep into yard work as he cleaned up much of the mess from the cabin's destruction and began replanting some of the bushes that were torn away around the rear of the house. He worked for several hours, lost in the ebb and flow of the manual labor, forgetting the access he had into the other two clones.

Soon the sun was setting and the air began to cool. Curtis worked the heavy soil with a small trowel he had found when suddenly he stopped.

Something just happened, he thought.

He brought his fingers to his mouth, brushing his lips lightly. *What was that?* Quickly he switched focus to #2 and saw Annie. She was leaning very close to him and Curtis' whole body trembled as he watched her close in again and kiss him a second time.

Even though he was in the backyard, he could feel the softness of her lips, the warmth of her skin. *Annie was kissing me. #2, you lucky bastard, you.*

I know, the thought came back quickly from 2.

Curtis listened as Annie spoke.

"I've wanted to do that for so long," she said. They were in her living room. She had stopped by the farm and invited Curtis over for some freshly made tea and homemade cookies.

"I've wanted to do that too," Curtis 2 said as Curtis mouthed the words sitting in the dirty flower bed. "I was just really scared. And nervous."

Annie reached over and took Curtis 2's hand. Curtis stood from where he was sitting in the dirt, looking down at his own empty hand but feeling Annie's soft fingers entwined in his.

"I think I love you, Curtis," she said softly.

"I know I love you, Annie."

Curtis smiled and looked up at the ship in front of him. He had finally said it. Finally said the words that had echoed in his heart for some time. He sent a quick thought over.

Kudos, friend.

A reply came back. *I'll take care of her. I always will.*

I know we will, Curtis shot back. He shrunk the window in his head and left the two of them alone. It was hard at first. He could feel Annie's head lying against his chest. He could feel the light touch of her hair against his skin; feel her body move as she breathed.

But he did not want to intrude. As much as he wanted to sit there in the yard and feel her touch against him, he had already made his choice.

He turned to finish his work when a large sound filled the yard. It was steam hissing from the underside of the rocket ship. Billows of smoky fog unfurled from the ship's body. He watched in awe as a small door appeared on the side of the largest cylinder. More steam billowed as the door slid slowly open, exposing the dark interior of the ship.

Curtis stood and watched for a few minutes. Then he went inside and washed his hands and face. He changed clothes and came back outside.

"AMMO!" he called. The dog came bounding out from the bushes. He ran to his master, barking at the steaming smoke and jumping around Curtis' legs.

"It's time to go, buddy." Ammo barked. He followed Curtis to the ship and then followed him through the door.

The door slid closed and disappeared. The outside of the rocket was smooth again. There was no sign that a door existed there a few seconds ago.

Part 2

Curtis 3 stood on the dock overlooking the San Francisco Bay. Ammo sat next to his feet, watching seagulls flit up and over the small crests topping the water. Curtis 3 was waiting for loading time. He had booked passage on a ship owned by the Care Coalition and was heading for North Africa. The Care Coalition was one of the biggest charitable organizations in the world and Curtis was glad he had hooked up with them. He had volunteered to help oversee the supplies for the boat and then make the long voyage down to Africa to dig wells for several of the small villages there.

In the past two years, he had traveled in the Lumina across the country, Ammo by his side, stopping and helping wherever he could. He helped rebuild houses for Hurricane Sandy relief. He helped build shelters for the homeless in New York City. In Arizona, he had worked for six months building low cost housing for low income families. He would spend the days hammering nails and laying brick, and in the evenings (and some nights) help food pantries serve hot meals or visit the nearby senior retirement home and volunteer there.

Wherever he was, he helped. No matter who needed it or what needed to be done, he would stop his traveling and start work. And through the whole thing, Ammo was with him.

They had been to every state, every major city, covering as much ground as they could possibly cover. The Lumina finally died six weeks ago, but by then Curtis 3 had decided it was time to head overseas and start work there. He had "talked" it over with his fellow copies and they agreed there were many places that could use a helping hand.

"I want you to serve," Curtis had said to him that night in the kitchen in the small cabin. "I want you to go out and do everything in your power to make the world a better place."

Curtis 2 had nodded and agreed. "I'll do everything I can to support you from here." And he had. Any extra money Curtis 2 made went into the spending account only accessed by 3. It became a little trickier to deposit money after Curtis 2 married Annie over a year ago, but the money was always there, on the first of the month, waiting.

Curtis 3 looked out across the bay. The sun was slowly rising out over the crisp, blue water. Small boats made their way across the inlet, looking for deep ocean to fish in. A couple of freighters barged across the horizon, destined for other harbors in other cities to empty their cargo holds of goods.

Curtis 3 looked at the beautiful scene but saw none of it. Instead he was seeing three suns, in a triangular array, shining brightly down on the purple sands of a very, very distant moon. He watched as the lowest sun, the smaller one, began to disappear below the horizon. He saw Ammo watching the suns, while scratching deeply behind one ear. The moon's surface was flat and empty. The purple grains of sand twinkled in the bright light of the suns.

Curtis 3 switched focus and now he saw something different. He was staring out a window at cornfields. It was late at night, the edge of the fields illuminated by the safety light Curtis 2 had installed a few weeks ago. He watched as Curtis 2 turned and looked back at the large bed with Annie's still form hidden by the covers.

You are up late, Curtis 3 sent.

Just enjoying the view. It's beautiful. Curtis 2 shifted at the window, enjoying the sight of the suns moving closer and closer to the horizon. *Where are you, Curtis?*

I am sixty five million light years from you. I think it is called the Zandar Quad. It is a fairly large system all revolving around these three suns, which in turn revolve around each other. Curtis turned back to the ship. It sat silent, tall and imposing against the flat moon. *Taking a break from the ship. It's comfortable but Ammo needs to stretch his legs a bit.*

Curtis walked across the fine sand, lifting small tufts of it with his sneakers. Ammo followed, sniffing the ground here and there for anything interesting. They re-entered the ship and Curtis took his seat in the small captain's chair.

The interior of the ship was bigger than it looked from the outside. In front of the captain's seat was a large viewing screen and below that the main controls for the rocket. The controls were extremely simple. A small lever handled propulsion and another lever handled braking. Everything else was controlled by the ship.

Curtis would spend hours looking at star charts and maps of the universe that were stored behind him on several large shelves. He had never seen anything like the charts. They were beautifully made discs which you held in the palm of your hand. A holographic display would project from the disc, showing a detailed map of that particular part of the universe. Curtis had spent days just looking through the star charts when the rocket first took off, mesmerized by the sheer number of planets and galaxies the universe held.

Once he decided where he wanted to go, he fed the disc into a slot on the main computer and punched in the destination. The rocket set course and, depending on where he was and where he was going, it never took more than a day to reach his target. Curtis knew it was almost impossible to travel that fast through space, but he also realized he was now beyond the human limits of understanding and thinking. What was deemed impossible before could now be a simple reality. He simply accepted what the cube was giving him. And enjoyed it immensely.

There was a small bunk located behind the pilot room. He never felt tired but liked to lie down and search through the charts. Ammo would curl up on his legs and watch his master work, staring at the red tinted displays as they dipped and swirled in the middle of the air. Sometimes Curtis would just lie and watch what the others were doing right then. He spent a lot of time sharing dinner with Curtis 2 and Annie. He loved watching her; the way she smiled at him, the way she chewed her food with her cute little mouth, how her freckles appeared darker after being out in the bright sun all day.

Other times he would watch Curtis 3 building shelters or digging sanitation ditches or just driving through new places. He finally got to see the Grand Canyon and New York City and San Francisco and Mount Rushmore, even though he was never physically there.

They never ate on the ship. They never felt hungry or tired. At first, Curtis worried if this would be too taxing on the beagle, but Ammo seemed very pleased to be with him. When they ventured out of the ship to explore, they never needed any kind of space suit or protection from the new environments. Curtis knew the cube somehow provided all these things and he never questioned it.

He slid a new disc into the computer and looked at the display. There were several places to visit in this quadrant, but he was really interested in a nearby nebula cloud. He had seen a few so far on his travels and loved to float in among the neon gases, and this one was the largest he had come across yet. He set the coordinates and felt the ship gently leave the small moon behind. He watched the suns disappear on the screen.

Curtis 2 slipped back into bed and carefully put one arm around Annie. She groaned softly and snuggled closer to her husband. Ammo glanced up from the floor and watched them for a few minutes. Then he went back to sleep.

Curtis 3 heard the call for boarding and grabbed his nearby backpack.

"Let's go, Ammo. Africa, here we come." They marched across the dock and headed for the gangway.

Curtis watched all of this and then reached over and took Ammo in his arms. He hugged the dog closely and the beagle responded by licking his face. Curtis took out the small red rubber ball, one of only two things he had brought onto the ship, and tossed it against the far wall. The ball bounced crazily and Ammo jumped from the cot and gave chase. Outside the ship, planets and stars raced past in a blur of light.

*****

"Where has all of this been going to, Curtis?" Annie asked him. They were seated at breakfast. Curtis 2 had been reading the newspaper until Annie had interrupted him with her discovery. He slowly sat the paper down, staring at the handful of papers that Annie grasped in her hands.

"Every month, Curtis. You've been doing this every month for how long? Even before we were married? And you never told me." Annie's nostrils flared and Curtis knew she was angry and hurt. "What is it for? Why have you been sending money to this account every month? You sent $500 last month. We don't have that kind of money. We just bought a farm, you idiot!"

Curtis 2 stood up from the table and reached over for the papers. He plucked them from Annie's hands, folded them neatly, and stuffed them into his shirt pocket. Annie stood shocked and watched as her husband sat back down.

He sipped a bit of orange juice and nibbled some bacon.

"Are you not going to say anything?!?" Annie cried.

"Why? You are so angry at me, for what? For depositing my money in another account? That's my money right. I earned that money. Just like you earn your money at the office. And you deposit it into your account."

"But we're married!"

"Yeah, and we share all the bills. And we pay all our bills. Yes, we bought this farm, at a hell of a reduced price I might add. Philip was very kind in that. But the money is not what this is about."

Annie sat at the table. "What is it about?"

"It's about how you don't trust me." Curtis 2 stared at his wife. "Have I ever done anything that you felt was wrong or hurtful, to you or to our marriage? Have I, Annie?"

"No," she shook her head. "No. You are the best man I know."

"Then why do you not trust me now?"

"No, Curtis, it's not that. I was just surprised. I was at the bank and she starts talking about the monthly deposit for this account and I have no idea what she's talking about. Then she shows me the information and it is something I've never seen before. And it's been going on for years. And the fact that you made a joint account between the two of us...I don't what's going on. What is it for?" She grabbed a napkin and wiped the tears from her eyes.

"I can't tell you," Curtis 2 answered, softly. He held up his hand to ward off her objection. "Do you trust me?"

Annie stopped her objection and sat still. After a few seconds, she nodded slowly. "I do."

"Good. Because if I die, if I keel over on the tractor tomorrow or an airplane crashes on top of me while I'm out picking beans, if something happens to me, I need you to keep depositing money into that account." Curtis watched his wife. Annie sat back in the chair.

"I don't understand, honey," Annie said quietly. "Can you at least tell me why it is so important?"

Curtis 2 sighed. "That money, when it really comes down to it, is about making a difference in a world that doesn't give two craps about itself anymore. That money helps people, helps those who can't help themselves, who are....forgotten by their own brothers." He looked down at the table and started picking at a spot on the surface. "It's an investment. Into something positive."

Annie nodded again. "Okay. That's good. I'm glad. But why can't you tell me exactly what it goes to?"

"I just can't. You wouldn't understand." And then under his breath, "Sometimes I don't even understand it all." He looked back up at Annie. "Just know that I love you more than anything in the world, anything in this God given universe. And I would never do anything to hurt us."

Annie got up from her seat and ran to Curtis 2. She cried softly as he held her.

"I know you wouldn't," she whispered.

Curtis rose from the cot and looked at the view screen.

Alpha Centauri stared back at him. He wiped a tear from his eyes.

"I'm sorry, Annie," he said to the bright galaxy. "I never meant to hurt you." He moved to the view screen and ran his fingers across the small clusters of stars grouped here and there on the outer rim of Alpha Centauri. He touched the stars but he felt her hair as Curtis 2 ran his fingers through it.

Under the hot scorching sun of North Africa, Curtis 3 looked down at the deep, dark hole his team had just finished digging. He could hear water gurgling from the dark depths. He wiped his arm across his sweaty brow and picked up one of the village boys who had spent the morning watching his crew carefully.

"We got water, little buddy!" he yelled as he swung the boy around. Ammo barked and ran around the new well as the other village kids ran to see what all the excitement was about. The little boy laughed and laughed as Curtis 3 swung him higher and higher into the air.

It was the third well they had dug in the past week.

Curtis 2 left the kitchen and went to the large barn. He grabbed the feed for the chickens and headed for their fenced pen.

I hope this is the right thing, what we're doing. Because it is hard as hell.

I know it is the right thing, Curtis sent back to him. *We know the love of a beautiful woman, a beautiful home, and 3 just helped a poor village find new life.*

2 caught a glimpse of the laughing children dumping tins of cool water over their heads. He smiled.

I know what we have built down here, but what about you? What do you think we will find up there?

I don't know, Curtis replied. *I used to think I would be shown some great answer to everything. But the more time I spend up here, the more I think the point is something else entirely. The things I've seen, we've seen, I don't know what it all means. Maybe it means nothing. Maybe I have no clue what I'm supposed to be doing up here.*

Curtis 2 shook his head at the stupid chickens swarming around his feet, pecking desperately at the small crumbs he threw to the ground. He left the pen and headed for the fields. He still had a long day ahead of him.

Curtis looked down at the star chart in his hand. There were still plenty of discs that were waiting to be read, and he came upon this one earlier. It showed a quadrant of the Scion 16 Galaxy. This galaxy was one of the ones outside the furthest studies of Earth. It lay 15.2 billion light years away, a large galaxy among many smaller ones.

This chart carried something curious. One of the planets was marked with a small symbol. He had never seen the symbol before on any of the other charts. It looked like a triangle that someone had twisted around on itself. There was no key to explain the symbol, nor any additional information regarding the planet. Most of the time, the charts would say something about what type of planet it was and the conditions on the surface. But this one only contained the symbol and nothing else.

Curtis punched the coordinates into the main computer. He felt the rocket shift slightly and then watched as the universe began to fly by. He turned to Ammo. The dog was busy licking himself.

"Billions of miles from home. First dog to ever go to space. Riding along at umpteen miles an hour in a rocket. And you still got to lick yourself." Ammo wagged his tail and licked his lips. Curtis laughed and turned back to the view screen.

RAW FEED STORIES

*****

The planet held life.

The ship had sat down on a large rocky outcropping overlooking wide grassy plains. There was a large herd of animals feeding and resting all across the expanse. A lake held the reflection of the two moons that floated serenely in the sky. Curtis watched as something flew down into the lake and landed on the water.

He tapped a button on the control panel and the screen switched to a close up view of the herd. They looked very much like buffalo; only instead of fur they were hairless. Their skin was scaly and looked thick, like rhinoceros skin only this was a yellowish color. The animals reached down and plucked large mouthfuls of the light blue grass that covered the plain. He watched as a young calf jumped up and down around its mother.

Curtis switched the view to the lake. The flying thing was indeed a bird but this bird had two separate sets of wings and a hideous face. Its eyes glowed a fierce red and he watched as the bird flapped its wings and took off from the surface. Immediately the water erupted as something huge jumped from beneath the surface and snatched the bird in mid-flight. Just as quickly as it arrived, this new monster disappeared back under the water.

Ammo howled at the screen. Curtis shushed him quickly and replayed what he had just seen in his mind.

"I'm pretty sure that looked like a dragon," he said. Ammo whined.

Go look outside.

The thought broke into the confusion in Curtis' mind. It was from 3.

Not sure if that is a good idea. Might be dangerous.

I don't think the cube brought you all the way up here just so a water dragon could eat you.

Curtis mulled this over. So far he had been protected from everything he had come across since entering the ship. *Why would this be any different?* He looked at Ammo.

"Let's go."

Ammo barked.

The planet's surface was very warm and comfortable. Ammo ran around the ship, overloaded with new smells. Curtis looked around. The outcropping they had landed on was made of an extremely hard red rock. He wiped one finger across its surface. It was gritty and very warm to the touch. *It's like desert rock from home,* he thought.

He walked around the edge of outcropping and found a worn path running down the side of the ridge to the flat plain below. With Ammo on his heels he climbed down. He saw several footprints in the worn rock, wide prints that looked like a dinosaur's tread, each toe topped with a long, sharp claw. He tried not to think about what type of creature made those prints.

They reached the plain and saw a small herd of the grazing animals nearby. Ammo growled and jumped, barking nervously at the large creatures. They paid him no mind. Curtis walked slowly towards them.

He reached down and grabbed a small tuft of the blue grass. Holding it before him, he slowly approached the closet animal.

He was only a few feet away when the animal turned and stared at him, watching him closely. Curtis slowly waved the grass back and forth. The animal took two steps towards him and snatched the grass from his hands. Curtis smiled and Ammo barked loudly from a few feet away.

Since he had dug the cube from the ground on top of

the ridge, Curtis had witnessed one amazing thing after another. What happened next was the most amazing thing so far. The animal uttered a series of sounds, bleats and brays much like a donkey. Curtis heard the sounds enter his head and then recognized that familiar shift he had felt before within his mind. The brays and bleats turned to words he understood. So that when the animal called at him, he actually heard:

"Can you quiet that thing up, please?"

Curtis fell backwards and landed on his behind. Ammo ducked his head into the grass and became still. The other animals in the herd were now all looking towards the newcomers.

In the kitchen of a large farmhouse deep in the Shenandoah Valley, Curtis 2 quietly dried dishes while his wife washed. Stunned, he dropped the glass he was holding. It shattered against the tile floor and broke into pieces.

"Oh my god!" he exclaimed.

"Curtis?!?" Annie stopped washing, worry etched on her forehead. "What is it?"

"It talked!" He turned to his wife, his eyes wide with surprise and anticipation. "It talked, Annie!"

On the rooftop of a small house in Nigeria, Curtis 3 looked towards the night sky. He hooted and laughed, thrusting his arms into the cool air.

"WE'RE NOT ALONE! WE'RE NOT ALONE, YOU BEAUTIFUL, LOVELY PEOPLE!" he yelled. Small lamps blazed out of the darkness as many of the neighbors were awakened by these exclamations. Dogs began barking and Ammo howled out across the small town. A woman turned from pulling water at the new well, and tried to understand what the American stranger was going on about now.

Curtis shook a fist at Ammo. "Shut it, Ammo. Now!" The beagle ran behind Curtis and peeked out from behind one shoulder. Curtis turned back to the mighty beast, which now towered above him. The rest of the herd began to circle around them.

"I'm sorry. He is very nervous. We are new here." Curtis stammered nervously. *I'm talking to an alien.*

"I understand. We do not like very loud things. If it could please be quieter, that would be appreciated. Where do you come from, stranger?" The large animal tilted his head and examined Curtis more closely.

"I come from Earth."

"We do not know this place. Which plane does it exist on?"

Curtis shook his head. He did not understand the creature's meaning, and now the rest of the herd was beginning to whisper among itself too. He was trying to pick up on all the conversations going on but it was proving to be too difficult.

"I don't understand what you mean. I come from the Milky Way galaxy."

The creature stared silently at Curtis.

Curtis sighed. "I come from a great many planes away. Very, very far away."

"And why do you come here, wanderer?"

"I just want to talk to you. To visit with you. On Earth, on my home, we think we are the only ones who exist. But now I've found you. And now I know that we are not alone. I just want to talk to you for a bit. That is all." Curtis moved to his knees and twisted some of the grass in his hands.

The large animal moved to one side of the man. It

shook its mighty head and snorted. "Very well. I will speak with you. And you are not alone. Just as we are not alone either. Even if we had never met you."

"I don't understand. What do you mean?"

"There are others. Many others live among the other planes. They visit us here sometimes. And these others in turn tell us of yet more who exist on planes beyond theirs."

Curtis' heart skipped a beat.

Curtis 2 dropped another dish, much to his wife's dismay.

Curtis 3 grabbed up his dog and they danced back and forth across the rooftop.

"There are others," Curtis whispered and the great beast nodded.

****

There were others and Curtis and Ammo visited many of them in the next four years. The "space buffalo" were called the Wuggians. They were a peaceful group of herbivores who were the only advanced race on the planet. Another million light years away and Curtis found the Fdelians, an amoeba-like people not visible to the naked eye. The Fdelians communicated through singing, high pitched sounds that could not be heard by the human ear. He found the Vidi, a group of giants the size of skyscrapers. Then there were the Kii, small furry creatures who mined on a large rocky planet 64 billion light years from Earth.

Everywhere he went, he found the most peaceful races of life. And he communicated with them all. They talked about their different worlds and unique cultures. They discussed politics (the Fdelians were very political) and farming (the Vidi grew large stalks of strange fruit the size of a bus). With every meeting and every conversation, Curtis uncovered two important pieces of information: none of the races knew anything about war, and none of them knew anything about the cube.

Curtis picked up a small disc and watched the star chart pop up. There were two planets marked with the twisted triangle, which he now knew meant the planets held life. He punched in the coordinates for the first one. With each visit he was getting further and further away from home, deeper and deeper into the vast void of space.

He felt Ammo's nose nudge his fingers. He looked down at the dog and smiled. Ammo licked his fingers and Curtis knelt and rubbed the dog's head. He was worried about the dog. They had been on the ship for almost six years. Add his Earth time and you had a dog that was approaching seven years old, or forty-two years in dog time.

But Ammo never showed any signs of deterioration. He still looked the same as the day he followed Curtis onto the ship. He had "talked" about it with the other two Curtis' and they were experiencing different scenarios. Both earthbound dogs were aging normally. Curtis 3 said that his Ammo hardly ventured out of the shelter anymore. He still liked to play with the neighbor kids but only for very short times. Curtis 2 stated the same thing. His Ammo very rarely left the house and he had stopped taking the dog hunting a long time ago.

And what about you? Curtis 3 asked one night. *Are you aging at all?*

Curtis had looked at his reflection on the viewing screen. From what he could tell, his facial features had not changed a bit. *No. I haven't changed.*

The ship hopped from warp speed and a small planet appeared on the screen. The disc had labeled it Star Deem VI, one of eight planets in the Star Deem galaxy. To his surprise, he saw the planet was covered with water. He brought the ship down through the atmosphere and skimmed the roiling ocean, looking for a place to land.

Miles and miles of water stretched out across the planet. Curtis saw nothing moving through the sky and could not discern anything beneath the ocean surface. Where was this life the disc had marked? He leaned back in the seat and watched the screen, periodically patting Ammo on the head.

Curtis 2 sat in the doctor's office and waited. Annie should be coming out anytime. He needed to get back to the farm and fix the guttering on the house. In the past few years, Green Valley Farms had become one of the largest organic producers in the state. Curtis hired several new employees and welcomed interns from neighboring universities, and with the extra help, was selling goods at farmers markets and organic food stores every day all across Virginia.

Annie entered the waiting room, thanking the nurse who had escorted her out. Curtis 2 could see right away that she had been crying. He rushed to her side.

"Not yet. Outside in the truck, please," Annie said softly as she wiped a tear from her eye with a wrinkled tissue.

Curtis walked her to the truck and they got in.

"What happened?" he asked. "I thought it was just a routine checkup."

Annie nodded. "It was. But the doctor found something this time."

"Oh God, its cancer isn't it?"

Annie shook her head. "No."

"Then what?"

"I can't have kids, Curtis. He said there is something wrong inside and that I won't be able to have children." She barely got the last part out before the tears came again.

She cried and cried and Curtis 2 held her, there in the parking lot of the doctor's office for a long, long time.

"It's okay," he soothed her. "We can always adopt. Or maybe do that surrogate mother thing." She nodded and wiped her eyes. "Or I can take the next one I see down at the market. There are some cute ones there." Now she smiled, and carefully touched her forehead to his.

"I love you," she said gently.

He took her home and wrapped her in a large blanket, sat her in her favorite chair, and ordered an intern to make her some hot tea. Ammo loped in from the hall and jumped up on Annie's lap.

"Anyways we got one kid already," Curtis 2 said, pointing at the old dog begging for attention. Annie stroked Ammo's head and they curled up together. Soon both were asleep, and Curtis 2 watched them. His two favorite things in the world holding each other: his wife and his dog.

Curtis leaned back in the captain's seat. He had merely observed the past few hours, not interrupting with his thoughts, just feeling the couple's pain and love deep inside of him. Kids. He never really thought about Annie and Curtis 2 having kids, but now the thought filled him with sadness and a pang of jealously. He hoped the others did not pick up on it.

Ammo jumped up on his lap and licked his face and Curtis gave the dog a gentle squeeze. They sat that way for a while until Curtis felt the ship slow down. He glanced at the screen and saw what he had been searching for the past several minutes: land.

It was not much land. Only an island in the middle of the large ocean. It was barren and rocky and the waves crashed along its shore violently. The ship found a suitable place to land, a flat surface of hard, black rock. It parked smoothly and Curtis and Ammo hopped out.

They were almost knocked down by the wind. Strong gusts pushed against his body, rocking him back. Curtis looked at Ammo. The dog was struggling to move.

"Ammo! Go back to ship! Stay inside!"

The dog barked once and tilted his head, as if to say *Will you be okay?*

Curtis waved him off. "Go back! You're going to end up in the water and I'm not going in after you!" Ammo barked again and returned to the ship. Curtis surveyed his surroundings.

The ground rose up severely in front of him. It was not too steep but climbing in this wind could be disastrous. He began to look for another place to explore when something on top of the rise caught his attention.

There was a small cave nestled in the rock. Curtis blinked against the wind. There! That's what had caught his eye. Firelight flickered in the opening of the cave.

Curtis made his way to the bottom of the rise and began to climb. It was torture. For every three feet he climbed, the wind would knock him back down two. But he continued on. Higher and higher, until just when he thought his energy was finally gone, he stumbled onto the entrance of the cave and sat there panting.

The air was warm here and the firelight flickered brighter now. Curtis could smell meat cooking. Oh what a smell it was! How long had it been since he had smelt food cooking, or even tasted food? Slowly, he crawled into the cave.

The interior was small, a round room with shelves carved into the wall of rock on either side. The fire blazed brightly from the center of the cave. Something sizzled, impaled on a spit over the fire. Curtis cleared his throat and a small figure turned to him.

It was a woman. Quite possibly the most beautiful woman he had ever seen.

No, that's not true. Annie is the most beautiful thing I've ever seen. But this woman was close. She stood from the fire and Curtis saw that she was very short, almost two heads shorter than him. She was dressed in a tattered gown, and rags were wrapped around her hands and legs for warmth. Curtis felt the familiar shift in his head as the woman spoke.

"Who are you?" she growled. "Why are you here?" She picked up a large staff that lay on the ground. The staff ended in a sharp point, and appeared to be made of some sort of metal alloy. She thrust the point at him, warning him to stay away.

"Please," he said. "My name is Curtis. I am just visiting. I found this planet, and this place. I saw the light and came to see what it was." He stepped closer into the cave and the woman pointed the spear at him.

"Stay back!" she cried. There was a sudden rush of air and Curtis stumbled backwards as the woman seemed to grow larger. He pushed himself against the wall, out of breath, staring in awe at the young maiden. She had not grown larger; it was an illusion cast by the large, colorful wings that had exploded from her shoulders and back. They were shaped like butterfly wings and seemed to hold every color conceivable. Curtis stared as the colors swirled within the shape of the wings.

"I don't mean any harm. I am a visitor to this part of the universe. And you are beautiful." He said the last part under his breath, but the woman caught it. She backed away from him and sat on the other side of the fire. Now he could see her face quite clearly. Her eyes were entirely white, no iris or pupils in them. Her skin was a dark tan and she had long, golden hair that flowed down across her shoulders. She folded her wings back into her shoulder but still held the staff tightly.

"You do not look like you are Grem. You look like you are Superion, like me. But where are your wings? And your face is different." She studied Curtis cautiously from across the fire.

"I am not Grem. I don't even know what that means. And I am not Superion. I am a human."

"I do not know human. And I have no need for visitors. The Grem made sure of that." The woman spun the spit over the fire, making sure the meat cooked evenly.

"What is a Grem?" Curtis asked. He made his way slowly to the fire and sat on the opposite side of the woman. He could not take his eyes off of her.

"The Grem destroyed this world. Do you think it was always just an ocean out there? No. We Superion made great cities of glass with tall white towers that stretched to our moons." The woman pushed a lock of hair back from her face. "Then the Grem came and destroyed everything. They came with their war machines and their battle armies. They cut our warriors down, and smashed our great cities. Then the waters rose and flooded this world. Now nothing can live here."

"Where are the rest of your people? How many of you

are left?"

The woman stared at Curtis, the fire burning deep in her milky white eyes.

"There is only me. I am the last Superion." She sniffed and tore off a chunk of hot meat. She took out a small glass dagger and began cutting the meat into small pieces.

"Why did the Grem destroy your world?" The woman offered Curtis a small cut of the hot food. He placed it in his mouth and chewed slowly. It tasted like spicy, smoked salmon. It was delicious.

"They came seeking It. We did not have It here." She tore into the food, rending the chunks with her teeth. "They did not believe. Called us liars. Invaded with their armies. They go to every world, always searching, always seeking, and always destroying everything in their path."

"What are they looking for?" Curtis' eyes were drooping. He was feeling quite comfortable in the warm cave. And the warm feeling traveled all across his body. He closed his eyes.

"They seek the Great Engine. The Life Giver. The God Motor." The woman fed more wood onto the fire and the flames leapt up. Curtis lay down beside the fire pit. He was extremely sleepy now.

"I know the engine," he mumbled. "I dreamed of it. They can't find...Have to...have to stop them."

As Curtis fell asleep, the woman leaned closer and caressed his face.

"You are a Cube traveler, stranger. And you are far away from home." She touched one finger to his lips. "You seek the Engine too. I will show you where it is."

She picked up her staff and stood next to the fire. In the dirt, she began to draw something. Curtis rolled to his side and talked in his sleep. He whispered her name,

RAW FEED STORIES

Annie, over and over again.

When he woke up, the fire was still burning brightly but the woman was gone. He rose to a sitting position and watched the flames flicker. He felt great. The tiredness had left his body quickly. *But where did it come from?* He had never felt that worn out during the whole trip. But it felt good to sleep, to remember what sleep was. And to dream. He remembered he was dreaming of Annie.

As Curtis stood up he noticed the scribbles in the dirt floor of the cave. He walked around them, trying to figure out the meaning of the circles until he realized what he was looking at.

It was a star chart. A large star chart. He had never seen one like this in the ship's archives. It was of two galaxies, one on either side of the map with a large empty expanse between them. He recognized the first galaxy from one of the ship's data disc. He had not visited it yet. It was quite a ways away. But the second galaxy was new to him. It was a small, spiral galaxy with three planetary bodies revolving around a small sun. One of the planets was marked with the triangle symbol. Curtis stared at it. *The Engine. That has to be where it is.*

He read the numbers along the edge of the chart. According to the figures, the expanse between the two galaxies was immense, larger than anything he had ever encountered. *How long would it take to cross that?* He wondered. *Would the ship do it in a day?* He figured with this much traveling it would take longer. *Perhaps a week, maybe more.*

He studied *the* chart over and over again, committing it to memory. Finally, he returned back to the ship and a dog that was happy to see him.

MICHAEL WHETZEL

*****

Curtis 2 turned the tractor off and called one of the interns over. He wanted to make sure the water pipes in the secondary greenhouse were repaired. As he was going over the details of the repair, he heard the screech of tires and the honk of a horn coming from the road in front of the house.

He ran down the drive. Annie burst from the front door, a look of worry on her face. A delivery truck was idling on the side of the main road and the driver was looking down at something on the asphalt.

Curtis ran up next to the driver. A groan escaped his lips and he fell to his knees.

"I tried to stop," the driver pleaded. "I couldn't stop in time. I'm so sorry."

Annie ran up behind Curtis and placed a hand to her mouth.

Earlier, Ammo had been at the rear door, begging to go outside. In the past year, the dog began to suffer from arthritis and one of the things that seemed to comfort him was sitting by the front porch steps in the sun. Annie thought nothing of it when she saw he wanted to go outside, and patted him on the head as she opened the door.

"Go rest, honey," she said. She watched him carefully (and painfully) hop down the three steps to the ground and then she turned back to the cherry pies she was making for the Women's Church Council meeting that night.

But now Ammo was lying in the middle of the road. And as Curtis 2 watched, his dog breathed one last breath and the light faded from his eyes. Ammo 2 was gone.

"No, buddy. No." Curtis 2 picked the dog up gently and carried him back to the front porch. The truck driver was apologizing profusely to one of the farm employees. Annie followed her husband, weeping softly.

Curtis 3 turned to his Ammo and studied the dog. He could feel Curtis 2's heavy emotions, and quickly 3 wiped his eyes with the back of his hand. They were in Burundi, one of the poorest places on Earth. They had arrived two weeks ago by small plane. Bouncing along the African horizon he held Ammo in his lap and watched the brush lands pass underneath the plane's shadow. They were here to help the coalition build a church, and oversee the food supplies due to come in tomorrow.

Curtis 3 knelt beside Ammo. The dog was whining softly under his breath, and his eyes watered profusely. As Curtis watched, a small trickle of blood dripped from Ammo's mouth. Curtis moved closer to the dog and held him in his arms.

"It's okay," Curtis 3 said. Ammo moved his tail weakly. *Are you seeing this?* He sent.

Curtis turned from the view screen and looked at his dog. Ammo sat next to the captain's seat. His head was lowered and Curtis saw bits of red drool slowly fall to the floor. He reached over and touched the dog on the head softly. *I know,* he sent back.

Are they all going to die?

I don't know. He turned back to the screen. It held nothing but blackness. He was on the edge of the first galaxy the Superion had drawn on the cave floor and now faced the large void that was marked on the star map.

Black was all he could see. There were no stars, no suns, and no asteroids floating around. Nothing. Empty, black space.

Dark matter. Pure, thick dark matter. He felt Ammo lick his fingers with a very dry tongue and he reached out and touched the dog's wet nose.

"It's almost finished, Ammo." He pushed the red button on the small control panel and the ship accelerated forward, heading towards the coordinates that Curtis had entered earlier.

Curtis left the seat and lifted Ammo from the floor. He carried the dog to the cot and lay down next to him. He gently stroked Ammo's back. Ammo thumped his tail and licked his lips. More red drool dripped onto the cot.

"I'm sorry, boy. I know it hurts. You lay here and rest. You can get better, I know it. You'll be okay." Ammo whined and then closed his eyes, asleep. Curtis kissed the dog on his nose and held him close.

*****

Curtis 2 and Annie buried Ammo on the side of Grayson Ridge, very close to where the cube had been found on that fateful day a long time ago. Curtis cried heavily as he laid the wrapped body of the dead animal in the grave and began covering it with dirt. Annie wept softly into her tissue, watching her husband work to bury the closest thing to a child they had ever known. Curtis 2 finished, and walking hand in hand, they hiked back to the truck and drove home.

Curtis 3 observed all of this while holding his Ammo in his arms. They were seated next to a small campfire on the outskirts of the village. Ammo was sick, had stopped eating, and did not leave the confines of their tent.

Ammo 3 held on for another ten days, his condition worsening every day, until the morning Curtis 3 woke to find he had finally passed away. The aid workers helped Curtis 3 dig the small grave and the neighboring children led a funeral procession through the dirt walkways of the village.

In a small unknown place in one of the poorest regions of the world, where dreams falter and hope wages a bitter war with death, Curtis 3 buried his best friend.

And through it all, the ship careened through blackness. Curtis sat at the screen watching it pass by. Ammo was walking around the ship, limping heavily, his tail drooping. He paced a route between the cot and the control panel. Curtis watched him limp slowly back and forth, wishing he could do something and knowing he was a slave to fate now. He knew it was only a matter of time before the beagle finally came to his end. He was glad he could be here for him, his best friend, his hunting buddy, his brother.

I wish Annie was here, he thought to himself. He focused on Curtis 2 but saw that the other man was working out in the fields with the hired hands. No Annie in sight. *She would know what to say to him. How to comfort him.*

Curtis waded through the seconds, until they became minutes, and the minutes became hours. Ammo stopped pacing and finally lay still on the smooth, metal floor of the ship. Hours ticked by, pushing day after day behind them, and the ship carried on through blackness. Curtis entrenched himself into the passing time. He ignored the windows into 2 and 3, instead focusing on the steady in and out of his dog's breathing.

A week passed. Then another. Man and beast, riding a ship of destiny, careening through the Great Void and waiting patiently for the veil of death to arrive.

And then with one final push, a gasping rattle of air

and life exhaled from the original Ammo, and the dog finally stopped breathing.

Eighty-two days after Curtis 2 found his dog dying in the middle of State Road 312, Curtis looked across the rocket ship's interior and saw the unmoving body of the most innocent thing he had ever known.

He went to the control panel and stopped the ship. It floated in the unending dark matter.

Curtis hit a switch and the side door of the ship opened onto the void. He picked up Ammo and carried him to the door. He stared down at the dog's closed eyes, ran his fingers over the soft furry snout one final time, and gently pushed Ammo out the door.

The dog floated serenely into the open darkness. Inertia carried him on and on and Curtis watched as Ammo grew smaller and smaller, until finally he was swallowed up by the unrelenting black nothing.

Curtis stepped into the doorway; his fingers the only thing holding him from falling into the abyss.

It would be so easy. To just let go. To float freely. No pressure, no pain. He stared into space, black nothingness reflected in his eyes. He now understood that if he left the ship for good, he would probably die. His body had sacrificed so much. No food. No water. No sleep. The only thing that kept him functioning was the cube. The cube that was now a ship. The cube that was now his life's blood.

Curtis screamed. He screamed with all his might, all his love, all his pain, all of his sacrifice that had filled him, fueled him, on this long journey. He let it all go into the deep dark Void.

Curtis screamed and Curtis 3 awoke screaming on a plane bound for Sierra Leone. He smashed himself against the small seats, trying to escape the horrible nightmare he was having. An attendant hurried down the aisle and several passengers tried to restrain and calm the crazy man.

Curtis screamed and Curtis 2 flipped the dinner table over in the farmhouse in Virginia. Annie dodged back against the wall, ducking the flying peas and barbecued chicken wings. She watched as Curtis 2 fell to the floor, sobbing and shaking.

She ran to him and gathered him in her arms, listening to him chant over and over again into her shoulder "Not again. Not again. Why do I have to lose him again?"

What is happening to him? She thought to herself. *Is he losing his mind?* She had been noticing things about her husband for years now. His long silences, his furrowed brow. Sometimes it seemed like he was somewhere else entirely and she worried so much for him.

"What is it, Curtis? Tell me, sweetheart. What is happening to you?" She rocked him on the kitchen floor, back and forth, back and forth. Slowly and softly, hoping he felt her love for him radiating from her body.

In the Void, Curtis stood at the door. He stopped screaming, tears flowing heavily down his cheeks.

And he began rocking. He opened the window wide into 2's mind and felt Annie holding him, whispering into his ear, and rubbing his back.

Curtis backed slowly into the doorway and closed the hatch tight.

He stumbled back to the captain's seat and sat there. He listened to Annie's voice, felt the tingle of her hair on his face. He could smell her perfume if he concentrated hard enough.

On the plane, Curtis 3 also opened the window into 2 and quieted under the grace of Annie's love. The passengers gave him a wide berth and the stewardess kept a wary eye on the man in seat 17. But Curtis 3 soon fell back asleep, and dreamed of nothing but darkness.

After some time, Curtis flipped the lever and the ship took off, swallowing light years and light years of empty space. He closed his eyes, and fell into a stage of semi-consciousness.

The ship moved forward. Ever forward.

Part 3

Curtis 3 heaved the sandbag up onto the growing barricade. He had been working since yesterday to build the retaining wall, pushing the others in his group well past their limits. There was a lot on the line.

Curtis 3 was in Haiti, in a small coastal town called Petit-Goave. He had spent the past month helping build a large school to replace the one that had been destroyed by fire. But with the approaching calamity known as Hurricane Laura scheduled to hit the coast any day now, the workers had stopped building the school and started sandbagging the road.

Willie, another volunteer with the Care Coalition, stepped in next to Curtis and helped him throw several full bags up on top of the wall. Laura was only a few hours away, and the group was working desperately to complete their work.

"What do you think, Curtis?" Willie asked. Sweat glistened on his brow as he shoveled sand into one of the burlap bags.

"I think if we get what they are forecasting, it's going to be a long night." Curtis stopped and chugged water from a large bottle. He passed it to Willie, who in turn took a long drink.

"Are you taking shelter in the rec center with the rest of us?" Willie glanced out at the still water in the bay. It was unbelievably calm, quite the opposite of the impending storm.

"No," Curtis answered. "I'll be at the school. I want to make sure the storm doesn't carry all our hard work away." He noticed the questioning look on Willie's face and waved it away. "Don't worry. I'll be okay. We built those walls a lot stronger than they look. We are too close to being finished to let the storm destroy it. I'm just making sure everything gets tied down and secured. If it gets too hairy, I'll join you at the rec center." Willie smiled at this and the men continued filling sandbags.

The hurricane hit landfall three hours later. The sky grew dark and heavy rain began to pelt the workers. The wind began to pick up and sandbagging became impossible to do. Curtis 3 called the men together and gave them final instructions. Then he told them to get to shelter. Small bits of hail started to fall and the men ran inland to get away from the storm.

Curtis 3 headed for the school. He ran up the walk, cursing the stinging welts of the falling hail under his breath. He reached the front entrance of the school and dove into the door.

It was a going to be a pretty large school, housing grades K through 10. The main building was almost finished, but the adjacent wings were only skeletons of what they would eventually be. *At least there's a roof on this part,* he thought to himself.

He double checked the large tarps covering the equipment they were using, and then went into what would eventually become the front office. This part of the building was finished and he settled in behind a small table and lit the oil lamp sitting on top of it.

Outside the wind howled, pulsing and pushing against the building. The hail turned to rain, and water began filling the streets and walks of Petit-Goave. In an hour, four inches had already fallen. By midnight it would close on ten inches.

Curtis 3 listened to the wind pound the side of the school. Turrets of water cascaded over the unfinished eaves of the annexes and the walk outside became flooded in minutes. In the recreation center at the top of the hill, families huddled close together inside the warm gymnasium as the storm attacked the city. Children clung to their mothers listening to the monster that attacked the mainland. Men, many of them aid workers, hung around in groups talking about the cleanup that would follow and the past storms they had experienced. Curtis 3 sat at the desk and thought about the long journey he had undertaken so long ago. He thought about reaching out to 1 or 2, but decided against it. 2 was probably just settling down for the night with Annie and he did not want to intrude. As for the original, they hardly had contact with him anymore. He would check in maybe every few months with 3, but even then it was just a small flicker. Just as quick, Curtis would disappear back to the ship. He had a lot more contact with 2 apparently. Curtis 3 couldn't blame him. He could feel how much the original missed Annie.

Twenty years had passed since the death of the Ammos. Twenty years and the ship still sailed the blackness of the Void. And Curtis was sailing along with it. Alone.

He should have cracked by now. How can one man experience so much emptiness for so long?

Curtis 3 grabbed one of the woolen blankets from under the desk and wrapped himself in it. He walked to the front door and opened it. The storm raged against the front entrance. In seconds, he was drenched and he threw the wet blanket to the ground.

It's unbelievable, Curtis 2 interjected in 3's head.

"It's fascinating," 3 answered. A great gust of wind pushed him back a few feet into the school and Curtis 3 laughed. He glanced down towards the sandbags. Already water was filling the areas on either side of the makeshift wall. It would only be a matter of time before the wall was completely submerged.

"I thought you would be asleep already," 3 said.

Wanted to make sure you were okay. The storm looks vicious on the television.

"Have you talked to him lately?"

Two days ago. I tried to convince him to turn the damn thing around. I think he should give it up. I'm really worried about him. I check in and he is just staring at the screen, watching the blackness. I feel him a lot in the back fringes of everything. He watches us. Listens for Annie. Sometimes....well, never mind.

"It's okay. I know." *Sometimes he was there at night, watching. I know.* Curtis 3 shivered against the wind and rain. He studied the road across from the manmade embankment. The water was already a good four feet deep there and steadily rising. He looked over the sandbags, hoping they would hold for just a bit longer. There were many outside in the storm still trying to fortify shelters and get to safer ground.

Go back! The thought was loud and violent in his head. *Go back! Turn back to the road!*

"What is it?" Curtis looked down into the flooded roadway. The storm had darkened what was usually a bright evening and he had trouble making out much of anything in the rising water.

There! Next to the guardhouse!

Curtis studied the small building carefully. The water was rushing against one side of it, pushing loose debris and broken branches against the wall. He watched for quite a bit. His breath finally caught in his throat. He saw what 2 was talking about.

There was a little girl hanging onto the debris covered

side of the guardhouse. She could not be any older than ten or eleven. She was clinging to one of the barred windows for dear life as the water pushed hard against the back of her neck and shoulders. He watched as she reached down with one hand and pulled something from the flood water. It was a boy, younger than the girl, sputtering and flailing his arms every which way. The girl was trying to pull the boy up to the bars, but was having trouble as the powerful waters kept pulling him back down.

Curtis 3 was off like a shot. He burst through the door of the school and sprinted, screaming for help the whole way down the small ridge to the roadway.

The freezing water shocked his system as he jumped into it feet first. He came up and pushed himself against the current towards the sandbag wall. The water was hitting five feet now, still below his head and shoulders, but not by much.

Curtis 3 grabbed the sandbags and hauled himself over the top of them to the other side. The water was fiercer now that he was in the main current. He looked over and saw the kids still clinging desperately to the window.

"I'm coming!" he yelled. The little girl heard him and looked in his direction.

The pull of the water was great here, but he fought against it. He reached the kids in no time and heaved the boy from the water. The youngster grabbed Curtis 3 around the neck and buried his head into his chest. Curtis 3 reached down and pulled the girl higher onto the window sill.

"Is this your brother?" The water was rising fast now and he could barely see the girl nod her head up and down. "You stay here! I'm going to take your brother over to the sandbags and then I'm coming back here to get you." The suction was becoming greater and he knew he would not be able to carry both of the kids across.

Curtis 3 made sure that the girl was holding on tight with both hands. She was safe for now but he would have to be quick and get back as soon as possible. He wrapped his arms around the boy and pushed his way back towards high ground. As he reached the sandbags, he could see lights bobbing through the trees.

Willie and two other aid workers stopped on the edge of the rushing water.

"Willie!" He yelled and the young man caught sight of him. Willie jumped into the water and Curtis 3 handed the boy to him over the sandbag wall. "There's a little girl over there. I'm going to get her. Be ready!" Willie nodded, rain water bouncing off his head and face.

You've got to hurry, Curtis 2 sent to him. *This water is coming up fast.*

Annie came out of the bathroom dressed in her nightgown. She usually was already in bed by now but was too excited to sleep. Tomorrow they were meeting with the adoption agency and it sounded like they had some really good news for the couple. They had been trying to adopt a child for the past fifteen years, but were always coming up short in the adoption process. Now with Curtis approaching what he called his "twilight" years, she knew this would probably be their last chance.

She walked into the bedroom to find Curtis standing outside on the balcony. He was staring at the horizon, almost pensive in the way he stood. She walked out and touched his shoulder, but pulled it back quickly. His muscles were tense and shaking. She came around and looked at his face. A thick sheen of sweat glistened across his brow and she saw his hands were locked in a vise-like grip around the balcony railing.

"Hurry. You have to hurry. There's no time," Curtis 2 was saying over and over again.

Annie touched his cheek and felt the full flush of fever against her hands.

"Curtis?" she asked. "Curtis? Are you okay?"

There's no time. You have to hurry.

The mantra echoed in Curtis 3's head over and over again. He pushed away from the wall and through the massive current of water. A large tree branch came out of nowhere and slammed into his shoulder. He cursed loudly and turned his body to let it pass, ignoring the pain throbbing in that area now. He had to use every bit of his energy now, not just his legs to get traction in the water.

Curtis 3 made it to the wall of the guardhouse. The rising flood and howling wind pushed him hard against the concrete wall. He leaned over towards the window. The girl was gone.

"No!" he yelled into the hurricane.

Curtis dropped his eyes from the view screen and blinked several times. Small bits of color flashed across his vision. *How long have I been staring at the screen?* He couldn't remember. He felt like he had stared into the darkness for ages, maybe even ever since he was born.

But now something was happening. His body shivered in the captain's seat. He was freezing and finding it hard to breathe all of a sudden. Curtis closed his eyes and dove into the window that was 3's.

Curtis 3 spun around in the water, trying to locate the girl. He began to make his way to the far corner of the guardhouse. But he was getting weak, his muscles were being pushed to their upper limits, and he kept slipping under the water.

Hang on. Concentrate. 3 pulled himself out of the water. He could feel 2 still watching, but this thought did not come from him. It came from Curtis. It came from 1.

"Long time, buddy," Curtis 3 gasped into the onrushing water.

Too long. You need to check the other side of the house. She could have slipped around the corner.

Getting tired, boss, Curtis 3 sent back.

"I'm going to try something. Just keep moving," Curtis said, his voice ringing off the walls of the empty ship. He kneeled onto the cold floor and began to concentrate. He pictured a warm ball of energy forming in his body and he sent it across the connection to his clone.

"Help me," he moaned as the ship continued its course.

Curtis 2 leaned forward against the balcony railing. He gritted his teeth. A large vein stood out from his forehead and he began to shake uncontrollably. Annie ran inside to call 911.

"Hold on. Hold on. It's coming. It's coming," 2 muttered as he sent a twin sphere of energy through his channel.

Curtis 3's body slammed against the wall again. The water rushed over his face and arms and he was pulled violently down. He tried to fight but fatigue had finally caught up to him. He felt himself begin to give in to the storm.

Suddenly, his eyes flew open in the dark flood waters and he felt strength surging into his whole body. What an amazing feeling! His heartbeat thrummed in his chest and he pushed himself straight up from the deluge of flood water.

Curtis 3 shot out of the water and bounced off the side of the guard house. He felt renewed. Quickly he paddled to the corner and looked down the opposite wall. The girl was there, holding on to a roof support, barely keeping her head above the torrent of water.

"I see you!" Curtis 3 yelled. He let the flood carry him down to her position and he grabbed the roof support next to the frail girl. He placed one arm around her and grabbed her small body tight.

Something huge toppled over into the roaring river behind them, a victim of the escalating winds. Curtis 3 turned to the frightened girl. "When I say let go, we are going to let go and let the river carry us clear of the house, okay? You let go of the roof, but do not let go of me."

The girl nodded and Curtis 3 forced a smile at her. He counted loudly to three and they let go of the roof strut.

The water grabbed them quickly and carried them past the guardhouse. Curtis 3 caught his footing, spraining an ankle in the process, and began pushing his way back across to the sandbag wall. He could barely make out Willie on the other side with the others, watching and waiting with baited breath.

You're going to make it. Stay calm. You'll make it now. Curtis 3 held the girl tightly and fought his way to help. Willie was smiling at him as they came within yards of the wall. The younger man started forward to take the girl when something caught his eye upstream. Willie stopped moving and opened his mouth to shout a warning.

"Look out!"

Curtis 3 turned, just in time to see the large hulk of the transit bus before it slammed into him and the girl, and buried them under the water. Willie yelled and tried to scramble across the sandbags.

But it was too late.

Curtis 2 fell to the hard balcony floor as the paramedics rushed from the bedroom. He began to convulse wildly. Annie screamed his name over and over from the lit doorway. Curtis 2 rocked his head back across the hard wooden surface with small thuds. The paramedics restrained him as they shot a sedative into his shoulder. Curtis 2 fell quiet and lay still.

Curtis shivered on the metal floor of the ship. Sweat dripped from every pore in his body. He coughed violently and felt something drip from his nose. He wiped it away with a finger, staring as it came away tinted dark red. Blood.

He tried to rise to his feet but huge bouts of coughing racked his body and he tripped and fell. Still he coughed and wetness erupted from his mouth and splashed to the floor. Curtis blinked at the puddle of liquid. It was dirty river water.

Inside his head, one of the windows of shared consciousness was closed.

Forever.

*****

Annie watched the water boiling on the stove and thought about the past four weeks. It had been one of the darkest times in her life. Her marriage to Curtis was wonderful, flooded with happiness and well-being. The only bad times she could think of were Ammo's death and the day she found out she could not have kids. That was, until now.

She looked through the kitchen doorway into the living room. It used to be the living room. Now it was a hospice room, and her husband lay on the hospital bed, staring at the ceiling. He did not move, could not move from what the doctors had told her.

At first the doctors thought Curtis had been the victim of a violent seizure. This was partly true, but the cause of the seizure remained a mystery. Curtis' body had gone into a form of shock. Annie had paced the waiting room, counting the minutes as they passed and the doctors tried to stabilize her husband. Finally, a young man dressed in scrubs came and told her that her husband's condition had finally calmed down.

"But there is a complication, Mrs. Yankey," the young doctor had said in the empty waiting room. "It seems your husband has suffered some damage to his brain as a result of the seizure."

Annie stared at the doctor as he continued. "We don't know the extent of the damage until we do some further tests."

"What happened to him?" she cried.

"We're still not sure. He's suffered some sort of traumatic episode. We found some....odd things also." The doctor glanced down at his clipboard, one eyebrow raised in thought.

"What do you mean?" Annie asked softly. *Odd things. I can tell you about all kinds of odd things regarding my husband, doc. Secret bank accounts, moodiness, daydreaming, talking to himself, dropping dishes and waking sporadically in the middle of the night. You have no idea about odd things.*

"We found something puzzling. His lungs and stomach contained excessive amounts of water. This seems like an explanation of what might have caused the seizures. But.....it wasn't raining and he wasn't near any water. We...We can't explain it. We hoped you might know something." He looked at her, waiting for the plausible explanation for it all.

"Water? He took a shower a couple of hours before it happened. That's all." She looked at the floor, confused.

"That wouldn't be enough to do any harm," the doctor replied. "We're going to run some tests. Try to gauge how much brain damage occurred. We'll let you know as soon as we know. Right now he is stable, but unresponsive."

And unresponsive he would remain. The resulting shock had robbed Curtis of his motor skills and left him in an apparent catatonic state. After two weeks of sitting around the hospital, waiting for a change in his overall state, Annie elected to bring her husband home.

They changed the living room into a small hospice and Annie hired a fulltime nurse to help take care of her husband's needs. She maintained supervision over the farm and waited patiently for her husband to wake up.

The pot finished boiling and Annie added the tea bags, letting them steep for a short time. The sun was dropping quickly in the sky and she watched through the window as the last of the farm's employees left for home. The nurse that came daily to help with Curtis had left already too.

Annie poured the tea into a small mug and walked into the living room. She looked down into her husband's eyes, wishing they would register her appearance but not reading any kind of recognition in them. The doctors had said that he probably could see and hear her, and so she spent most of her free time talking to him or watching the television with him before turning in for the night. She now slept on the couch, wanting to be near Curtis, not only because she missed him but in case something changed.

Like he dies, she thought to herself. She quickly pushed the thought away. The doctors had no idea how long

RAW FEED STORIES

Curtis would hold on for. He was eating his food through an I.V. and growing weaker with each passing week.

"Hey, sweetie," Annie said quietly to her husband. "Do you want to watch the news together?" She pushed the button that raised the bed to a sitting position and moved Curtis so that he was able to see the T.V.

Annie switched the news on and sat down to enjoy her tea. The weatherman was just finishing up with this week's forecast. Cold fronts were beginning to move in and Annie made a mental note to check over the upcoming winter preparations for the greenhouses. She sipped her tea, enjoying the comforting warmth.

"Looks like cold weather is coming soon, Curtis," she said to her husband. "I'm glad you found those other two year-round markets to sell at before….." Annie stopped herself and let her voice trail off. She sniffed and turned her attention back to the news.

They were talking about the hurricane that had hit Haiti a few months before. The island was still reeling from the effects of the terrible storm. Annie had donated several hundred dollars to help with the relief efforts. The storm had claimed over forty lives and the devastation in many of the small towns was tremendous.

She watched as the reporter went over a story regarding an aid worker who died while trying to save a little girl. Apparently, the volunteer managed to save the girl's younger brother from the flood but perished when he was trying to save the girl herself. The town was placing a small gold plaque in honor of the volunteer's heroics. The television cut to a shot of the plaque placed in the rebuilt sidewalk in front of a newly built school. The etched writing was too small to read but the large square held a picture of the volunteer, a man surrounded by several smiling Haitian children.

Annie dropped her mug of tea to the floor. She screamed loudly and turned to her husband lying in the hospital bed.

The T.V. closed on the picture of Curtis 3 and then cut to a report regarding an armed robbery in Texas.

Annie tried to get up from her chair but her legs were too weak and her head was overcome with a hazy cloud of confusion. *Not possible. I'm seeing things. It's not possible.*

She made her way to the computer in her office and accessed the internet. Quickly, she found the story regarding the dead volunteer. The computer screen held an enlarged version of the picture she had seen on the television. The man's name was Curtis Yarborough. He was a lifetime volunteer for the Care Coalition. He was the exact double of her sick husband who lay in the living room.

"It can't be," Annie muttered to herself. But it was. The same hair, the same bright smile, even the way the man was folding his arms across his chest. Everything was a match to Curtis.

This man drowned trying to save a little girl. She checked the date of the man's death. *He drowned the same day my husband had his seizure.*

And then something else came back to her. She remembered what the young doctor was telling her in the emergency room. *His lungs and stomach contained excessive amounts of water.* But he wasn't near any water.

"But this man was," she said out loud in the quiet house. "This man died from water."

This Curtis drowned. And my Curtis almost drowned.

"What is going on?" she whispered as tears began to fall from her eyes. She turned, staring at the corner of the hospital bed that was visible from the office.

*****

Curtis was suffering.

He sat in the captain's chair and stared at the unchanging darkness on the ship's screen. But he was not seeing the screen. Instead, he was in Curtis 2's consciousness, trying to catch a glimpse of Annie. She had just looked down at Curtis 2, making Curtis' own heart jump, but now had disappeared.

Curtis poked around 2's mind a bit, trying to find some semblance of the clone's thoughts. They were scattered and incoherent. Ever since 3's death, Curtis had tried to help find Curtis 2 and bring him back to life. But his efforts always ended in vain. He would catch small parts of random thoughts, everything from bits of songs to old memories, but nothing was Curtis 2. The man's mind had simply splintered. And Curtis began to spend more and more time within 2's window of reality.

It was better staring at the living room of the farmhouse or the television, then returning to the black void that awaited him on the ship. Curtis would stare out of 2's motionless eyes, watching the days unfold in the house. He would see Annie working in her office, or the nurse changing the bedspreads. Sometimes he could feel Curtis 2 being wheeled out onto the front porch in a wheelchair. Those were the best times because Curtis could see the farm stretch out before him. He would see the sun setting over the tall peaks of the Blue Ridge Mountains, and Curtis would be racked with homesickness.

But he never turned the ship around. He kept the same

course, straight on into the Void.

At night, he would come back to the small control room and watch the dark unfurl more and more before the rocket ship. He was afraid to be in Curtis 2's head while the man slept. Curtis 2 dreamed of Curtis 3's death over and over again. And Curtis had no intention of reliving that moment.

Curtis felt the effects of 3's death all the time. His body had grown extremely weak ever since that night, and he was accustomed to furious bouts of coughing, falling to the floor and grasping his sides from pain. He felt feverish constantly and sweat clung to his clothes and body.

But when he was inside 2, when he could feel Annie nearby, all the pain and discomfort went away. He only focused on her, her touch, her voice, every second he tried to soak up. This made the limitations of 2's condition infuriating.

Curtis watched as Annie passed before his sight. She was holding some papers and her eyes were full of tears. He held his breath as she knelt over Curtis 2.

"I don't understand, Curtis," Annie said gently. "I don't know what it means. I'm going to go to the bank tomorrow. I'm going to check the accounts again." He felt her touch his face gently. "I wish you could tell me what it means."

Curtis tried fervently to move Curtis 2's head. He pushed with all his mental power, trying to force the catatonic man to say something, do anything. But nothing happened and Annie left his line of sight.

Curtis came back to the ship and flopped onto the cot. He felt something sticky on the side of his head and touched his ear nervously. There was blood inside his ear canal. He wiped the blood on his chest. A wave of nausea washed across his body, followed by a jagged coughing fit. He fell from the cot, trying to stop the violent hacking. As the last cough escaped his lips, Curtis rolled under the cot to the cool, dark corner of the wall.

I'm in a bad way. I don't think I'm going to make it.

He passed out just as a light began to blink on the ship's control panel.

*****

The next day, Annie went to the bank. She talked with one of the account managers, and after explaining her husband's condition for the umpteenth time, finally got the information she was looking for.

Now she was sitting in her car holding a detailed list of account withdrawals. It was from the mystery account Curtis had set up so long ago. The listing told the date and location of each withdrawal. She read the paper in astonishment.

Money had been taken from the account in locations all across the world. In the beginning, the money was accessed right here in the United States, but for the past fifteen years it was withdrawn all over the globe. Zimbabwe, France, Central America, Australia, and Africa were all listed on the paper. The last entry was four months ago in Haiti. Annie's hands begun to shake.

Curtis was sending money to someone who looked exactly like him. Who was the man at the other end of this account? She had been putting money into the account for the past four months, on the first of each month, like clockwork. But the money had stayed there ever since the stranger's death.

She started the car and headed for home. Her mind was racing a million miles an hour but no matter how she looked at everything, she could not make sense out of any of it.

Annie pulled into the driveway and went into the house. The nurse was changing the linens on the bed and had moved Curtis to his wheelchair. Her husband stared at the wall, not moving. She bent down and kissed his forehead.

The nurse finished with the bed and Annie dismissed him for the rest of the day. She threw the papers on the desk in the office and went out to the bed where Curtis now lay. She stared down at her husband, smoothing the sheets back and fixing the collar on his night shirt.

"Did you have a nice day, sweetheart?" she asked. She took his hand and squeezed, hoping he would squeeze it back. There was no response.

"I had a bad dream, Annie," Curtis responded from underneath the cot. He had heard her voice in his head and woke up, focusing on the fuzzy window in Curtis 2's mind. "I dreamt I was lost in the dark, and I couldn't find my way out. And you were gone. I couldn't find you. I couldn't see you anymore. I called for you, but you couldn't hear me."

"Look at your hair. We need to comb it. When was the last time we combed this mess?" Annie grabbed a small black comb from the nightstand and began gently pulling the tangles of hair apart. "I think we need to get you a haircut, honey."

Curtis closed his eyes again and breathed deeply against the cold ship floor. He could feel the teeth of the comb slowly working its way through his hair. He pushed his way further into Curtis 2's conscious, soaking up as much of Annie as he could.

He reached up and felt the hair on his head, wondering

if he did need a trim. But then remembered his hair had not grown any since he had left in the ship.

Annie finished combing her husband's hair. She placed both hands on either side of his face and gave him a small kiss on the nose.

Curtis pushed more into 2's mind. He wanted, needed, desperately to be with Annie now.

"Annie!" He yelled into the empty ship. He was still lying under the cot, oblivious to the red light blinking on the control panel.

Annie bent over her husband's face and stroked his forehead. "I went to the bank, Curtis. I saw the withdrawals from the account." She wiped a tear from one eye and then continued. "Who is that man who died in Haiti? Why does he look like you, sweetheart? How are you two connected?" She stroked his face softly, wishing for a reply.

Curtis rolled from under the cot and onto his knees. He hugged himself tightly and willed all his energy through the connection he shared with the clone. He could feel heat pulsing through his body and across his skin.

"Annie."

"I wish you could tell me what is happening." Annie started to cry uncontrollably and tears fell onto Curtis 2's chest. "I miss you so much. I don't care what it is you were doing. I just want to understand what happened to you" She smothered her face in her husband's chest and sobbed. "I miss you so much."

Back on the ship, Curtis began shaking. His eyes rolled into the back of his head and drool ran from his mouth. But still he focused everything into the connection and pushed the energy through just as he did for Curtis 3 during the hurricane.

Annie smoothed her face against Curtis 2's chest. "I'm so alone, Curtis. Please come back to me, sweetheart."

"Annie." It was barely a whisper but she heard it. Annie picked her head up quickly and looked down at Curtis. His eyes had rolled back into his head, showing the pinkish discoloration of the whites. He was shaking, and his mouth kept opening and closing.

"Curtis!" Annie screamed. She turned to grab her cell phone but felt a hand wrap around her wrist. Annie gasped and looked back into Curtis' eyes. They were clear and normal and looking right at her. "Curtis!" She grabbed his face with her hands, laughing and crying all at the same time.

"I'm sorry," Curtis said from the ship's floor. He tried to reach up and touch Annie's face but the connection wasn't strong enough. "I'm sorry for everything."

"No! It's okay! Please don't say that," Annie cried. She kissed him on the forehead and smiled warmly at him. Curtis began to shudder. "What's wrong? What's happening? Let me call the ambulance, please."

"No. Not much time." Curtis slowly climbed up into the captain's chair and swiveled around to the front of the ship. He barely saw the small flashing light in the fuzzy vision of Curtis 2's sight. "I don't have much time."

"Don't say that, Curtis. You stay here with me." Annie hugged his shivering body close to her and kissed his flushed cheeks. "You are going to be okay. You have to stay here with me. Please."

"It's so cold here. So dark." Curtis hugged his legs up close to his chest. Blood began to flow from his nose and ears. Fever racked his body and bile rose in his throat as he tried to talk. But he was seeing Annie, could feel her touch now. All the pain was worth it.

RAW FEED STORIES

"I should have never left you," Curtis 2 moaned in the warm living room. "I should have never gone on the ship.'

Annie's face tightened. "What are you talking about, Curtis? What are you saying about a ship?"

Curtis began to lose his focus. The small flashes from the light were beginning to intrude on the mental connection. He glanced down at the panel. The red light was blinking quickly now. It was the alarm. It flashed when the ship was approaching its set coordinates.

"I can't hold on anymore, Annie." Curtis leaned forward looking into the darkness on the viewing screen. He was tired; his body having burned through the last of its energy reserves talking through the connection. He searched the screen with eyes that were barely open.

"Curtis!" Annie shook her husband as his eyes began to close. "Curtis!"

"I love you." It was barely a whisper but she heard it exhale from Curtis 2's lips. And then there was nothing.

Annie hugged her dead husband's body close to her.

Curtis leaned forward in the chair and squinted at the screen. He wiped the blood from his nose with the sleeve of his shirt. His eyes watered and he blinked the moisture quickly away. His vision clearing, he studied the bright star glowing white in the middle of the screen.

It's the small galaxy. The one on the end of the Superion's star chart.

Curtis smiled weakly. "I made it," he said to no one. Then he promptly vomited on the floor of the rocket.

*****

The planet the Superion marked with the "life" triangle was solid white from the dense clouds covering its surface.

Curtis stopped the ship right outside the planet's orbit. Behind the white planet was a bright sun and another planet to the right of the screen. A third planet, the smallest of the group, could be seen on the opposite side of the sun. It was exactly like the chart had shown.

Curtis dropped his eyes from the screen and looked at his hands. Ever since he felt Curtis 2 slip away, they had been shaking nonstop. He opened and closed all of his fingers at once, trying to push the numbing sensation from them. He had managed to stop his nose bleed, but the coughing fit that followed had pulled something loose deep inside his body. He could feel it rattling around in his chest.

There were no more windows inside his head. Only his own conscious was open to him now. His heart hurt, not knowing if he would ever see Annie again. He sniffed and fought the tears that threatened to come back and focused on the planet in front of him.

He pushed the lever on the panel and the ship dived steadily towards the white planet. Within seconds it penetrated the thick clouds and speared its way through. Breaking through the heavy fog, Curtis was met with more whiteness. He shook his head, thinking that he was still in the planet's outer atmosphere, but the readings on the panel showed that he was approaching the outer crust.

Curtis straightened the ship and relied on his instruments to guide him to the ground. He shot the rocket parallel to the planet's surface, finally recognizing the second layer of brilliant white.

The planet's surface was completely flat, and covered with thick white grass. He watched the grass flow seamlessly as the ship's draft pushed the stalks back and forth. For miles all Curtis could see was whiteness. He flew the ship a hundred feet above the ground and began looking for a place to land. The pure white color met his eyes everywhere, showing no breaks in the terrain. It was almost blinding.

He had flown on for almost an hour before something different appeared on the horizon. There was a large circle of dark red with a smaller circle of white in the center. Curtis guided the ship to the colored spot and sat down next to it. He staggered to the hatch and stumbled through the door, falling hard to the soft grass below. His head was swimming and the violent coughing returned, spattering small flecks of blood on the white grass. He waited for the fit to pass, and then pushed himself to his feet. He was moving mostly on adrenaline now.

The red color he had seen was flowers. But they were unlike any flowers he had ever seen before, even in all the galaxies he had visited. They stood taller than Curtis, their stems resembling the trunks of small trees. Every stem was topped with a huge deep crimson flower. Each flower's petals were open wide. The center of each petal held a small, orange sun. Curtis stared at the suns, his face lit by the flickering glow of the hot orbs.

He pulled his attention away from the flowers and stepped in between the tall stalks. As he made his way to the center of the large circle, the flowers tracked his movements, watching him through the burning gaze of the suns. He swallowed, his throat dry and rough and continued on into the unique forest, the hairs on his arms and neck standing on end.

The white circle he had seen from the air was a small round meadow, topped with the same white grass that covered the planet, only shorter. Seated on a large ebony rock in the center of the meadow was a man. The man was young, like Curtis, and dressed in a bright white robe that matched the planet's surface. Curtis stumbled from the circle of flowers and fell to his hands and knees. He looked up at the stranger.

"Hello," the man said kindly.

"Hello," Curtis gasped.

He watched as the man left the rock and came over to help him up. Once on his feet, Curtis leaned against the man, who lead him over to the rock and helped him take a seat. As soon as his body touched its ebony surface, Curtis felt the weakness and dizziness leave him. He took a deep breath and faced the stranger.

"Thank you," he said. "You are a man like me?"

The man smiled and shook his head. "I'm afraid not. I am only appearing this way for your benefit. My true aspect is not safe for human eyes."

"You know I am human?" Curtis asked. "You know about humans?"

"Yes, I know all about you. I know all about every being that lives across the universe." The man stepped in front of Curtis and sat down in the plush grass. "As I also know about the Cube and the ship and everything else it does for you."

Curtis stared at the stranger for a few minutes before speaking. "You made the Cube, didn't you?"

The man smiled. "Very close, but not quite right. I didn't make it. I harvested it. When it was ready, I picked it much like you would pick an orange back home. And after I picked it, I sent it off."

"What is it?"

"It is a gift. A great gift."

"From whom?" Curtis felt better than he had felt in quite some time. He could feel the rock humming against his body. It seemed to be feeding him energy. "Who is the gift from?"

The man paused and looked at Curtis. "Who do you think it is from?"

Curtis licked his lips and ran a hand through his hair. "I think it is from the Engine," he finally said.

The man nodded.

"Who are you?" Curtis asked.

"I am a guardian. My people are responsible for the growth and care of the Cube. I serve the God Motor, or as you called it, the Engine." The stranger waved one hand through the soft white grass. "It takes generations of our kind to raise one Cube. I am the most recent incarnation."

"There is only one of you?"

"Yes."

"How many cubes have been harvested?" Curtis' brow furrowed. "Have there been others like me?"

The man smiled and nodded again. "You are the third Cube traveler."

Curtis bit his lip. He looked around at the beautiful flowers and then turned back to the man.

"But why? Why send the Cube? What's it all for?" He cried in anguish, his voice carrying across the meadow. The flowers shuddered slightly at the tremor of his voice and the suns glowed brighter for a split second, all in unison.

"The Cube is a gift," the man answered. "It is designed to share everything that the Creator has made with someone special." The man spread his arms wide. "To give you everything you want."

"But why?!?"

The man stood from his seat and looked at Curtis patiently. "Because, Curtis from Earth, you are loved."

Curtis turned and stared at the ground. His shoulders sagged and he sighed. "I've lost everything. Threw it all away to come here. I thought it was for….." His voice trailed off. He looked up at the man. "I didn't get what I wanted."

The guardian nodded. He knelt down and looked Curtis in the eyes.

"When you got on the ship, way back when," the man said, "what was it you wanted then? What did you hope to find?"

Curtis spoke up loudly. "The truth. I wanted to find out the truth. About everything. About why we live and why anything is the way it is. About….I don't know….."

The man nodded again, his eyes never leaving Curtis'. "The truth. The truth is different for everyone. What is true for one living thing is different for another. What fuels us to live, to do the things we do every day of our lives, that is truth." The man's face broke into a small smile. "All the places you have visited, all the diverse beings you have talked with, they are all so different, right?" Curtis nodded.

The guardian continued. "And they all focused on different goals, dependent on what they thought was important for each of them to survive and exist comfortably. It is never about the why, but about the driving force behind the why."

"I don't understand."

"Think about all those different races, each one so unique from the other. Most unaware of the other's existence. But they have one thing in common, one shared trait that bonds the entire universe together."

Curtis blinked his eyes. "There was never any war, or hatred. Everywhere I went, I found peaceful beings. They were filled with…"

The stranger's smile grew bigger. "They have the capacity to love."

"Love." Curtis stated it clearly. The idea filled him with warmth. And then another thought popped into his head. "What about the Grem?"

The man's smile left his face. "The Grem. Yes. The Grem seek the Engine too. I'm sure they want their own answers to their own truth. But even the Grem, a strong race of warriors, even they know something of love. A mother for her child. A soldier for his comrades-in-arms. A general for his troops."

"But why create something as harmful as the Grem? They destroyed worlds seeking the Engine."

The man's face softened. "Love is at its most powerful, at its strongest, when it accepts everything. Even the ugly, and the different, and the weak, and the flawed. Even those who would destroy you."

Curtis stood up from the rock. The humming stopped immediately. "My planet, my people, we destroy each other all the time though. We are just as bad as the Grem, aren't we?"

"Your people also know a lot about loving something, don't they?" The man stood up and looked to the dense clouds overhead. He was searching for something. Without turning away, he continued talking to Curtis. "Love encompasses all. Even the bad. And always the good."

Curtis watched the man quietly. "I'm dying, aren't I? I'm going to die."

The man turned from the clouds and looked at Curtis. "Death. The bane of existence." He turned back to his cloud watching. "Pain in the behind, isn't it? But really, with all you have seen and experienced, all that you feel inside of you now, every little second in the *three* lifetimes you forged through," the man paused and grinned, "do you really think something as little as death can stop all of that?" He clasped his hands behind his back. "Death is just another experience. Another step."

"Towards what?" Curtis asked.

The guardian stopped his search of the clouds and began walking away from Curtis to the opposite edge of the clearing. "You should leave now. They are here," he called back over his shoulder.

"What am I supposed to do now?" Curtis called after him.

The guardian turned and looked at Curtis. "The Cube is a gift. It will give you whatever you want. So what do you want?"

There was only one thing in the world Curtis wanted. It flashed into his mind so fast he felt dizzy. *I want to see Annie again.*

"So what are you waiting for?" the man chuckled. "You got a long way to go and you're running out of time."

Curtis watched as the stranger disappeared into the red flowers. He turned and ran back through the way he had come, back towards the ship. As he broke through the other side of the flowers, he was met with a horrible noise. Explosions erupted on the horizon, tossing chunks of white earth into the air. Curtis watched stunned as several dark shapes dropped from the dense cloud cover. They were huge flying warships, black as night, with huge guns shooting volleys of fire. The Grem had arrived.

Curtis ran to the ship followed by the sound of the Grem attack. He strapped himself in and hit the controls. The ship began to rise from the planet's surface. Curtis leaned back against the seat. His head was throbbing again and he felt the weakness return to his body. He willed his body to fly the ship back up through the cloud cover. As the rocket ascended higher and higher, he watched the Grem warships bomb the surface of the planet. The large red circle of flowers disappeared under a ball of flame and then the ship burst through the heavy atmosphere, and he lost sight of the ground.

The surrounding space was filled with the Grem armada. Curtis slammed the accelerator forward and drove the ship through the Grem warships, dodging their powerful guns. He pushed the ship through the blockade and turned it back towards the planet.

The Grem armada covered the planet's surface, peppering it with artillery. They flew everywhere dropping bombs and firing their powerful guns, ripping the crust of the planet to bits.

Suddenly, everything froze. The Grem froze in mid-air and fireballs from the explosions paused in their eruption. Curtis watched as the planet and the area surrounding it seemed to collapse into itself, like some great black hole. A huge ball of bright light filled the view screen, blinding him. He squinted through the flashes of spots before his eyes as he screamed against the bright light.

The Grem had disappeared. The planet was completely destroyed. In its place sat the Great Engine that had appeared in Curtis's dreams. It glowed a metallic bronze in the rays of the galaxy's small sun. And then it was gone. In a burst of light, it zoomed away.

A coughing fit racked Curtis' body. He waited for it to pass and then reached into his pocket and pulled out the second thing he had brought from home. It was the diagram of the Engine he had drawn from his dream. That time seemed so long ago. A lifetime away. He stared at the thin scribbles of pencil and then returned it to his pocket. He turned the ship back towards the black, empty void.

Curtis punched in new coordinates and felt the engines begin to accelerate into the thick dark matter.

He hoped he had enough time.

*****

Annie walked out onto the front porch and sat on the weathered rocking chair. She sipped the hot tea from her cup and looked out at the farm. It was late summer, her favorite time of year. The farm was quiet, all the employees having gone home already. She did not know any of them anymore, not after she had sold the farm to the university right after her retirement. She still owned the house, would never sell that. She wanted to stay here forever.

Annie was sixty-eight years old. She never remarried after Curtis 2 died, instead she threw herself into the farm, turning it into a school and then eventually selling it to the university when she was ready to quit. Now she enjoyed just watching the crops grow, and sitting on the porch. During the week, she volunteered at the town library and helped organize the Sunday luncheon after church. She tried to stay busy, but her favorite time was when she got to sit quietly on the porch and remember.

She would sit and rock in her chair, daydreaming about her and Curtis in their younger years, walking around the farm, holding hands. Ammo would run ahead of them, chasing rabbits and digging holes, until Curtis would chase him down and scold him for being messy. And then lifting the dog in his arms and forgiving him for everything the beagle had done. She would daydream about Curtis building the large greenhouses over next to the barn, see him working in the afternoon sun, and her bringing him ice cold tea and ham sandwiches. He would stand up on the ladder, smiling down at her, his skin tan from being out all day in the sun.

Everywhere she looked, she could see her dead husband. That was how it had been for the past twenty-two years. Annie was haunted by his ghost and by the mysteries surrounding his life. After he died, she stopped looking into the other man who died in Haiti. She pushed everything about the talk of the ship and her husband's weird behavior away. She wanted to forget it. She only wanted the good memories of Curtis.

She would never admit it to anyone, but she wondered if Curtis had developed a mental disability. It saddened her to think he may have been suffering from delusions and she had not helped him in anyway. She felt so much guilt at not being able to understand everything. It hurt so much inside, until she had to push all of that away also.

She took another sip from her tea and daydreamed again. She could see him standing in the front yard smiling up at her. He was telling her about the new crop of corn, and the deer he had seen on the edge of the fields. The daydream was strong and it pulled her deep into it. She smiled in the evening air, her eyes unfocused, her tea getting cold.

A loud THUMP pulled her from her fantasy and she glanced out into the yard. *Oh,* she smiled, *I'm still daydreaming.* Curtis was standing in the yard, looking at her. It was the young Curtis, the one she fell in love with so many years ago. She smiled down at him and then looked past him to the ship that had made the loud THUMP when it sat down in the large front yard. Steam billowed from its cooling engines. A door was open on one side, displaying the ship's dark interior.

"Hello, Annie." It came very quietly, carried by the breeze across the yard to the house.

Annie dropped her mug, spilling the cold tea across the porch. She slowly got up from her seat and walked to the top of the steps, holding the porch railing for support.

"It can't be," she whispered.

Curtis began to sway weakly back and forth. He stumbled a step and then regained his balance. "I finally found you."

Annie somehow made it down the front steps. She stared at the ship and then back at Curtis. "You said you never should have left on the ship." It was the only thing she could think to say. The only response she could muster.

"No. I shouldn't have." Curtis collapsed to the ground and rolled over on his back. He began coughing and spitting blood. Annie ran and knelt slowly next to him. She gently placed one hand on his chest.

"Tell me," she said. She pulled a handkerchief from her apron pocket and wiped the blood from Curtis' lips. "I'm going crazy, aren't I?"

Curtis shook his head and smiled. "No. I was the crazy one."

She stroked his forehead lightly and Curtis sighed. There was no filter this time. Her touch was for real.

"Tell me," she said again.

"I found something in the woods that day with Ammo. It was a small cube. It turned into that ship." Curtis breathed deeply. His lungs were hurting badly. Annie held him up and he continued. "There were three of us." Curtis looked at Annie. "And we all loved you. Three times the love and you still deserved so much more."

Annie laughed and then started to cry. "What did you do? You crazy, stupid guy. What did you do?" She smiled down at him.

"I should never have left you. I should have been the one to stay here." Curtis stopped as his body shook violently. They waited for it to pass and he looked back up at Annie. "I don't have long."

Annie nodded. "What do you want me to do?"

"Do you still trust me?"

"Always."

"I've seen everything. The whole universe and beyond. I've been everywhere, found others." Curtis' voice began to rise in excitement but was cut off with more coughing.

"There are others," he continued. "They're good. I went through the dark too, Annie. I was in it for so long. But on the other side I think I found God."

Annie held the dying man close and listened.

"So many beautiful things out there. Spiral galaxies, pink nebula clouds, comets so brilliant they burn your eyes. The beings are so perfect and happy." A spasm racked his body and Curtis' nose began to bleed. "So beautiful. But you are the most beautiful thing I have ever known."

Annie smiled. Curtis reached up and stroked her cheek. "I should have been the one to stay with you. I should have sent him on the ship. I'm sorry."

"It's okay. You're here now."

"Take it. Take the ship and go. It will protect you." His breathing began to turn raspy. His eyes began to flutter. "Take the ship and see everything. My gift to you."

One final time, Curtis's eyes opened wide and he stared clearly at Annie. She held his head in her hands, her tears falling against his face.

"See everything. Be loved."

Curtis took one final deep breath, closed his eyes, and was gone.

Annie held him for a long time. Then she laid his still form gently against the cool grass. She got up and walked across the yard to the ship.

Cautiously, she peeked into the doorway. She hesitated, looking back at Curtis, and then out across the farm she had cherished for so long.

Annie entered the ship.

The door closed.

SPECIAL PREVIEW
Bonus Chapter from the Black Rain Journals

The Student
Day 1

WEDNESDAY WAS THE WORST AT Valerie Clements High School. It was even worse than the typical Monday. Tina abhorred Wednesday's class curriculum, hated it with every ounce of her being, despised it more than school itself, and hissed and growled her way through it every week.

The sole reason for this hatred spawned from one thing and one thing only: Gym class. She hated gym class, hated the act of gym, hated the sweaty jocks who turned it into nothing but a big pissing contest, hated the teachers urging everyone to get up and get active. But the one thing she hated most was "dressing out."

Changing in the dressing room into the horrible yellow and green gym suits was horrid. Tina wanted to be anywhere else in the entire world, anywhere except for the girl's locker room at Valerie High.

She hated the way the other girls looked at her. They seemed to always be scrutinizing each other's bodies, trying to figure out who had the biggest boobs or shaved their bikini line. It was uncomfortable and just skeezy. And now, on this particular Wednesday, Tina was going to be an even bigger target for their focus.

She reached into her gym locker for the yellow T-shirt and threw it on the bench. She took off her jean jacket and white sweater. Underneath she wore a red bra, a bit risqué for high school but tame compared to the other thing she was displaying this morning.

"Oh my God! I can't believe you did that!" Marian Hensley squealed from behind Tina. She pointed at Tina's shoulder and squealed again.

"Damn it, would you shut the fuck up?" Tina turned on the girl. She could feel the other girls' eyes crawling all over her shoulder where the tattoo was.

Carly Seinz piped up from the back of the room. "The goody two shoes being a bad girl again?" The others around her laughed. "Got a little ink to go with that nose ring, little Tina?"

"Why don't you come over here and I'll break *your* fucking nose for you, Carly." Tina glared at the girl, whose mouth now hung open with shock.

Tina felt Marian touch her shoulder. She jerked away and stared at the girl. Marian pushed her horn-rims up onto her nose.

"You're not old enough to get one of those. It's illegal," the mousy girl said.

"Not if you know someone who knows someone," Tina smirked.

The girls all around the locker room whispered and tittered about the new tattoo.

RAW FEED STORIES

"I can't believe she did that."
"Isn't she supposed to be valedictorian?"
"Somebody should tell Principal Hough."

Tina pulled the gaudy gym shirt over her head and bent down to tie her sneakers. She was smiling inside. *Let the little wombats get all worried. I don't care.*

The tattoo, which featured the Valerie High mascot, a bald eagle, being eaten by a large rabid wolf, was concealed from sight again. But it had already done its job.

*****

Tina suffered through gym class, trying her best to half-heartedly perform crab walks and jumping jacks. At the end, the teacher sent the class out to the track to walk laps for the remainder of the period. Tina walked in the rear of the group, away from the others. She did not want to be a part of the class, or even the school for that matter. She was smarter than all of them, her I.Q. tests were off the charts and she was ranked first in her class. School was easy for her. That was, the actual work was easy. The social side was what she hated. All of the ass kissing and backstabbing, she wanted nothing to do with it. It was stupid to lower your self-esteem just in the hopes of being popular.

She was getting quite tired of it.

She looked at the large group of teens walking in front of her, split into smaller groups depending on popularity. There were the jocks pushing into one another and trying to pull each other's shorts down in front of the girls. Their lack of maturity was sad. They were followed by what Tina referred to as "The Valley Girls," the teen princesses who wore designer clothes and hung out at the mall. They were followed by the Goths, the Middle-Earth geeks, the Pocket

Protectors, and the Lonely Hearts Club. And then there was Tina. A conglomeration of all the groups before her (except the jocks), Tina looked upon this small minded group of students and felt absolute disgust.

None of them knew what life was really about. None of them knew how hard it was. How sad it could be. How deeply repressive it was. They existed in their little bubble worlds, tick-tocking the days until the next summer vacation.

They knew nothing about what life could do to you. How a father could die from the drugs he chose over the family he had waiting at home. How a mother who was rotting in prison could forget about her little girl. How the aunt she now lived with spread her legs for a different asshole every single night. How some of those assholes tried to seduce a sixteen year old and how that girl would have to lock herself in her room for protection.

Carly Seinz doesn't have a fucking clue, Tina thought to herself. She glared at the kids in front of her.

"Fuck them. All of them can suck balls." Jesse Copperstone turned to her as Tina said this from the back of the group. Tina glared at the short boy with his acne covered face.

"What the hell you looking at, Jesse?" Jesse quickly turned away and quickened his pace.

After gym, Tina had Advanced Sciences. She actually liked this class. It was one of her favorites. Being an advanced class, there were only eight students in the whole class, and the teacher was one of the more popular ones. She took her seat at her desk and watched Mrs. Fanner drawing diagrams on the board.

"Tina, how are you today?" the teacher asked without turning around.

"Just another sucky day in this sucky school," Tina replied. Mrs. Fanner finished the last graph and turned to the teenager, a small frown on her face.

"I hate when you talk that way," the teacher said. "I know you are smart enough to express yourself a lot more eloquently than that."

Tina shrugged. "That was pretty eloquent, I thought."

Fanner smiled. "I'm sure. Have you thought about what you are going to do for your science tech project?"

"I thought we agreed I wouldn't do it. Don't really have the time."

"I don't remember us agreeing to anything." Mrs. Fanner took a seat at her desk as the rest of the class filed in. "But since you are the highest grade in the class, I think you should be the one to represent the school." One of the lower classmen entered the room and handed Fanner a note. She took it and looked at Tina before opening it. "I want you to think of something and we can talk it over at the end of the week, okay?" Tina nodded.

As Mrs. Fanner read the note, Scott Snee waved at Tina from across the room. Tina turned to him and Scott stuck out his tongue, wagging it back and forth at her. Tina glared at the boy with disgust. She watched as Scott, a jock who just happened to have some brains too, made a fist and inserted the index finger from his other hand into it over and over again.

Tina flipped him the bird. Scott grinned stupidly and nodded his head. The others in the class started laughing.

Mrs. Fanner looked up and cleared her throat. The noise died down. "Tina, they want to see you in the office."

The class was filled with hoots and titters. Mrs. Fanner calmed them down and then nodded at Tina to go ahead.

Tina walked towards the door flipping double birds behind her back as she went.

What the hell do they want now, she thought as she walked slowly down the white tiled hallway. She entered the office. One of the secretaries vacantly pointed for her to go in.

Principal Hough sat behind his huge oak desk, talking on the phone. He nodded at Tina and motioned for her to take a seat. Tina plopped down in the plush leather chair as the older man sat the phone in its cradle.

"Tina Meyers," Hough said as he picked up the manila envelope on his desk and flipped it open. He began reading from the papers inside. "Grade point average of 4.8. Advanced studies curriculum, Tech Science award. Math Award. Advanced English certificate. 1540 on your PSAT's and a tested I.Q. of 152." He stopped and glanced at Tina over the open folder.

"I'm great, aren't I?" she responded and smiled.

Principal Hough continued reading,

"Since coming to Valerie High, you have collected 2 suspensions, 19 detentions, and another 16 warnings. You were in 3 fights, 2 with Mallory Thomas and one with a person who doesn't even go to this school but occurred on school property."

Stupid Griff, Tina thought to herself. *I can't believe he actually came here looking for me. So I kicked him in the nuts. Big deal.*

"Last week," Hough recited, "you told Scott Snee, and I'm quoting here, that he was a 'closet homosexual with repressed feelings and really should talk to his father regarding therapeutic, ahem, circle jerks.' End quote."

"I was just trying to help the guy out. You should see how much he struggles in gym class. With all those sweaty boys running around in their little yellow shorts, Scott was close to losing control. You should probably talk to him. He's in Advanced Sciences right now. You want me to go and get him?" Tina got up from the chair.

"Sit down, Miss. Meyers." Principal Hough's nostrils flared. Tina sat back down. "Anyone else and they would have been suspended indefinitely a long time ago. But because of your outstanding academic record, we were tolerant." Hough leaned back in his chair. "But now, I am thinking our tolerance may have reached its limit."

Tina stared at the principal. He looked at her for a few minutes and then leaned forward again,

"Let me see your shoulder."

"What?!?" Tina exclaimed.

"I want to see your shoulder. Now."

"I have to take off my shirt."

Hough nodded and waited.

"I'm not taking my shirt off so you can sit there and get a massive boner, creep."

Hough's eyes widened. "I would never take advantage of any student in any way...."

Tina cut him off. "And yet here I am, alone, in your office, and you want me to take my shirt off."

"I want to see that tattoo, young lady." Hough's face was getting red and small flecks of spittle shot out from between his lips. "Now!"

"Not happening. What I do to my body is my business. I don't care how much you fantasize about me. I'm not showing you a damn thing, pervert." Tina got up from the chair. Hough came around the desk and grabbed her wrist.

"You have disrespected this school for long enough, little lady. I will not have it anymore. Now let me see that tattoo." He made a grab for her shirt, balling it in his meaty fist. Tina turned and flung one foot into his crotch.

Hough went down. Hard. His eyes bulged from his head and all the air whooshed from his mouth in a great torrent of wind.

Tina bent down and looked at the man's tight face. "If you ever touch me again, I will rip those tiny wrinkly things you call balls right off your body, asshole." She poked him in the middle of his forehead with her pointer finger for emphasis. "And you can take your precious school and go fuck it all week long, I quit." With this last part, Tina bolted from the office.

The secretaries were looking at her, shocked expressions on their faces. Tina glared right back at them.

"Just so you know, he asked me to take my shirt off in there. I am leaving this school now. I do not want to be here if the school continues to employ child molesters." *There*, she thought. *That should make the rounds by fourth period. By then everyone will know what a skeez Hough is.*

Tina thrust her chin into the air, walked back down the hall, past Mrs. Fanner's classroom and straight out the front doors. She walked down the 32 front steps (she had counted them many times before) to the street level. She never looked back. And never felt better.

*****

Valerie High was right on the outskirts of Greensboro's commercial district. The streets were fairly busy, even in midday when most were at work. Tina walked down the sidewalk, taking the familiar route back to her apartment. She didn't want to go back there, but right now, she wasn't sure what she was going to do. Her aunt was probably there, and if she was there that meant one of the boyfriends was there, and that usually meant trouble for her. Any way she figured it, Tina knew that leaving school was the first step in a major change that was now happening,

I'm going to leave home too. I'm not staying there anymore. I have enough money for a bus ticket out of here. She was not sure where she would go. She had an uncle that she never really saw much of. Maybe once or twice a year. But her uncle was always very nice to her, and pleasant to be around. He had a nice family, two small kids and a wife who was very pretty. He had invited Tina for a visit countless times. And Tina figured she could finally take him up on it. Either way, she was done with school and home.

She turned right and headed down Trasker Boulevard. The apartment was located in the Middlebrook Development community five blocks from the high school. She watched as the cars rolled along Trasker, wondering where each one was heading and if it was better than where she was going. She stuffed her hands into her jean pockets and kicked a crumpled soda can across the walk.

A car pulled slowly up next to her. Early model Ford Mustang. Red. The window silently lowered and a young teen boy stuck his head out. It was Griff.

"Good morning, sunshine," Griff grinned at her. The sun shined off his crew cut and the zippers on his black leather jacket jangled against the Mustang's door. "You're looking mighty fine."

Tina kept walking. "I told you I did not want to see you anymore, dickwad."

"Aww, baby. Don't be like that?" Griff stopped the car. Tina turned onto her street and he got out of the Mustang. "Come on. Let's go back to my place." Griff was eighteen and a high school dropout. And a mistake. A big mistake.

He grabbed Tina's elbow and spun her around.

"Hey!" Tina wrenched from his grip and snarled at the boy. "Don't touch me!"

"Aww, come on. That's not what you said before."

"Look, dummy. I slept with you one time. And I wouldn't have done it if I knew you were going to be such a needy, little piss-ant about it. So take your little dick and go away."

Griff's face turned red at the insult. "You seemed to like it when we were together."

Tina rolled her eyes. "Please. You got less game than a pee-wee football team. I thought it would be fun but now it's over. Get lost!" She spun back around and started to march away. Griff grabbed her arm again.

"I don't think so, little Tina."

She slapped his hand away and he pushed her down.

"You little whore. You go sleep with all your aunt's boyfriends but you can't give old Griff the time of day. You're a whore just like her." Griff sneered down at the girl.

"Hey! What's going on over there?" They turned at the voice, Tina from her spot on the sidewalk. It was the manager from the Bistro across the street. He was walking their way. "You leave that girl alone or I'm calling the cops!"

Griff turned back to Tina. "To be continued." He ran back to the Mustang and peeled off. The manager reached over and helped TIna up.

"Are you okay? Do you want me to call the police." There was concern in his eyes.

"No. Thank you. I'm okay. Just a school friend who is a little upset. I need to get going now." The words came automatically. But Tina was thinking about what Griff had said. *You're a whore just like her.*

She broke away from the manager and picked up her pace. The manager followed her with his eyes, shaking his head in wonder, before going back into the bistro.

*****

Tina lived in an apartment complex at the end of the street. She reached the edge of the parking lot and plopped down on the curb. She was shaking.

I just quit school. Griff is chasing me everywhere. I don't want to go back home. What am I going to do?

"Hey, Tina."

She looked up at the sound of her name. It was Mr. Jacobs, one of their neighbors. He was a retired aeronautical engineer and one of the few people Tina actually enjoyed being around. He was across the lot, waxing his silver Corvette, something he did weekly. He was in his normal T-shirt, shorts, and sandals. Tina always thought his skinny old man legs were funny.

"Hey." She got up and walked over to the old man. "Waxing again I see."

Jacobs smiled. "Yeah. When you get old you get bored." He wiped a small place on the hood and snapping the towel with a flourish, threw it into a small empty bucket.

"No school today?" he asked. A hint of a smile touched the side of his mouth as if he already knew the answer to the question.

But Tina did not answer. She looked at the ground.

"You quit?" Jacobs asked. She quickly looked up at him but still did not reply.

He read her face, nodded, and then picked up the small

bucket containing the wax and sponge and headed for the apartment complex's large side yard. There were picnic tables arranged here for the tenants to use during warm weather. Tina followed him and sat across from her kind neighbor at one of the tables.

"That's a pretty big decision, right?" Jacobs continued.

Tina finally answered. "No, it was pretty easy. I don't belong there."

Jacobs frowned. "Everyone expects so much of you because of how smart you are." It was not a question, but an observation. He looked at her keenly. "You probably stick out like a sore thumb. Get a lot of special attention from the teachers and others kids."

"I don't want it. I never asked for it." Tina looked across the yard away from Jacobs. She trusted him. She felt like he listened to her and tried to understand what she was going through. She never told him everything though. Especially not about her mom's boyfriends.

"And that is why you get into so much trouble at school? You get tired of that other spotlight."

"I don't deserve special attention," Tina countered. "I'm not special."

Jacobs sighed. He reached over into the bucket and brought something out. "You know, I've known you for what, five or six years now? You are one of the few people I can actually talk astronomy with. You also understand engineering. Believe me, when I bring that up at the tenant picnics the others start getting all nervous and mousy and turn the subject to last night's episode of The Bachelor. But not you. You actually like talking about it with me."

Tina just looked at the older man. She chewed her lip nervously. *I don't want to go home.*

"I trust you. So I am sharing a deep, dark secret with

you." He opened his hands, displaying the secret thing he had pulled from the bucket. It was a pack of Marlboro Reds.

"You smoke?" Tina exclaimed. "But I thought..."

"That I was just an old goody two shoes?" Jacobs grinned. He produced a small Bic lighter from his pocket and lit one of the cigarettes. He pushed the pack across the table. "You look like you could use one too."

Tina hesitated. Then grabbed a cigarette and lit it with Jacobs' lighter. It was not her first time; she had snuck many of her mother's Newports from her purse.

She inhaled the smoke and felt it calm her a bit. Then she laughed. "What other secrets do you have?"

Jacobs shook his head. "Oh no. I'm not telling you anything else. Especially not about the special plants I got in my closet." Tina laughed even harder and Jacobs joined her. It felt good to her to laugh. It helped push the horribleness of today away for a bit.

They finally quieted and smoked in silence for a few minutes. Jacobs broke the silence first.

"That school sucked anyways."

Tina was surprised by this comment. "Why did you say that?"

"Because it's true. It's hard going to a school where everyone in the place is basically a dumbass." Jacobs lit another cigarette and motioned for Tina to help herself. She grabbed a second one.

"I'm not going to pretend I know what all your problems are, Tina. And you might be surprised at what I can assume." Tina was actually not surprised by that. They had known Jacobs for quite a while. He knew her aunt and had met many of the sleazeball boyfriends who came by. She had also told him all about her parents.

"You quit school. That, I think, is probably going to be an important first step," he continued.

"First step into what?" Tina asked.

"Into your growth. Into adulthood. It's coming. You might as well face that fact. Age runs down on you so quickly, sometimes it kind of leaves you behind at the same time." Jacobs stared down at the weathered surface of the picnic table. He suddenly looked older than his sixty nine years.

"So now, what are you going to do?" he asked.

Tina looked at him and puffed on the cigarette. She stubbed it out on the picnic table's surface. "I know what I don't want to do. I don't want to go back into that apartment. Ever again."

Jacobs nodded. "I figured it was bad in there. I just, I couldn't figure out a way to help you."

"It's okay. It's not your problem." She flicked the dead cigarette stub into the nearby parking lot.

"But I think I can help you, Tina. There's a way. If you are really interested."

She looked at him, confused. "What is it?"

"There's a school. It's a specialized school, much like a university, only they start taking students when they become teenagers. It's a private school for gifted students. And you are gifted."

Tina shook her head. "It doesn't matter. I can't afford a school like that."

Jacobs waved her off. "There is a lot of opportunity for scholarships and grant money. I could help you with that. I taught there for a good while. I would write you a recommendation letter. You would get in. It's not a question with your marks and intellect."

Tina sat stunned.

"The school is not large at all. And the teaching is very specialized. If you show an aptitude and interest for something, they help and encourage you in learning more. And if you redirect that focus into something new, they would not mind. The teachers would encourage that also. And," he paused a bit here, making sure she was listening, "there are no social cliques. Everyone, all ages, share one large classroom and the school's resources."

"It sounds....sounds really cool," she said quietly. "But my aunt would never let me go. She would lose the support money from welfare services and...." Again Jacobs waved her off.

"Let me handle your aunt." His voice dropped an octave and the old man's facial features became very stern. "I don't think welfare services would take too kindly to how a teenage foster child has been treated. I'll talk to your aunt. Don't worry about that."

Tina continued to chew her bottom lip. *It sounds like a good chance. I can finally get away from all of this. I can be on my own like I want to.*

"The scholarships and such won't cover everything. You're old enough that you can get a part-time job to help ease some of the burden," Jacobs said. "As for the rest, I'll take care of that for you."

Tina was dumbfounded. Here was this nice man, someone she did consider a friend, offering to pay for a special school for her.

"What's the catch? I'm not sleeping with you, dude. You know that right?"

Jacobs paused for a second, and then brayed laughter and slapped the top of the picnic table. He was laughing so hard tears were starting to run down his cheeks. Tina began to feel uncomfortable. The laughing fit lasted a few minutes and then finally passed and Jacobs wiped his eyes with the tail of his shirt.

"Oh God. Sorry." He dried his eyes and then looked at the young girl staring at him. "I know that, Tina. And I'm sorry I laughed. It's just I totally saw everything from your point of view for a second. The old man offers to get the young pretty teen out of her shitty life in exchange for a good jump every now and then. I know how it looks now."

"So what then? What's the catch?"

"There is none," he answered. "I never married, Tina. I never had any kids. The only relative I have is a younger brother who owns a car dealership in Nebraska. I see him maybe once every three or four years. He's kind of an asshole, a real conceited prick, if I must say so. When I pass from this life, right now he will inherit all my things. I'm sure you know I did pretty well for myself. A lot of government work, NASA contracts, they all add up to a nice payday." Jacobs rubbed his hands through his gray hair.

"Suffice it to say, I got a nice chunk of change saved up in the bank. I live a pretty simple life. Not many bills, nothing lavish except that stupid ass Cadillac I fret over every week. The truth is I don't want my hard earned money going to my dumbass brother. I would rather put it towards something fruitful. Right now, I think I want to invest it in you."

"I don't know....." Tina stammered. She wasn't used to this, someone else giving her something. Especially something as huge as this. *Opportunity,* rang through her head.

Jacobs did not wait for her to reply, "My brother will just buy something stupid like a boat or a bunch of timeshares. But you, you can make something of yourself. You can go out and become something important, use that intellect you have been gifted with. And when you are rich and famous, then you can pay an old man back." Jacobs smiled and Tina smiled too.

"I don't know what to say," she responded. "I'll do it. If you think you can convince my aunt then I will go...." She stopped.

Something was wrong.

Blood started to gush from Jacob's nose. The dark crimson liquid ran down over the pale skin of Jacobs' chin.

"Are you..." Tina started but the words never came. A lightning bolt of pain struck inside of her head and she screamed in agony, covering both ears with her hands. The lightning ended in pain which began to undulate through her head. She could feel the pulses shiver through her teeth. Her jaws immediately clamped shut.

Something was talking to her. Through the intense pain a voice began to take shape. Words formed inside her head, pounding across her conscious. She fell from the bench and rolled over to her back, snapping her head against the ground, trying to lose the awful sensation.

The voice was speaking and Tina did not recognize the words. They were strange and garbled and.....and mechanical. It sounded like an alien robot trying to say something through a wall of white noise.

And then it stopped. Just as suddenly as it began, the sound disappeared and the lightning left her head. But the pain remained.

Tina lie motionless on the grass, weeping. Her nose was bleeding and her ears were thumping over and over again. She moaned and tried to move her feet. Little by little her body began to respond again. She eased herself carefully to her knees and then stood, swaying dramatically.

Tina looked over to see Jacobs lying faced-own on the ground. She slowly walked over and reached down, grabbing his shoulder.

"Mr Jacobs? What happened?" Tina rolled the old man over. His eyes were wide open, unmoving. Blood covered the lower half of his face where it had erupted from his nose. It dripped from both ears, dark and runny.

Jacobs was dead.

Tina looked up to call for help. Across the street, bodies laid still on the sidewalk and in the road. A car had run over the curb and crashed into one of the apartment buildings, the front end a battered mess. Across the complex she could see the basketball courts. More bodies were sprawled over their flat surfaces.

"Holy shit!" Tina screamed.

A large rumbling erupted beneath her feet and she was thrown violently to the ground, Cars began bouncing in the parking lot and she heard glass breaking as their windows shattered. She rolled over and tried to stand but the ground was shaking too much.

Fucking shit, it's an earthquake!

She quickly crawled under the picnic table and covered her head with her arms. Tina peeked between her hands and watched in horror as the shops across from the apartment complex disappeared into the ground. A huge cloud of dust and smoke billowed into the air. A large crack ran across the parking lot and several cars fell into it, the sound of crunching and twisting metal added to the chaos.

Tina screamed and then screamed again as she watched one of the apartment buildings collapse. Brick and concrete showered the area and she could not see anything. Something large landed nearby and she felt the table move.

The quake subsided. Car alarms blared and Tina could hear someone screaming in pain nearby.

She tried to get up, but found she was too weak to move. Breathing was hard as the air filled with dust from the collapsed building,

Tina turned to her side and vomited. Once and then twice more after that. She shut her eyes tightly, unable to see through the cloud of dust.

As the world ended, Tina huddled underneath the picnic table and cried softly.

Want to know more? Pick up THE VOICE, *Book 1 of in the Black Rain Journals, the new science fiction series from Michael Whetzel.*